THE A. R. F. WEBBER LIBRARY

Those That Be in Bondage: A Tale of Indian Indentures and Sunlit Western Waters

THOSE THAT BE IN BONDAGE

A Tale of Indian Indentures and Sunlit Western Waters

A.R.F. WEBBER

With an Introduction by Selwyn R. Cudjoe

Calaloux Publications

Copyright © 1988 by Calaloux Publications

All rights reserved. Except for brief quotation in a review, this book, or parts thereof, must not be reproduced in any form without permission in writing from the publisher. For information address Calaloux Publications, P.O. Box 82-725, Wellesley, Massachusetts 02181.

First published 1917 by The Daily Chronicle Printing Press, Georgetown, Demerara, British Guiana

Calaloux Publications paper edition first published 1988.

Printed in the United States of America

International Standard Book Number 0-911565-05-1
Library of Congress Catalog Card Number 88-71567

To the Memory of

THE LATE

LIEUT. T. GORDON DAVSON
Of His Majesty's Royal Horse Guards,

Who, prior to giving his fair young life in a cause of righteousness on the blood-soaked plains of Flanders, gave to the world some proof of the capacity of Colonial genius in "The Druid's Prayer," and "Saints and Sinners;" those enrapturing Valse conceptions whose touching chords of symphony, and pulsing peans of joy breathe so completely of the love and temptations of these children of the hills, and the plains, and the sunlit western waters, whereof this book is writ.

A. R. F. Webber: West Indian Nationalist and the First Novelist of Trinidad and Tobago

by Selwyn R. Cudjoe

> We truly must remember
> The good points in his life,
> We refer to Albert Webber
> And his career of strife
> He was a man of many parts
> (Though most on a grade),
> And always won the people's heart
> By the game fight he made.
>
> By cast of die he won or lost
> It did not matter which,
> His sunny smile will melt the front
> Or bridge the hostile ditch;
> And as he lived he surely died
> Without the least preamble,
> Proving however occupied
> The game of life's a gamble.
>
> Z, "A. R. F. Webber"[1]

On Thursday, June 30, 1932, the *New Daily Chronicle* of British Guiana (present-day Guyana) carried a stunning announcement. It read: "Sudden Death of Hon. Albert Raymond

Research on this project was made possible by two Wellesley Faculty Research Grants. I thank Tommy Payne (Guyana National Archives), Joan L. Christiani (Guyana National Library), and Jennifer Welshman, granddaughter of Webber, without whom this project would not have been possible. This article is part of a larger work on Webber that is in preparation by the author.

[1]This poem, written by a reader who merely signed his or her name Z and dedicated to the memory of Webber, appeared in the *Daily Argosy* on Friday, July 1, 1932, two days after the death of Webber.

Forbes Webber: Brilliant British Guiana Politician." The death of a man who seemed to be in the best of health, was relatively young (he was fifty-two years old), and enjoyed tremendous popularity among the mulatto middle strata (creoles) and the black masses of Guyana came as a great shock to the community and represented the passing of a very important symbol of the people's resistance to colonial domination. This announcement marked the end of one the most distinguished politicians, lecturers, journalists, and literary men of Guyana and the West Indies. He was also the first novelist that Trinidad and Tobago produced, and he played an important part in shaping the early literary and journalistic discourses of the English-speaking Caribbean.

Over the years, however, Webber has been lost to the pages of West Indian literary and cultural history. References to Webber's work have been at best tangential, at worst, woefully ignorant. In his "Year by Year Bibliography," Kenneth Ramchand lists Webber's novel *Those That Be in Bondage* (1917) but does not quote from it. Anthony Boxhill, in his explication of the beginnings of West Indian literature, notes, almost woefully but incorrectly, that after Webber wrote *Those That Be in Bondage* "nothing more" was heard from him.[2] Today none of Webber's books is in print. There are two existing copies of *Those That Be in Bondage* and only one known copy of *An Innocent's Pilgrimage* (1927).[3] The bulk of his other work consists of his impressions of his visits abroad that take the form of a series of articles in the *New Daily Chronicle* and a printer's copy of his only book of poems.[4] Rediscovering Webber, it seems to me,

---

[2] See Kenneth Ramchand, *The West Indian Novel and Its Background* (London: Heinemann, 1983), and Anthony Boxhill, "The Beginnings to 1929," in Bruce King, ed., *West Indian Literature* (London: Macmillian, 1979), p. 42.

[3] There is one copy of *Those That Be in Bondage* in the National Library of Guyana and one in the possession of Jennifer Welshman, a granddaughter of Webber. Also, one copy of *An Innocent's Pilgrimage* can be found in the University Library of the University of Guyana but page 89 is missing. There seem to be a number of copies of his *Centenary History*, which is listed in the Library of Congress.

[4] These works are in the possession of Jennifer Welshman.

is a matter of utmost importance because it takes the written history of the creative literature of Trinidad and Tobago back by ten years (that is, if we posit C. L. R. James's "La Divina Pastora" [1927] as the beginning of creative literature in Trinidad and Tobago), it enriches the scope of West Indian written literature, and it gives us a new understanding of the interrelated nature of the West Indian nationalist struggle for liberation.[5]

His Life and Times

A. R. F. Webber, as he was popularly known (his family called him Allie), was born on New Year's Day 1880 in Scarborough, Tobago, to James Francis Webber and Sarah, née Hope, and christened in the Wesleyan-Methodist Church by the Rev. A. H. Aguilar on February 1, 1880.[6] The second of five or possibly six children (Frederick, George, Elenora, Ivy, and Clarence, who might have been illegitimate), Webber was educated in Tobago and served in the Roman Catholic church as an acolyte before immigrating to Guyana in 1899 at the invitation of his uncle, S. E. R. Forbes, a partner in the firm Crosby and Forbes, large traders at Bartica and in the gold fields in the interior of the country. Crosby and Forbes was the first firm for which he worked. A few years after his arrival he left his uncle's firm and joined British Guiana (Puruni) Gold Concession, becoming secretary to the company in 1906.

Some years later, Webber branched out into Water Street, Georgetown, the business center of the society, as a clerk at J. I.

[5]C. R. L. James "La Divina Pastora," appeared in the *Saturday Review* on October 15, 1927; Alfred Mendes's *Pitch Lake*, generally regarded as the first novel published by someone from Trinidad and Tobago, was published in England in 1934.

[6]Although all the newspapers accounts at the time of his death give Webber's birth year as 1879, his birth certificate gives his birth as 1880, and Edith, his second daughter, confirms this fact by noting that her father was fifty-two years of age when he died. This mistake seems to be replicated even on his "Certificate of Cause of Death," which notes his age as fifty-three (he was in his fifty-third year when he died), cause of death as "cerebral hemmorrhage," and the duration of his death as ten minutes.

Chapman, a post that he held for a short while. Later he became secretary of Peter's Mine, a prosperous gold-producing company that ended its gold-mining operations in 1909 when the great boom in the balata and rubber industries led to the "ever-increasing cost of wood fuel" and, as a consequence, "a wane in corporate activities in the gold industry."[7] After he left Peter's Mine he joined Mara Mara Gold Company. It was during this period (1899 to 1910) that Webber gained an enormous amount of knowledge of Guyana's interior, which proved to be of great value in his subsequent political, literary, and journalistic activities. In this period, Webber, a self-educated man, also sought to improve his formal education, particularly his knowledge of the English language, by studying under Mr. Richards and another master who taught at Queens College in Georgetown.

In 1910 Webber joined the advertising department of the *Daily Argosy* as an advertising agent and later became an advertising clerk at Bookers Brothers, the largest conglomerate in the colony. Both of these positions, according to the *Daily Chronicle*, "gave him valuable knowledge of publicity methods which stood him in good stead as the politician and journalist which he subsequently became."[8] In this period, he also did freelance work and polished his writing skills. In 1919 he was appointed editor of the *Daily Chronicle*, succeeding C. W. Marchant, and served in that capacity until 1925, when the newspaper went into liquidation. Such a position conferred immense influence upon Webber because the local press was perhaps the most important instrument of political advocacy at that time. As one correspondent to the *Daily Chronicle* noted on October 6, 1921, "the masses looked largely to the press for political guidance." In 1921 Webber became the secretary of the Sugar Planters' Association, publicity secretary of the Georgetown Chamber of Commerce, and, at one time, editor of the latter's official journal. It is safe to say that at that moment of his career

---

[7] A. R. F. Webber, *Centenary History and Handbook of British Guiana* (British Guiana: Argosy Co., 1931), p. 335.

[8] *Daily Chronicle*, June 30, 1932, p. 4.

Webber was close to and apparently courted the favor of the members of this commercial class. For example, three members of the Electives, R. E. Brassington, F. Dias, and M. Nascimento, were directors of the *Daily Chronicle*, and Brassington supported Webber's candidacy when he ran for election in 1921.[9]

In 1923, however, Webber made an interesting political move. Although his paper supported another candidate, Webber supported the Hon. Nelson Cannon, auctioneer, valuator, and stockbroker, when he ran in a by-election to fill a seat that was vacated when one of the members of the Council resigned. In this election Webber seems to have broken with the dominant mercantile interest as he and Cannon set themselves up as "the champions of the masses" and opponents of the government. According to Harold Lutchman, out of this election association there "emerged one of the closest and enduring political partnerships up to that time in the colony."[10] In fact, they became so successful as a team that in 1926 they formed the Popular party, the first political party in the history of British Guiana.

When the *Daily Chronicle* went into liquidation in 1925, it seemed only natural, given Webber's journalistic and political interest and Cannon's political concerns, that they should found a new newspaper to promote their mutual interests. This they did, forming the *New Daily Chronicle*, the first number of which appeared on January 17, 1926. Webber became the editor, a position he held until his departure from the paper in 1930. On the occasion of his death, the *Daily Argosy* noted Webber's success as an editor and remarked: "Few men could have passed from a stool in a commercial house to the editorial chair of a responsible local journal and achieve the measure of success which crowned the efforts of Mr. Webber."[11]

It was in the *New Daily Chronicle* that Webber really became

---

[9]See Brassington's letter of support for Webber's candidacy as it appeared in the *Daily Chronicle*, September 9, 1921.

[10]Harold Lutchman, *From Colonialism to Co-operative Republic: Aspects of Political Development in Guyana* (Rio Piedras, Puerto Rico: Institute of Caribbean Studies, 1974), p. 82.

[11]*Daily Argosy*, June 30, 1932.

an advocate of the common people. His hard-hitting editorials, his advocacy of the rights of the masses, and his support of the trade union movement and the right of Guyanese citizens to self-government made him truly a man of the people. Clarence David Kirton, born in 1910 and a journalist for the *Daily Argosy* at the time that Webber edited the *New Daily Chronicle*, argues that Webber was "a forceful journalist who championed the cause of the masses. He was very critical of those in high places (the expatriates) and ran a very popular paper."[12] Edith Mae Forbes Dummett, his second daughter, noted that "he used the papers as a weapon in his struggle against the plantocracy."[13] Certainly by 1926 Webber had emerged as one of the "foremost political thinkers in the country," and the *New Daily Chronicle* was at the forefront of "progressive political thinking" at the time.[14]

In spite of the popularity of the *New Daily Chronicle* and its journalist success—perhaps because of it—the paper was denied advertising revenues, which made it difficult to operate. Webber, however, wanting to devote more time to politics and mining, left the *New Daily Chronicle* in 1930 and joined R. V. Evan Wong's stone quarrying business. Later he became instrumental in the formation of the Colonial Tanning and Refrigerating Company (of which he became the manager), which later acquired the Demerara Leather and Boot Factory, Charlestown, and the Meat Factory that developed from it. It was while he was journeying to the gold fields of Bartica that Webber died. When Webber's will was probated on July 29, 1932, his assets included five thousand shares in the Colonial Tanning and Refrigerating Company, some shares in the Rupuni Development Company, and two insurance policies with Demerara Life and Manufacturers Life of Canada respectively. His shares of these enterprises could not have counted for much, nor was the value of the insurance policies very great for Webber's daughter re-

---

[12]Interview with Clarence Kirton conducted at the Guyana Archives, Georgetown, Guyana, January 1, 1987.

[13]Interview with Edith Dummett, née Webber, conducted at West Hill, Toronto, February 7, 1987.

[14]Lutchman, *From Colonialism to Co-operative Republic*, p. 84.

members her father leaving very little monetary assets to his family at the time of his death.[15]

It was in the area of politics that Webber's influence was felt most keenly in both Guyana and the West Indies. As his daughter Edith noted, "He loved politics more than anything else and loved to serve the underdog."[16] He began to serve his people officially from October 18, 1921, when he was elected as a financial representative in the then Combined Court for the County of Berbice, a position to which he was reelected in the general elections of 1926. With the change of Guyana's Constitution in 1928, which Webber strongly opposed, Webber was given a seat as the Honorable Member for Western Berbice in the new Legislative Council and elected for that division in the general elections of 1930 "against the stern opposition of a prominent resident of the constituency in the person of Mr. Peer Bacchus."[17]

Webber, a tireless worker for West Indian integration and self-government, opposed the Guyanese plantocracy intensely. In 1926 he went to England as one of the colony's delegates to the first West Indian Conference, a journey that he described in *An Innocent's Pilgrimage* (1927). The other delegates were the Hon. John Hampdem King, Sir Alfred Sherlock, and the Hon. Francis Dias, with G. C. Green acting as secretary. From 1926 to 1928 Webber served as a member of the Georgetown Town Council as a representative of Kingston Ward. In his capacity as a legislator, Webber fought strenuously to preserve the self-governing aspects of Guyana's constitution. On January 5, 1928, in an editorial in the *New Daily Chronicle*, Webber vigorously challenged what he claimed was the *Daily Argosy*'s assertion that the people of Guyana were in favor of "abandoning all of its rights and privileges, and handing over its administration to imported officials directed by unknown masters 4,000 miles

---

[15]*New Daily Chronicle*, July 30, 1932; interview with Edith Dummett, February 7, 1987.
[16]Interview with Edith Dummett, February 7, 1987.
[17]*New Daily Chronicle*, June 30, 1932, p. 4.

away." He called upon the people to organize "such spectacular demonstrations in every town, village and hamlet in the colony as will leave no manner of doubt as to the temper and determination of the country." Further, he called upon the people vigorously to assert their sense of national pride so that the secretary of state, who had the responsibility of administering the colonies, would have no doubt "that the fourteen men who stood together in the Combined Court as one man on Tuesday last do not stand alone."

It was as a member of the Combined Court that he led the opposition to the proposed changes in Guyana's Constitution in 1928 and was largely responsible for the preparation of the Electives' memorandum in reply to the Report on the British Guiana Constitutional Committee that was composed of Roy Wilson, chairman, and Harry Snell. In pursuit of this goal, Webber (together with the Hon. E. G. Woodford, K. C. and H. C. Humphreys) led a powerful constitutional delegation that went to London to see the secretary of state for the colonies to preserve the integrity of the country's constitution.

In 1930 Webber made his last trip to London with Albert Crichlow, secretary of the British Guiana Labour Union (BGLU) and one of the fathers of the trade union movement in the West Indies, as a delegate from that country to the British Commonwealth Labour Conference. As early as February 5, 1926, Webber had praised the work of Crichlow when he wrote in an editorial that "Mr. Crichlow has done his bit in the work of trying to get at the people, teaching them to unite for a common purpose, helping them to use their own brains to think for themselves, and guiding them in the performance of the far more important function of acting to secure the measure which should be meted to them. . . . 'Tis an age of democracy in which we live and to which men and institutions alike will have to conform." When a branch of the BGTU was established in New Amsterdam earlier in that same year, Webber commented almost rhapsodically, unconsciously taking his theme from "Poor Ole Joe," the Negro spiritual that celebrated the passing of slavery days,

Gone are the days when our fellow creatures will accept with a calm stoicism the severest buffets of an unkind Fate without murmering; gone are the days when our fellow creatures will submit to be led along paths which their eye of reasoning cannot discern; now, instead, they contest against Fate every inch of her onward march and will only be content to bear with adversity when not necessity, but expediency and calm counsel warrant such a course. Thanks to this union, the hitherto "disorderly rabble," the prey of the plans of well-ordered but mischievous minds, has now been converted into the semblance at least of orderliness, and, however feeble, their voices can now and must now be heard.[18]

Such, then, was Webber's enthusiasm for the welfare of the workers of the colony. When he accompanied Crichlow to London in 1930, the main objective of the delegation, according to Ashton Chase, "centered on getting the Imperial Government to help finance public works in our country so as to relieve unemployment."[19] In a way, this trip demonstrated Webber's continuing support of the union and his commitment to the working people of the country since the trade union of that day represented the struggle not only for greater benefits for workers but for social reform as well.

When Webber died, the *New Daily Chronicle* noted that "he was one of the greatest critics of Government at times"[20] and one of the most prominent West Indians of his time. More important, Webber's association with the trade union movement led his antagonists from the white planter class to term him a socialist. He was one of the country's best debaters, and his contributions in the Legislative Council were marked by "ardour and good humour." Perhaps he earned that sobriquet because he spoke out continuously for the interest of the colored middle strata and the laboring masses that resided at the bottom of the society.

[18]*New Daily Chronicle*, February 5, 1926, p. 4.
[19]Ashton Chase, *A History of Trade Unionism in Guyana, 1900 to 1961* (Demerara: New Guyana Co., 1964), p. 76.
[20]June 30, 1932, p. 4.

Writer and Journalist

Without a doubt, Webber was one of the most prolific contributors to early West Indian literature. Although we do not have any of Webber's works before 1915, when he wrote "What of the Night?" it is clear that Webber had a fairly long writing apprenticeship.[21] When in 1916 Webber accepted an invitation from the editor of the *Chronicle* to submit an article on the colony's industries in the place of one that was to have been written by Cecil Richter, who was out of the country at the time, he was well prepared to carry out that task. "The Rise and Wane of the Colony's Industries," the piece Webber submitted, launched his literary career and remains the first piece of his work that we have. As the editor of the *Chronicle* noted when Webber's article was published, "It would have been difficult for us to choose a more vigorous or better informed writer."[22] Its academic rigor and its lucid and liquid prose clearly indicate that Webber had indeed written in some capacity before and was thoroughly at ease in the literary/journalistic milieu of his time. Undoubtedly, Webber was offered the position of editor of the *Daily Chronicle* in 1919 because of his advertising experience, his journalistic skills, and his writing ability.

As an author, journalist, and legislator, Webber wrote many editorials and weekly columns in the *Daily Chronicle* and the *New Daily Chronicle* and made many contributions in the Legislative Council. Webber wrote four books, *Those That Be in Bondage: A Tale of Indian Indentures and Sunlit Western Waters* (1917), *Glints from an Anvil* (1919), *An Innocent's Pilgrimage* (1927), and *A Centenary History and Yearbook of British Guiana* (1931), and innumerable articles. His notebook indicates that Webber was in the process of preparing his other travel writings ("From an Editorial View-Point" and "New York vs. London," two series of articles that appeared in the *New Daily Chronicle*

---

[21]See A. R. F., *Glints from an Anvil* (Georgetown: Daily Chronicle, 1919).
[22]"The Rise and Wane of the Colony's Industries," *Chronicle*, Holiday Number, August 1916, p. 58.

in 1928 and 1929) for publication at the time of his death. Patrick Hastings Daly, a Guyanese historian and the writer of the longest article on Webber, called *A Centenary History and Year Book* Webber's "most notable contribution to Guianese [sic] Literature." Tommy Payne, archivist of Guyana, called it "the most authoritative history written about Guyana up until that time and for many years afterward."[23] In many ways, he was as revolutionary in politics as he was visionary in his writings, and he did much to clarify the conditions of the working people of Guyana. His writings served as one of the true barometers of the conditions of the working people in the society and gave them great encouragement to carry on their struggle for freedom.

"Those That Be in Bondage"

A year after "The Rise and Wane of the Colony's Industries," Webber's first published article, came the publication of *Those That Be in Bondage*, dedicated to the memory of "the colonial genius" of Lieutenant T. Gordon Davson, whose works, Webber argued, "breathe so completely of the love and temptations of these children of the hills, and the plains, and the sunlit western waters, whereof this book is writ." It is clear from reading "The Rise and Wane of the Colony's Industries" that Webber empathized with the suffering and deprivation of the East Indians, conditions that he had known on a firsthand basis because of his travels throughout the country in his varied capacities. In "The Rise and Wane of the Colony's Industries" Webber had pondered upon "the higher value set on males in recruiting, and consequently, the existence of a disproportion of the sexes" within the Negro community.[24] In *Those That Be in Bondage* he would use the theme of the disproportion between

[23]P. H. Daly, *Story of the Heroes, Book 3* (Georgetown: Daily Chronicle, 1943), p. 330; correspondence with Tommy Payne, January 8, 1987.
[24]"The Rise and Wane of the Colony's Industries," p. 58.

the sexes as his point of departure to examine the condition of bondage in a colonialist-capitalist society.

Those That Be in Bondage, a difficult philosophical text, is one of the great historical romances in the literature of Trinidad and Tobago particularly and in the West Indies generally.[25] Although the work begins somewhat as a realist novel—that is, it sees the psychology of its characters as being shaped by the socioeconomic environment—it slips into a romantic narrative mode in which the hero is portrayed as existing in a state of melancholia, preoccupied with his own thoughts and ego and detached to a certain degree from his social and political environment.[26] Indeed, the fundamental conflict of the hero is resolved only when he recognizes the pull that the demands of the social and political world have upon him and the manner in which the latter shapes his destiny. The work, however, oscillates between romanticism and realism and signifies a transitional

---

[25] Michel Maxwell Phillip, Trinidad's most distinguished legal mind of the nineteenth century and a man of "varied intellectual power and breadth of culture," as C. R. L. James called him, is the author of *Emmanuel Appadocca: A Tale of the Buccaneers* (1854), the first known romance of Trinidad and Tobago. Jose M. Bodu called it a work that "showed signs of constructive powers and a great command of language." See C. L. R. James, "Michel Maxwell Phillip, 1829–1888," in Reinhard W. Sander, *From Trinidad: An Anthology of Early West Indian Writing* (London: Hodder and Stroughton, 1978), p. 268; and Jose M. Bodu, *Trinidadiana* (Port of Spain: A. C. Blondel, 1890), p. 83.

[26] Nathaniel Hawthorne defines the romance as having "a right to present that truth [of the human heart] under circumstances, to a great extent, of the writer's own choosing or creation" and its attempt "to connect a bygone time with the very present that is flitting away from us" (*The House of the Seven Gables* [Boston: Houghton Mifflin, 1924], pp. 13–14.) Boris Suchkov defines the realist novel as going "deeper and more fully into circumstances and character, and examin[ing] the connection between them, revealing their mutual influence." Thus, he argues, romanticism "grossly inflated the individual and imparted universality to his inner world by isolating him from the objective world. Realism, on the other hand, examined life as an integral whole, within which relations and links were causally conditioned by one another" (*A History of Realism* [Moscow: Progress Publishers, 1973], pp. 64, 77). Webber was aware of Hawthorne's work and makes references to it in *An Innocent's Pilgrimage*. See *An Innocent's Pilgrimage* (Georgetown: New Daily Chronicle Printing Press, 1927), p. 20.

mode of discourse between the oral literary culture of the colonial society and the nascent written literature that began to flower in the 1930s.

Although the focus of the text shifts in the course of the narrative, it examines the dual nature of bondage: its physical and spiritual dimensions. The author is concerned with the alienation of the overseer from the rest of the society but also with the enslavement of men to man-made systems. His characterization of Harold as Savonarola alerts the reader to the tyranny of the social system and the reactionary nature the church played in the society.[27] In a way, his story is about the rebellion against particular dimensions of bondage that keep the human being enslaved. At one level the hero rebels against the specific colonial bondage; at another level, he rebels against social institutions that keep men and women in human bondage, and these are the central concerns of the text.

Set in Guyana, Tobago, and Trinidad between 1890 and 1913, the historical romance traces the lives of two generations of Waltons as they work out their destinies in those societies. Chapters 1 through 6, the first part of the text, examine the life and death of John James Walton, "sugar oracle and Planting Attorney" for one of the largest sugar plantations in Guyana, and his brother-in-law, Edwin Hamilton, bred on the English sense of "fair play" and reared "far from Colonial influences." He is the perfect gentleman, the romantic stereotype untouched by the inhuman influences of colonialism and racial separation. Thus it is not inconsistent that he marries Bibi, "that smooth-skinned, bare-toed East Indian young lady,"[28] the quintessence

---

[27]Girolamo Savonarola (1452–98), a Dominican preacher and reformer, was a champion of the people who believed in direct democracy and "sought to introduce a spiritual revolution through moral reform." His advocacy of these positions led him into conflict with the Roman Catholic church, and he was hanged and burned for his opposition to the church. Edith Dummett notes that Webber, as a boy, was an acolyte in a Roman Catholic church and believed in many of the church's doctrines. In that encounter, he may have garnered a dislike for the rigidity and bondagelike nature of the Roman Catholic church, which he sees as one of the major repressive organizations of society.

[28]*Those That Be in Bondage: A Tale of Indian Indentures and Sunlit Western*

of rustic beauty, whose "strong Caucasian features had brought many men to her feet with all manner of proposals" (*Bondage*, p. 25).²⁹ Through this marriage, a daughter, Marjorie, is born and the rest of the text is taken up with the romantic love that develops between Harold Walton and Marjorie on the idyllic island of Tobago.

Harold, who eventually becomes a priest in the Dominican Order, breaks his vow of celibacy when he becomes romantically involved with Marjorie. In the end, he returns to British Guiana, becomes involved in the "Brickdam Cathedral fire," as A. J. Seymour terms it, and when his offer to assist in rebuilding the cathedral is rejected by the pope, he leaves for England to begin a new life. Such is the romantic dimension of the text.³⁰

In the first part of this text, Webber is concerned with four aspects of the colonial system, all of which are worked out in the second part. First, he is concerned with "the great tragedy" that grew out of the system of indentureship and the way it affected the lives of all it touched.³¹ He examines the conditions of the whites in the colonies, in this case the overseers, who "deteriorate in mind, morals and manners" (*Bondage*, p. 7) once they are separated from the corrective (civilizing) influences of the mother country, a condition that is also examined in Jean Rhys's *Wide Sargasso Sea* (1966) and Herbert de Lisser's *The White Witch of Rosehall* (1929). In this sense, Webber's work is very much in the tradition of other West Indian novels that

---

Waters (Georgetown, British Guiana: Daily Chronicle, 1917), pp. 6, 4 (hereafter cited in the text as *Bondage*).

²⁹Jeremy Poynting sees such depictions as continuing what he calls "the prurient estate stereotype" that is found in similar novels. See "East Indian Women in the Caribbean: Experience, Image, and Voice," *Journal of South East Asian Literature* 21, No. 1, p. 141.

³⁰See A. J. Seymour, "The Literary Adventure of the West Indies," *Kyk-Over-Al* 2, No. 10 (April 1950): 36.

³¹This text is rich in historical incidents. There are allusions to the activities of Crosby, the immigrant agent-general, "who was a tower of strength and righteousness to immigrants" (*Bondage*, p. 12), the Des Veoux Commission, which was sent from England to look into the conditions of the Indians, and so on. See Webber's *Centenary History* for a historical account of these activities.

examine the debilitating effect the plantation economy of the Caribbean had upon Europeans.

Second, he examines the arbitrariness of plantation ways. Singh and his family exist at "the big Crosby's will" and must pick up and leave all of their worldly possessions behind when "big Crosby" gives the command. As the narrator notes of the East Indian immigrants,

> Since their enforced sojourn in this far-away land, [they] have created out of nothing, but their thews and sinews, a rice industry which feeds the whole country and the neighbouring islands in the Caribbean. Every immigrant of any thrift or industry—and which is not—has his rice bed. When an order such as this comes, rice beds must be abandoned, or sold for what they could fetch: and what ever does a forced sale realize? The humble home such as many have been made, with its kitchen garden and feeble conveniences, must be left behind. Kith and kin, shipmates of the long lonely voyage of "an hundred days" from far away India, friends and associations, must all be said goodbye to. (*Bondage*, p. 15)

Third, Webber is concerned about the unjust treatment of the colored people of the society. His being colored probably made him very interested in discrimination against them. He argues that the racist attitudes "of those that control the destinies of the industry" prevented any "coloured creole" from being appointed to a management position. "They may have every qualification under the sun: they may be as able as Attila: but they may not aspire to such appointments" (*Bondage*, p. 52). The young Europeans who were recruited to fill management positions, no matter how unqualified they were for those positions or how little they understood the conditions of tropical agriculture, were always preferred over local black persons of merit. "That the best material is not always obtained is only too apparent in the wastrels so frequently met within the colony's industrial life" (*Bondage*, p. 53). As a result of such racist behavior, the narrator argues, the industry strangles itself, and as, Harold notes in the second part of the text, because no generations of planters had been "bred in the atmosphere of agriculture and sugar . . . [no] inventions [were] recorded for the last hundred years." He concludes: "Each generation sees a scratch team of raw Englishmen, who have never seen a cane field in their lives—and often not even a hop or a potato field—or rawer Scotsmen, and of broken Creoles. Death or dismissal closes all the effort and study of their minds; they bequeath their thoughts to no offspring; the barren die, and those few who rise to positions of affluence and are blessed with sons see that they take to the learned professions, to the Army or Navy, and to every other walk of life except planting" (*Bondage*, p. 204).

Fourth, the text is concerned with the conflict between Eastern and Western ways of perceiving the world. Edwin, idealizing the Eastern aspects of Bibi's origins, becomes resolutely opposed to her acquisition of any "westernizing" tendencies. His chief aim, according to the narrator, is to "order her surroundings in a somewhat similar manner to those which would have been hers had her fiery old grandfather not disinherited his daughter. . . . Thus was ensured unto him his wife as a never-ending source of delight; never once had he felt that indescribable feeling of disappointment in seeing anything like *gaucherie* in any effort to ape the manners and customs of her Western sisters" (*Bondage*, p. 59).

In the end, the romancer/novelist seems to suggest that a person is the master of his or her fate and should not be controlled by any creeds. Freedom from physical bondage (colonialism) or spiritual bondage (in this case, that of the church) are to be struggled against when or where they occur. As Dr. St. Aldwyn cries when he foils Harold from taking his life: "You are the architect of your own fortunes and master of your destiny. Don't forget it! No man can be master of anything, unless he takes masterful precautions to be master" (*Bondage*, p. 214). Only with such control and balance can one begin to construct a temple that reflects one's own native genius. This is the synthesis toward which the text moves.

Those That Be in Bondage represents a transition from the oral literary tradition to the novel and thus can be defined as a transitional piece. It stands midway between the folk tales and the more developed West Indian novel and inaugurates a tradition of exploring the dawning social and political consciousness of a people that continues in works such as Ralph de Boissiere's *Crown Jewel* (1952), V. S. Naipaul's *A House for Mr. Biswas* (1961), and Earl Lovelace's *The Dragon Can't Dance* (1979). Although the work is somewhat rough in its contours it is, nonetheless, a very precious achievement. A. J. Seymour notes that the work suffers from "the shapelessness of being successive episodes" and argues that "the characters are not fully round, although they have vitality, and, in the Eighteenth Century manner, the author keeps interjecting moral comments. Four chapters are merely descriptions of Tobago, in the best guide book fashion, there is the account of a riot on a sugar estate and many instances occur of the florid oratory and rhetoric that are characteristic of Webber the politician."[32]

Those That Be In Bondage is a difficult book that raises some troubling philosophical questions about the nature of existence and the need of men and women to struggle against conditions that keep them in bondage. Seymour calls the work "significant in its criticism of the plantation system," and Peter Ruhomon in his *Centenary History of the East Indians in British Guiana, 1838–1938* quotes from it on two occasions to dramatize the cruelty that the East Indians suffered under indentureship in British Guiana.[33] It is an important work, however, in that it inaugurates a national tradition of resistance and, in many important ways, begins to articulate, in literature, the aspirations of West Indian peoples.

Conclusion

Much more work needs to be done to recover Webber's work. It represents an important era in West Indian literature

---

[32]Seymour, "The Literary Adventure of the West Indies," p. 38.

[33]Ibid.; Peter Ruhomon, *Centenary History of the East Indians in British Guiana, 1838–1938* (Georgetown: British Guiana Daily Chronicle, 1947), pp. 124–25, 197–98.

and tells much about that period in our social development when we began to grapple with our emerging self-consciousness as a people. In his politics, he stands shoulder to shoulder with illustrious West Indians patriots such as T. A. Marryshow of Grenada, Captain Arthur Cipriani of Trinidad, Cecil D. Rawle of Dominica, and Peter Watt Sangster and A. G. Nash of Jamaica. He worked with, corresponded with, and visited all of those patriots in the cause of West Indian freedom. One of the earliest advocates of a West Indian federation, he was a pioneer in the cause of freedom of the press in the West Indies, doing much of the spadework in preparation for the first West Indian Press Association that was formed in Barbados on January 23, 1929, of which Herbert de Lisser, the Jamaican author, was named president and Marryshow and Webber were named as members of the Management Committee. Webber's work was so important in the formation of this organization that the *Port of Spain Chronicle* noted on January 24, 1929, that Webber "has shown himself to be fertile in ideas and his work for the West Indian Press Conference [Association or Union] will not be soon forgotten."

Although his *Centenary History* stands out as a landmark in the history of Caribbean intellectual thought (A. J. Seymour places it within the same category as Eric Williams's *Capitalism and Slavery* in that it seeks to correct the biased historical accounts of non–West Indians who wrote about the area),[34] his contributions to early West Indian journalism, his sketches on his travels, and his intellectual-activist posture make him one of the most important figures in the history of West Indian literature. An editorial in the *Trinidad Guardian* on July 2, 1932, entitled "From Office-Boy to Politician" captured something of the phenomenal achievement of Albert Raymond Forbes Webber:

> The death of the Hon'ble A. R. F. Webber in British Guiana removes from intercolonial public life one of its outstanding personalities. It would perhaps be too sweeping a generalization to

---

[34]Seymour, "The Literary Adventure of the West Indies," p. 40.

say that Mr. Webber was Demerara [British Guiana], yet he did represent that colony in the field of politics, enterprise and journalism in such a way that Demerara could not be mentioned without mentioning his name, too.

Mr. Webber was born in Tobago, and received part of his education there. Later, he went across to Demerara and began his commercial career as the proverbial office-boy. He ended it as the director of a big commercial company, a member of the Legislative Council and a vice-president of the West Indian Branch of the Institute of Journalism.

For a Tobago boy to go to Demerara and there become famous, is in itself, somewhat unusual. The drift from Tobago in the ordinary way, is toward Trinidad. The attractions of Demerara were, no doubt, somewhat greater in Mr. Webber's young days than they are today but to go and stay there and get on there shows that all things are possible to the man who strikes his own line and does not drift with the tide.

The editorial goes on to call Webber "the finest ambassador among local popular politicians" and argues that Webber's sudden death robbed "the British Americas of a tried and experienced politician at a time in our history when more than ever men of goodwill and ripe judgment [were] needed upon the political stage."

And Webber was colorful. When he was buried, his grave was strewn with red roses, a testimony to his flair for life and the joy he took in living. Therefore, when Z, the anonymous reader, wrote in 1932 that "as he [Webber] lived he surely died / Without the least preamble," he was only partially correct. On December 19, 1929, Webber had already offered his epilogue in a poem that he wrote that captured his essence and, in a way, anticipated the way he would have liked to be remembered when he passed from this life. It is fitting to end a discussion of Webber's life with this untitled poem:

I
No sunset and evening star for me,
Nor twilight and vesper bell.
Let me fall on the raging battle field
With banners gaily flying,

In full throated battle cry
With drums a throb and bugles calling.

II

Give me not a forgotten soldier's fate
To lie a log in a stagnant pool.
'Tis better to fall with ideals high,
Tossing buckler and pennon bright
To those that will seize with exultant cheers
For the crowds on rush to final victory.

III

Though I go with work undone
The world's work is never complete
'Tis better to leave the fields aglow
And a following with falchions flashing bright,
Than to wait and watch the fires grow dim,
And steal away in the still and darkening night.

Georgetown
19th December 1929[35]

S. R. C.

Wellesley, Massachusetts
May 1988

---

[35] *New Daily Chronicle*, December 20, 1929.

Selwyn R. Cudjoe, an associate professor of Black Studies at Wellesley College, is the author of *Resistance and Caribbean Literature* (1980), *Movement of the People* (1983), and *V. S. Naipaul: A Materialist Reading* (1988).

FOREWORD!

My ship this day have I launched without ceremony or apology. As best I could, with my own hands, have I rough-hewn her timbers, then driven them and tightened her seams. Her colours are Vermillion and White and Royal Purple, and to her mast-head are they nailed. She carries neither charter Party nor grappling irons, and, so, must steer her course as even I, the shipwright, have had to steer my own. Fair fortune, give her no mill pond to sail upon; but may she carry hope and cheer to any shipwrecked mariners encountered on the boundless main. May she also weather the gales, and breast waist-high the most tempestuous sea which her course may challenge, while sailing to the West.

A. R. F. W.

Georgetown,
    Demerara.

THOSE THAT BE IN BONDAGE.

CHAPTER FIRST.

" Jim, what are you going to do?"

" Me? Just one other before dinner: but see that he does put more Gin than Angostura."

" My goodness, man, I am not talking about your comfortable self, but of my troubles."

Thus opened the first skirmish, and so spake the fair chatelaine of the House of Walton: Walton the Big man. John James Walton: forty, hale and hearty—Sugar oracle and Planting Attorney of the firm of Rickets & Co., whose vast sugar plantations spread from the Mahaica River on the sea coast of British Guiana to far up the Corentyne River on the Dutch border of the same.

British Guiana! so few do know thee—except colloquially as " Demerara," the home of grocery crystals. Few stay-at-home people realise that you are a vast inheritance—and the only one—of some 100,000 square miles, snugly stowed away on the shoulder of the great South American continent, and the natural highway to the upper reaches of the fertile but turbulent Amazon. But these are things beyond this time of writing, and the scribe must his tale unfold.

To-day but a fringe on the sea coast of this magnificent domain is beneficially occupied, and that almost entirely by the dominating interest of sugar growing. Sugar-growing to give to the world the famous Demerara crystals: something to be proud of and to enjoy; and something to be imitated by rotten German beets, which destroy the bees that venture to feed on its sugar. This is the great work —the original not the imitation—that John James Walton spends his life time on; while he divides up his recreation between his swizzles and the petting of his pretty and affectionate spouse. This is the great work that has created for its well being a system of labour immigration, alike the wonder of economists and the anathema of Cobden school purists, from far-off India, across two oceans to the shores of the sunlit Caribbean.

Walton watched his under-managers and heard their tales of woe: he watched his canes and argued about seedlings; but he saw not the great tragedy that grew at his feet; a tragedy born of that system of immigration which was at once his pride and his worry. A tragedy deep as night, warm as the sun in his cane-fields, and subtle as the centuries whose guile and song have changed but little the hearts of women and the fancies of men.

At the check-up from his wife, recorded above, " Honest John," as he was known to his intimates, sat up. He turned the leaves of his memory back: he weaned himself from the half-pleasant contemplation of a swizzle, ill-made enough to give cause for an honest grumble, well made enough to enjoy; and turned to the wholly unpleasant subject which his wife would hark back to. His mental comment being, " Women are so worrisome." He had hoped to " jolly along " the subject with her until it reached the limbo of forgetfulness, or, at least, the easy toleration he had seen so many others win. Aloud he replied:

" Well, Marion, what would you have me do? I have selected the best-managed estate under me: old Rapfuller is the best planter alive. Things are run so on " Never Out " that the boy will learn more about the great work of agriculture and sugar making there, in six months, than perhaps he would in six years on some of the very much larger estates, where each subject is so very much farther away from the other. The boy, I tell you, is all right! What about the swizzles we spoke about?"

"Swizzles *we* spoke about?" echoed Mrs. Walton, "I did not hear myself in that conversation. Anyway, I'll ring, and then perhaps you will listen to me."

Walton rolled in his Berbice chair: that science of comfort; so called because it was first "practised" in the colony province of that name; being "invented" by an old soldier of India in the evening of his days, which he had spent in Berbice as a planter. "Honest John" took down one leg, from the chair's comfort-giving arm, and put up the other on the far side. He was clearly cornered and had to be rustling up the old arguments—getting the old brain away, as he would put it, from facts to fancies, —so he needs must roost himself in comfort.

"Look here, Jim," she persisted, "You know I am uneasy about the boy. I have not a word against old Rapfuller—except, perhaps, that if he had less of lean and lanky sisters, and more of plump and pleasing nieces, the road might be easier."

"Jim," as she called him in imitation of the fat grey mule which he sometimes rode and which owned to the name of "Big Jim," grumbled that he did not know what the lean and lankiness of "old Raps'" sisters had to do with it, and, moreover, if they had not been lean and lanky, Mrs. Walton might have been someone else's wife. Marion, however, was not taking any such red herring trail, but headed straight back.

"Jim," she espostulated, "you are not giving the matter sufficient consideration. Edwin, I have no doubt, is learning a great deal about planting; but what I am worried about is that he seems to be learning a great deal about other things too."

"Learning! and he from a Public School!" was all that poor Walton could ejaculate; and then he turned to contemplate the rosy sparkle and swallow the tempting swizzle, which by then was by his elbow.

Even that caustic comment could not deter my lady: she knew her mind, and that mind she was determined to speak.

"I have heard," she resumed, "on the best authority, that he is far too much wrapped up with that smooth-skinned, bare-toed East Indian young lady. And I do hate these entanglements when a boy is young."

Walton squirmed piteously, and remembered two bright eyed Eurasian boys, well placed in the local Civil Service, by an invisible hand: carrying another name than his own, but recalling some of the roystering days of his youth, under a dead and gone worthy whose only demand of conduct was that his staff should ride in "for orders"—sober, or seemingly so—under his verandah window in sun or rain at 5.30 every morning. Then, as now, the overseers, or "staff," were fed from the manager's table, because they "cannot be trusted with their board allowance." Outside of that their domestic concerns in those days were their own. Cut off from marriage under this rotten system, they found their wives among their neighbours', or, perhaps, shared another with some complaisant immigrant. For, despite Des Veoux —the civil servant originator of a great Commission on the treatment of immigrants,—some immigants will remain complaisant, and even invite such relationships, for the gain it brings them.

"Well, you know, my dear," the now fairly uncomfortable Jim replied, "the boy is young. Like the measles or teething, with sympathetic management, he will get over it. I'll tell 'Old Raps' to have a quiet look at the situation and keep me posted. And, moreover, I do think after all this dry-earth talk I am entitled to another swizzle before sitting down."

Saying which Jim suited his action to his word and took the reins in his own hands. The proximity of dinner revived his drooping spirits, and soon his cheery voice was heard echoing down the spacious verandah demanding " another rosy," and bespeaking a special " pony one for the missy, yeh!"

During dinner the subject cropped up and up again; and " Honest John " carefully repeated his plans. If things were really going to bad, "old Raps" would know. " Old Raps " was a wonderful man, and one to be depended upon in every respect. If it became absolutely necessary he would remove the boy to some other Estate; or get the indentures of that particular family transferred to some far away plantation. He would send the boy back to England. As " Honest John's " heart expanded under the pressure of good food and wine, and the charming influence of his wife, who made a capital hostess, whether company was present or not, he threw himself with zest into the plans for saving his wife's younger brother: for such, in fact, was the much discussed "boy." So, by the time dinner was through, he and his wife were well at one on the subject nearest her heart. As they rose and adjourned to the verandah, Mrs. Walton heaved one last sigh and gave voice to her hope:

" That the day would soon come when there would be more marriages and giving in marriage among sugar estate overseers; when there would be more of a social and home life among them, in keeping with their own walks in life."

Poor woman; she could not grasp the rotten economic conditions which made her hope a vain one, and condemned all overseers, irrespective of inclination, to a life of enforced celibacy: without the freedom from temptation of the cloister, or the safeguard of vows.

" Honest John's " counterpart of his wife's sigh and voiced hope, was the lighting of a cigar and the registering of a solemn, but, inward wish that she would drop the subject. For, he was resolved that Planting Attorneys had quite enough worry, chasing after seedlings, and agitators, and Immigration Circulars, without being hamstrung by their own wives over overseers and *their* domestic affairs. " It's all these agitators " he finally, and still inwardly, commented with charming inconsistence: as though agitators had anything to do with the subject.

Little did " Honest John " dream that a solution of this self-same question would make easier many of the subjects dealt with in those tantalising circulars. At least, a better class of youths, on the average, would be found among the recruits for the rank and file of the staff; and the few Europeans imported under indenture would less frequently find themselves among the flotsam and jetsam of the city.

That same evening Walton, loyal in every respect to his petted wife, decided that early next morning he would set out on one of his tours of inspection and spend some time at " Never Out " in spying out the land himself.

Meanwhile, Edwin Hamilton, the subject of all the worry, slowly wove the mesh of his fate around himself and a generation ahead, amid the gibes and good natured sallies of his brother" celibates." Young and impressionable, on the threshold of his twenties, a little bookish by heart, he had dabbled in Socialism; he had flirted with Darwin and with Mendel, and had been captivated by Eugenics. Whilst, originally, he had set out in the study of Darwin and Mendel for their influence on the calling which he had been encouraged to make his own, they ended by influencing his whole outlook on the question of sex.

Had Edwin's temperament and learning been carefully measured by some accurate instrument, he would have been the last person to be sent on a sugar estate, where the whole atmosphere reeks of sex and its trying complications. Reared far from Colonial influences he was too prone to think a man " a man for a' that "; and a girl just a girl, without reference to the hue of her skin, or her immediate position in the world's economics. Bred in the atmosphere of an English public school, he had absorbed to a hypersensitive degree its spirit of fairplay, until it obsessed him and dwarfed his every other instinct. With such a spirit, "expediency" has no place, and "the balance of convenience" may as well have been expressed in unknown characters.

The problems of sex on a sugar estate are the problems of that immigration system on which the very existence of the sugar industry, and consequently the whole industrial life of the colony, may be said to be at stake. It is a paradox, but one easily understood by the initiated, that in a world where the female element so largely preponderates, the proportion of females among the 100,000 immigrant population in British Guiana is frightfully meagre. This develops a fierceness of sentiment, on questions of sex, which is horrible to behold. While there are immigrants, like some men of every community, who are complaisant with respect to their wives and daughters for their own gain, those are but the exceptions, and the remainder fiercely resent any poaching of such a nature. Wife slayers are hanged by the score: here a woman may be seen noseless, or, another, with both her hands loppd off, bcause some fiercely jealous lord and master had been wronged. Fierce, perhaps, as much because of the wrong that has been done him, as because of the difficulty with which he is faced in filling her place, with that freedom of choice, that would obtain under less strained conditions of proportion.

Add to all of this that other disturbing factor, thought of by Mrs. Walton as the absence of social life among overseers—the lords of the pay, comfort and very existence of the immigrants. These overseers, barracked under a most unholy system, under conditions worse than soldiering, what wonder they deteriorate in mind, morals and manners. Denied the soldier's right to married privileges and quarters, they must borrow or steal a wife. If the borrowed or stolen wife is the property of an immigrant, discovery means serious disaster; this, as is inevitable with human nature, supplyng the element of danger and romance that make an irresistible appeal to adventurous spirits.

Then again, an overseer may not quit the confines of his plantation, or entertain any friends on it to lunch or dinner, until he has obtained the sanction of his manager, to whom every detail, and even, possibly, every reason has to be stated. Thus, denied mastership of his table, board or leisure, it is little wonder if the overseer finds scope for the practice of the most clamant instinct of the human race on underlings and immigrants.

Such in brief are the conditions which make sex, and the complications arising from the attempt to force celibacy on overseers, such a burning immigration question.

Such was the atmosphere in which Edwin Hamilton found himself at twenty-two—lord of his hours of meditation, but not of his physical liberty; lord of the liberty of scores of immigrants, but not of his own. The very readiness with which " Old Raps " gave him leave to " quit boundaries," was in itself an embarrassment; for less favoured and less deserving ones were not slow to chaff him about his favoured relationship, and the privileges it brought.

Though no saint or milksop, Edwin was temperamentally unfitted for the post-prandial gatherings at overseers' quarters, which had for their chief object the decanting of gin. As a consequence, he was more and more thrown back on his books, and on his dangerous wanderings in ethics.

True to his promise, John James Walton was on the spot next morning; when, after patiently listening to " old Raps' " varied outbursts, and running commentaries on everything and every person, from the Brussels Convention to Biology; and from the Governor to the grooms, he cautiously veered round to " the boy."

" Old Raps " was doubtful and dutiful. The boy was good. The boy was always at orders. The boy would do: but those damned books were making a fool of him. He, " old Raps," was quite against drink as the " boss " knew—he always retained the affectionate name, of the old days, for Walton,—but if somebody would bring

IN BONDAGE.

the boy to dinner drunk once only, he would feel more sure of him.

The " boss " did not agree. He hoped the boy would remain straight. He had seen that "once" drunk at dinner, develop so disastrously, so many times, that he hoped " old Raps " would get proof of the boy's sanity in some other direction. He had no doubt that Edwin wanted bringing out in some way, and he would try to get him in town oftener.

" But the fact is, old man," he added, " the boy is just a little afraid of me, and never seems comfortable even in town when I am in the house."

" Well, you know boss," ventured " old Raps " " that's the discipline of the place: we have to break them all in early "

" Yes, I know," replied the " Big Man," but I like the boy, and his sister is devilish fond of him. What I am really anxious about," he added after a pause, " is this Afridi's daughter."

" Boss, to tell you the truth, I don't think his planting career will come to an end over that girl: but his social life may."

Walton put down his swizzle untasted. They had just reached the first rung of the ladder leading to breakfast, and Walton had never yet been known to set down a swizzle untasted under similar circumstances. Then he sat upright. A more fiery, and, it might be added, wiry man would have emptied the chair of himself and viciously swear. " Honest John," deliberate to a fault, replaced his untasted swizzle on the tray, sat upright, and subconsciously pinched himself to be sure he was awake. He then jerked out:

" What the devil do you mean?"

He did not mean to startle old Rapfuller, neither could he; and he could no more stop the old man, once started going, than he could stop one of his triples, as they spun his glorified crystals, by looking at it.

"Boss, I will just here say that the boy is not going to be rounded up in any illicit tangle with the girl, such as will bring his planting career to a stop. If he does do anything he will marry her, sudden like, before any of us are alive to his plan."

Saying which he reached over for the big man's swizzle, and breaking into the more friendly creolese, said:

"Boss, le' me brew dat swizzle up again fo' you."

So forceful is the action of suggestion that even Europeans, long resident in the tropics, will occasionally break into the not unmusical broken English of the creole.

The big man drank 'dat swizzle'; and, then with a great deal of emphasis said:

"Raps, I will be damned if he will! At least, the boy is fond of his sister, and will remember her feelings."

"But he can't marry her, boss," interrupted old Raps.

"Don't be silly old man, and don't try to be witty. It doesn't suit your grey hairs. I allow your joke, but still believe that he thinks too much of his sister to make such a devilish mistake. I think you must be mistaken. Anyway, I am glad nothing is wrong as yet. It would be a pity to have his career ruined."

It must be here explained, for the reader's information, that where Indians are under indenture, any planter found guilty of illicit intercourse with an East Indian, whether the Indian be free or bound, married or single, jeopardises his situation and makes himself liable to be perpetually banned from being employed on any plantation employing indentured immigrants. This policy, though it fell into abuse in some generations is to-day being rigidly enforced.

"Boss," answered old Raps, "I am sorry, and hope I am mistaken; but you know when old Raps is done thinking a thing out he is never far wrong. That boy Hamilton may be fond of his sister: he may be afraid of you; but mark me, neither of you is in control of him any longer. I have studied him; and I have tried the bit in his mouth, and he don't take it, that's all."

"I admit the soundness of your judgment in many things," said Walton, "but I should like to hear a little more detail before I decide what to do. On what do you base your conclusions?"

"First," replied old Rapfuller, "because if anything were really wrong I should have had a dozen or two informers on hand already. As you know, they are a plentiful breed, and always anticipate events well ahead. Secondly, the boy's visits to that yard are always timed to meet the girl's father at home. Thirdly, the father is very frequently in Hamilton's room: they seem to have struck up a queer friendship betwen them. And, lastly, the girl herself does not seem to mix freely with her own 'matties,' male or female."

"Your ground is not as strong as I thought it was, old man. Then, you have heard nothing from the boy himself over this ridiculous marriage proposition?"

"No, sir, and, I say again, I hope I am wrong. Old Singh, you see, is a type by himself. I often wonder how he became an immigrant; he is not very communicative, but it seems that he came, or was driven out, of some up-country Indian Native State and crossed 'the big pawnee' either in pique or as an act of safety. He does not put on any airs, but the other immigrants seem to respect him as a sort of pundit; and probably he appeals to some sense of chivalry in Hamilton, which will surely lead to anywhere if the boy is really moony on the girl."

"I tell you what," at last Walton summed up, "that old Afridi and his girl have got to go. I shall immediately see the 'big Crosby' on my arrival in town, and work the oracle: then I'll put my wife on the boy."

"Crosby" represented everything by way of immigration to the planter; and everything itself to the immigrant. There is a certain pathos attached to the rendering of this

Official's title. Officially, the department charged with the welfare of the immigrants is the Immigration Department; its head is the Immigration Agent-General, and his outlying representatives are Immigration Agents; but throughout the length and breadth of the land the whole is grouped under the generic title of "Crosby." The head of all is "the big Crosby," and his agents "little Crosbys": and wherefore? It is because at one time in the long ago there lived an Immigration Agent-General who was a tower of strength and righteousness to the immigrants, and his name was Crosby: a veritable protector of immigrants was he. Interred in some forgotten corner of a village churchyard, his virtues uncarved in stone and untold in monumental marble, his memory is carried as a living factor in the hearts of the people. So shall it live forever, as long as there remains a solitary immigrant in a land of exile.

CHAPTER SECOND.

As has been seen by the previous chapter, the rough conclusions of old Rapfuller had not been without their influence on Walton., or, as he was known on that Estate, " J. J. W." It is sometimes a peculiarity that men in Walton's position accumulate quite a number of soubriquets, each differing in familiarity or affection according to the giver. To hs wife and some of her lady friends he was " big Jim ": to some of his associates, " Honest John ": to his subordinates, " the Big Man," " J. J." or " J. J. W." and to some others who laid a different sort of claim, just " the Boss." Among these latter, as we have seen, was Rapfuller. Walton had long grown accustomed to pay a lot of heed to the rough and ready conclusions of " old Raps"; and it is surprising how influence of this kind from a subordinate entendrils itself around a man's heart until it reaches even unto the most intimate channels. In this case it had been no exception and the homely words of the older man had travelled from the understanding to the heart of the younger.

That day " The Big Man " had been uncomfortable: " The Big Man " had been ill at ease. As he travelled from one Estate to the other, he revolved and re-revolved the subject in his mind. He clearly looked for a bad half-an-hour from his wife, what time he had to report "old Rap's" conclusions to her: for from force of example she had also grown to pay great heed to the words of the older man. Nevertheless, he had decided to face it like a man, and get done with it as soon as possible.

Two days later Walton, at his wife's breakfast table, pitched headlong into his story. Mrs. Walton, wise in her generation, had said not a word on the subject to her lord and master, since his return; for she had learnt, what so few women seem to know, that the easeist way to freeze a confidence was to "nag" into a subject before the confessor is ready to open up.

"Marion," he said, "I am afraid old Rapfuller has given me some thought over the boy; but, worse than all, he thinks the danger lies in marriage, rather than illicit relationship."

At this Marion was too aghast to speak immediately, and could only gasp "Marriage" in a tone which clearly heralded the close approach of tears.

"Well," cheeried her lord, "I don't think you should take it on too seriously. In the first place I don't agree with Rapfuller; and, in the second, if things are really taking that guise they should lend themselves very much better to our plans than otherwise. You can prevent a marriage faster than you can stop illicit intercourse." After which oracular announcement, he added: "And you can, no doubt, do something towards interesting him in someone else, as a counter irritant." This last with some feeble attempt at wit.

By now Marion had recovered her senses somewhat, and feebly suggested that "the boy" should be sent back to England. However that suggestion was soon abandoned; chiefly because it would mean closing his career as a planter; and, next, it would be necessary to get Edwin's acquiescence, which would in itself be a very doubtful proposition.

At last it was resolved that Walton should proceed with his plans for the removal of the old Afridi and his family from "Never Out"; and that Marion should do her share by way of throwing her young brother among the young and eligible maidens of the capital and cathedral city of Georgetown.

Back once more in good humour with the world and himself, Walton ventured the remark that if he had so much trouble with her young brother, the Lord only knew what was in store for him when their own toddling youngster left his petticoats and nursery rhymes behind. "I however beg to state," he added, "that I am going to have more say than you in his upbringing; and I am not going to let you apron-string him, as you are determined to do the boy." But his wife was too engrossed in her plans to pay any heed to his banter, or his threats.

True to his word, "Honest John," bon vivant and sugar king, soon had the departmental machinery on the move for the removal from "Pln. Never Out" of Singh, his wife, and his daughter. No offence was alleged, none had to be proved: simply that it was the will of "the big Crosby.' The immigrants, since their enforced sojourn in this far-away land, have created out of nothing, but their thews and sinews, a rice industry which feeds the whole country and the neighbouring islands in the Caribbean. Every immigrant of any thrift or industry—and which is not—has his rice bed. When an order such as this comes, rice beds must be abandoned, or sold for what they could fetch: and what ever does a forced sale realize? The humble home such as may have been made, with its kitchen garden and feeble conveniences, must be left behind. Kith and kin, shipmates of the long lonely voyage of "an hundred days" from far away India, friends and associations, must all be said goodbye to: and why? simply because it was "the big Crosby's will."

The move soon got noised ahead, as the will of the "big Crosby," but Singh, the wily old Afridi was not to be deceived: inside his skin he knew and felt the reason, but he muttered that the will of Allah was stronger than the will of "the big Crosby." And evidently, Sngh was no stranger to these forced marches. The wife of his fortunes, who, it was said, was not the mother of his daughter, was loud in her vociferations, but she was quickly silenced. Meanwhile, certain formalities had to be fulfilled before executive force could be given to the order, and events moved rapidly in the interval.

With Marion Walton also to think was to act, and she forthwith set about plans for a "nice little dance," at which she would set out all that was fair and loveliest to divert her brother's attention from his romantic Asiatic attachment.

Hurried notes here and there soon filled her morning room with a goodly number of Georgetown matrons and misses; ostensibly to lunch, but really to discuss dates and other etcetera of the dance that Mrs. Walton had informed them she desired to give, as "there had been so few of late," and she had been "somewhat remiss in doing her share," etc.

With such a congregation of the elect it did not take long to fix things: dates were soon decided, programmes brought into being, and invitations lists scrutinized again and again. All wondered that Mrs. Walton should include the names of two colonial daughters of Portugal, whose forebears had hailed from the lovely mid-Atlantic island of Madeira; and by careful small trading, thrift and husbandry had left a fortune of no mean dimensions: this had perhaps entitled the daughters to, but had never hitherto won for them, a place on the visiting lists of the elect, such as Mrs. Walton proposed now to confer. None, however, ventured to remark; as, after all, it was Mrs. Walton's house, and Mrs. Walton's party. Mrs. Walton, however, had her reasons and those were private: She knew quite as well as anybody else that their inclusion was unwarrantable under the canons of ordinary visiting lists; but she also knew that their charms were far and beyond any to be found among the girls of the elect. The more than hint of oriental beauty which marked those sisters, she also hoped, would appeal to that taste which was apparently developing in Edwin; and, moreover, she was barring no weapon in her fight for supemacy against the " little baretoed " East Indian.

Days passed, during which Walton eventually caught the enthusiasm of his wife and threw himself heart and soul into all her plans for the coming event. No expense was to be spared, was his order. Carpenters were called in and decorators set to work. Alas, poor Marion! She saw her charming informal little dance blossoming into a great function by the house of Walton. Her frantic protests were of little avail. " Honest John " pleaded that he could not help himself; it had got talked about: His Excellency the Governor had mentioned it to him; and he should not wonder if he signified his intention to be present. And, as the Louisiana Sugar Commissioners would be in Georgetown that week, he thought that they would be bound to extend an invitation to them.

Thus Marion, quite distracted, saw herself being gradually transformed from something between a fairy Godmother and a match-making sister into a straight-laced hostess at a brilliant society function.

What philosopher of current events will venture to say whether it is a distinct preordination of things which orders certain currents to flow to that end; or, whether it is a mere chance happening, quite free of predestination, which sets the currents that eventually disperse to the East or the West, with equal impartiality. In other words which is cause and which effect? Perhaps, after all, it is a lack of human perception which imposes failure or nullity on given policies or precautions and not any illimitable predestination; else were man's free will an empty dream. Here, at least, we see that Mrs. Walton may well have foreseen, after her admitted neglect of similar functions, that she could not hope to start in, from her social eminence, with anything like a "small informal party," without giving offence in too many quarters to be slightingly thought of, or lightly ignored.

His Excellency, a hoary old bachelor, did signify his intention to be present, and with him General Funston, from Jamaica, inspecting the Local Forces. With the latter was his daughter, who was reputed to be very beautiful, and as high spirited. Current gossip credited her with never missing a dance which it was practicable for her to attend; and, to give his young guest pleasure, no doubt, decided His Excellency in extending his semi-Vice Regal patronage to the function. General Funston's daughter had carried many of her father's glittering A.D.C.'s to trouble; but her heart remained her own; and her father was as proud, as sure of her.

The night came at last; and there was nothing to be desired in the way of success—save to Marion's own little plans. As a hostess, she was resplendent: her plump alabaster arms, glittering under countless lights, were a sight to make men envious of Walton. Her ample bosom, swelling into graceful curves, would have awakened the enthusiasm of Canova; and her head, well poised with the grace of a silver pheasant, carried its wealth of hair as regally as a diadem. The colour and texture of Marion Walton's hair, her friends declared, defied description. It was wavy and of that sheen of raven so rarely met in pure-blooded Europeans, yet often found in colonial families— a sure index of some negro-blooded ancestor. Of a type which in old Colonial days would have been called Octoroon or Quadroon, and possibly carried some social ostracism if known, these women, in grace and loveliness, surpass their pure-blooded sisters by streets. To-day they all pass for white, and none are the worse or the wiser for it.

General Funston's daughter herself could trace her ancestry with ease to a manumitted slave of mixed blood; and, this ancestry may, peradventure, have accounted for her inordinate love of dancing; for these children of mixed blood are emotional to an extreme degree. Yet, with it all, in this assembly of fair women she glittered and shone like a star among the best of them. The lustre and sparkle of her eyes had been many a man's undoing, and her charm and grace had been household words on whatever station her war-scarred father had served. For, losing her mother at an early age, she had stood by him and marched with every beat of drum from country to country, and from field base to field base.

Nor was Marion Walton any exception to the beauty and grace of this type of woman. Few men could look on her unmoved. What wonder if she found herself placed perpetually amidst a cavalcade of devoted admirers. Walton being one of those good natured men who are pleased, not wounded, by the admiration excited by their wives.

Under such circumstances what time could she find to devote to her brother's match-making? She did her best, and introduced him here and there: but of what avail? Her husband was out of the running as an ally to her: his mere presence in " the boy's " company being enough to depress the atmosphere; and, wise man, he stayed out.

One of poor Marion's " lovely sisters " had been early monopolised by the gay and glittering A.D.C. to His Excellency the Governor; and his fate was later sealed with great satisfaction to the high contracting parties, but a good deal less to " the gods " of the upper circle. Even rumoured was it that he had earned the Governor's displeasure: and, certainly, his job knew him no more, after a little while. The other sister caught hard on with a youthful Barrister-at-Law, who, fresh from his Inn and the winning of his first laurels in the local Courts, lost his heart and liberty to Mrs. Walton's second weapon; and, bold buccaneer that he was, he stood not upon the order of his dancing, so left his fair partner little chance to further their hostess's schemes.

Meanwhile Edwin Hamilton was of the throng yet " out of it." Rusty in his dancing; temperamentally unsuited to frivolities, he was poor company at best to the majority of boys and girls. Lacking intimacy with most of the former, Edwin felt almost in a state of boycott; chaperones regarded him as a " penniless overseer " with none of the possibilities of equally penniless Civil Servants, or youths of commerce, regarded from a matrimonial standpoint. Such being the unfair conditions under which overseers exist and move and have their being, that half of their wages are docketted and paid over to their managers, as board allowance, against which the overseer has neither voice nor right to be heard. By the time an overseer has spent the morning of his days, and reached a management, his economic status has changed visibly; he in turn preys on other overseers, and he may then marry or be sought in marriage. But then, as likely as not, he has reached the sere and yellow time of life and has also formed " connections " which cannot be lightly thrown off; connections which accommodated themselves to the status of his " morning," but of a class which no self-respecting chaperone can regard but with disgust. Therefore, on the whole, is it voted that overseers as a class must be turned down. Little cause for comment is it then, that most that is best and cleanest, in intellect and capacity, in young colonial life carefully eschew the calling of a planter; and the colony and the " profession " are poorer accordingly.

What wonder then that before the night was half started Edwin was heartily sick of it all. His heart did beat a fraction or two faster when General Funston's daughter was borne past him by her cavalcade of admirers, and her glittering eyes rested on him for more than a moment. Her quick sense of perception had readily noted the lonely pensive stranger within the gates; and her tender heart had gone out to him in sympathy. Her glance must have conveyed it all, for Edwin felt a burning desire to get near her. Then, as he looked after her and noted the group of men around the brilliant colonial, a bitterness seized him: full throated and oppressive; and he sighed for the life of the city; for fair women, and intellectual men, who could think of something beyond the varying degrees of emptiness of a Gin flask, or the wilful obstinacy of a riding mule. He saw hanging on the sweep of Miss Funston's trailing drapery a junior class clerk of the Civil Service, of good family: but neither family nor income, if his board allowance were considered, one whit better than his own; he saw a young Inspector of the semi-military police, all too conscious of his spurs: with an income of as microscopic a nature as his own; then a young medico with a ditto ditto income, and a high Church dignatary with a large and ample income, but a ditto ditto wife. In a second it all passed: longing, and bitterness, and all; as he thought of Mendel and Quelch—as yet unknown much beyond the confines of Demerara plantations—; of Darwin and the natural selection of species: and, inevitably, of Bibi the fair skinned daughter of the Afridi immigrant: her indeed of whom his sister thought and spoke, as the "little bare-toed immigrant." Why he should think of her at that stage, he gave little heed; because, certainly, Rapfuller's conclusions about matrimony had not yet taken form in Edwin's mind. Then, last of all, he thought of his sister: that sister who to him had been as a little mother; and as he thought, she gave being to his thoughts, and appeared in the flesh before him; having given temporary slip to her crowd of admirers.

"Well, boy," she greeted "how are you enjoying yourself and what are you doing?"

"Quite a crowd of questions, Sis," he replied, "Tell you the truth, I was never great on these city functions; and, if I had not received a hint from 'old Raps' that 'J. J.' would have been annoyed, I assuredly had backed out of your great fight."

"Oh, Edwin," she cried, "I do wish you would give up your bizarre way of thinking of things," this with a sharp *double entendre*, pointed one way at the Afridi's daughter; "This thing is not a fight, even though I may be a fright."

"No, no, you are not that," gallantly replied her brother, who carried devotion and worship of his sister to extremes, "but I do wish I was out of it all: fight, plight, or fright; I only feel like flight."

"Nonsense," cried his sister, "you must dance. Will you not dance if I get you a partner?"

"Dance," he answered mischievously, "oh yes, I will dance: if I stood a chance of getting one with General Funston's daughter."

"Of all the cheek!" was all Marion could gasp. Then she added. "Why, boy, you should have got in that game very early if you wanted a dance with her. Anyway, I will see what I can do with one of her partners."

"Oh, don't, don't," cried Edwin, "I am not nearly serious."

But his sister was off and away, intent on her thoughts and intentions. "The idea," thought she, "good intentioned as Eloise is, she has nearly broken many a man's heart: still, if he falls in love with her, time will be gained, at least."

Now General Funston's daughter was as good as she was charming, and when Major Smith, the Deputy Inspector-General of the aforementioned military police, and devoted knight errant of Mrs. Walton, asked that young lady to permit him to provide a substitute for himself in the person of young Hamilton, her hostess' brother, as he, the D.I.G., had been suddenly called to certain departmental matters, she readily agreed, and felt pleased in the idea of the pensive-browed boy opening his heart to a little of the music.

Oh Puck, you spirit of mischief, standing by and twirling your thumbs, you must have shrieked with delight and cried again: "What fools these mortals be." That dance forged another link in the long chain of tragedy.

Let us bridge the intervening dances, and suffice it to say that Edwin was nervous to a degree, when Major Smith led him to the glittering presence. When the strains of the waltz floated through the room and Eloise Funston laid her finger tips within his arm, a flood as of mighty waters rushed to his brain, beat at his ears and temples, and then his heart stood still. With scarcely growing consciousness he placed his arms around her supple waist and joined the throng of whirling dancers. Lack of practice: the touch of a charming woman, whom he more than admired, close to his bosom, all went to upset him, made him ill at ease, and put him out of step. Never had he waltzed so miserably in all his life; not even in the most gauche days of his boyhood. With charming manners his partner sought to set him more at ease with himself; as she readily felt that his blunders were chiefly due to extreme nervousness. She ventured the opinion that the crowded room did not lend itself to perfect dancing, and, later, that the band occassionally seemed to lose all count of time; but the kinder she became the worse he grew. He knew only too well that the room was not uncomfortably crowded, and that the perfectly trained band was too well conducted to lose count of time; and, worse, that her excuses were signs and symptoms of her consciousness of his defects. Soon their waltzing became nothing but a travesty, and a procession of sorrow. Fortunately, Marion, who had watched the pair cautiously, saw the trend of affairs and, conveying a hint to the band, brought the waltz to an untimely but welcome end, at least as far as two of the dancers were concerned.

Then Edwin fled: fled as though he carried the brand of Cain upon his brow: vowing by all the Gods of his fathers that never another Georgetown function would see him again. Marion sought him in vain: and was left to explain his early absence to her husband as best she might. For, no one else missed him, except Eloise Funston: she turned at every passing step to welcome the " pensive browed boy;" but he was instead riding hard for 'Never Out.' For some strange unexplained reason Eloise enquired not for her partner, but looked in silence for him that cameth not.

When Marion, after the departure of the last guest, found herself alone with her lord she told him, and he laughed hugely. Laughed as much to see how little progress Marion had made with her matchmaking, as because he also remembered a similar plight of his own in the long ago; but he said nothing, for the other actor had not been Marion, but someone of whom she was jealous to that day.

"Marion," he said finally, "You will have to get after 'the boy' again, because you have neither netted nor apron-stringed him."

And Marion heaved a sigh of agreement and withdrew.

CHAPTER THIRD.

It is not to be supposed that a girl like Bibi could live on any sugar plantation without creating a great deal of dissension. Nor did she: her charms were too manifest to the most casual observer. The soft clear tint of her skin proclaimed her parentage to be far beyond that of the average East Indian immigrant, and her plump little form was an additional cause for the unrest among the male element of Pln. " Never Out." Her bold luminous eyes and strong Caucasian features had brought many men to her feet with all manner of proposals. For, no matter what may be written to the contrary of the sexual abuses under the present system of Emigration from India to the British Colonies, the fact remains that a woman, under any circumstances, can remain mistress of herself. True it may be that crooked proposals may carry many advantages to the woman, and possibly to all of her connections: but that is also true in more or less degree in every walk of life. But, while it is quite true that this question of sex relations between the various grades of labour is a very vexed one, there is no such question as forced relations, such as may be imagined under any aggravated system of White Slave Traffic.

This Afridi's daughter, it could be said with accuracy, had received offers of one kind or another from practically every able-bodied male on her own plantation—with the exception of Edwin Hamilton—and many from neighbouring plantations. Some of her refusals were curt and scornful: some resolved themselves into passages of wit and badinage with the proposers; all according to their respective stations. But all bore the same impress of finality, and all took their refusal with more or less grace, except Abdool Karim, a handsome type of his species, who occupied a position of driver on Pln. " Never Out." Karim was hot-headed and educated above his station. It was even said of him that he indulged in some of the fancies of advanced Indian Socialism, and, distasteful as this was to the Estate authorities, they had already given him his rating as a driver, and it was not deemed politic to disrate him, until they had a more serviceable peg to hang a reason on. He alone of all the rejected suitors put in words the general feeling of all, and that was, that she was favoured of the Sahib Hamilton, hence her stubborn refusal of all overtures. Indeed the temper of his metal and his intense jealousy led him to make accusations that were wholly unwarranted. He clothed possibilities with the bitterness of fact, and boldly accused her of living in hidden relationship with Edwin.

The warrior spirit of generations of Afridis, which coursed through her father's veins sprang into being in the daughter's. Without a moment's warning Bibi flew at the throat of her accuser and before Karim had time to recover he was stretched full length on the earthen floor of the little hut which old Singh had made his home. There could be little doubt about the ultimate outcome of such a struggle; but old Singh, arriving on the scene immediately, put an end to what must have otherwise terminated very disastrously for the woman: for these primitive natures exhibit none of the chivalry which is usually found in more developed minds, where a struggle with a woman is concerned; Karim thereupon took his departure, swearing vengeance on Edwin —not the woman. This occurrence took place quite a

IN BONDAGE. 27

week before the dance referred to in the previous chapter, and was common property all over the estate; clothed in every variety of fantastic detail. Those who know the East Indian character will readily realize how prone they are to romance around every conceivable subject. Indeed it may be said that ' to lie ' is the East Indian immigrant's vital breath. But when it is considered that he is the child of centuries of tyranny and oppression: when it is remembered that lying and chicanery are perhaps the only weapons available to the defenceless and the bitterly oppressed; we may perhaps spare a tear for this failing of his race.

Through all these wars and rumours of wars, Edwin, it might be said, heard of them least of all. His handsome pensive face stilled the idle jest, and froze the would be spoken confidence, at its source. And, " The Ameer," as the old Afridi was generally known, half in respect and half in chaff, who alone may have ventured on the subject, had pledged himself and daughter to secrecy: at least as far as Edwin was concerned.

Like similar cases in every walk of life, Edwin was alone blind to his favour with the " little bare-toed " Immigrant. While the whole plantation voted that he had but to ask to receive: and some even affected to believe the bitter accusations of Karim, Edwin alone remained diffident, and, indeed, careless of prowess in that direction. Thus his relationship with the cause of all this trouble and unrest had never progressed beyond the casual friendship so accurately stated by old Rapfuller.

Edwin, as a matter of fact, even abhorred the loose relationships practised all around him by his fellow overseers, despite Immigration circulars and all the dangers incidental to flouting them. It must not be assumed, however, that Edwin gave no thought to the fair Afridi; but never had he yet considered her either with a view to irregular association, or yet of matrimony. Many a night had he thought how ill-suited every immigrant on the Estate was to become the husband of this refined girl of the hills;

for refined she was, even though she was bare-toed and worked like Ruth in the fields. When once the evil in him had whispered to try his fortune with her in an irregular association, his innate chivalry, and the thought of her father's humble dignity, stopped him; and finally he put the thought from him in the firm belief that she would have none of it; even though he made the proposal ever so temptingly. When on another occasion some imp of himself, as he called it, had hinted to him to marry the girl boldly, he had laughingly put the thought from him with the mental comment that "he was not quite prepared to make a fool of himself." If, thought he, they were thousands of miles away from his relations or associations; or in the bosom of some impenetrable jungle or mountain fastness, where he could live and die unknown, then perhaps he could think of a worse fate than Bibi as a wife. But in British Guiana, with his immediate associations: with his sister, and his close "sense" of local feeling on the subject of "colour" marriages, the idea could not be entertained.

When he had heard of the rumoured removal, of "The Ameer" and his daughter from 'Never Out,' Edwin did so with mixed feelings. Sometimes he would rejoice and be glad of heart, for it would solve in one way his interest in the daughter by cutting off all intercourse between them. At another he would be sorrowful, and sad of heart: he reasoned with himself that he was fervently sorry for the old man; and thereto he traced his sorrow. For the old man it meant new associations: new friends to be made, and only God knew what sort of a task-master for his daughter. As the old man said, frequently, for himself it did not matter, for he had been accustomed to much: but at least at "Never Out" he had never had occasion to complain about the treatment of his daughter; and she was the apple of his eye and as the breath to his nostrils. Later on, again, Edwin would hope that other counsels would prevail against the threatened removal, for rumours and agitators had been busy, and the temper of the immigrants had grown ugly on the subject.

Nor had Abdool Karim been idle during these days; he secretly hoped that time would be his successful ally, and consequently viewed with grave apprehension the removal of the "Ameer" and his daughter to far beyond his reach. Still as a 'driver' on the Estate he had to preach his doctrines with care and caution, lest the authorities should gather wind of his machinations, and dismiss him from his lucrative employment—lucrative in more ways than one: for to prey upon the labourers under them is the perquisite of the 'driver.' All must pay tribute for favours past or to come: the men must pay with silver, or service, and the women in pain and person: and so has it been for generations.

Karim, to serve his ends, did not hesitate to advance it, as secretly as he could, that transfers were being invented to prevent the immigrants from acquiring independence; for sacrifices of provision beds and even of stock have to be made at each transfer. "The Ameer" had provision beds and his industry and influence had excited the envy of the Sahibs. Went he also further and, with the native chicanery of his race, completely reversed his fomrer accusation against Edwin and "The Ameer's" daughter. Now he alleged that this particular removal was also influenced by the Sahib Hamilton who had worked it through his relationship with the "big Sahib" (Walton) in order to spite "The Ameer," because his daughter would not agree to his improper advances.

All these doctrines did he advance, as suited the temper of his immediate hearers, and neither were they without result. There are no people so easily inflamed as the ignorant, and none so susceptible to the teachings of a prophet as those in an alien country or serving under bondage. Such then was the state of affairs and feeling on Pln "Never Out" on the afternoon of the day on which Edwin left the Estate, and set out to face the music and tread the mill at his sister's City fight.

When Edwin fled at mid-night from the ball-room of his sister's handsome city residence he had but one thought —to get as far as ever he could from Georgetown and all it held, and that immediately. The first thing that caught his eye, as he emerged from the lower verandah was a motor bicycle: evidently left there by one of the revellers who had apparently selected that method of making an early exit and getting to his destination, probably some distance away, without much trouble. Edwin stood not on the order of the proprieties, for in the frame of mind in which he found himself he would have, without hesitation, appropriated the war chariot of Julius Caesar himself; so it did not take him long to appropriate that lonely motor bicycle and head it for "Never Out."

Opening his valve and throttle to the full, he just raced out of the City. Fortunately, at that time of night, traffic in Georgetown had practically ceased, and Edwin reached the East Coast road without misadventure from his reckless riding. The violent exercise of the motor and the need for alert attention soon called Edwin from his obsession back to earth, and, as he cleared the suburbs of the city of his disgrace, as he put it, he slowed down to a more even pace and gave rein to his thoughts.

After all, thought he, an overseer was utterly out of place in the social world: he had not felt so uncomfortable as he did that night, even long before he danced with Eloise Funston, for a mighty long time. He confessed to having felt himself a distinct species from every other fellow in the room. There were some half-a-dozen fellows that he had chummed it with in their boyhood days, yet they had been as far from him as any of the others. There were two rollicking fine girls with whom he had come back on the Mail Steamer from England. As he remembered the joyous time they all three had experienced at sea, his heart turned to bitterness when he remembered how coldly they had taken his advances that night, what time he sought to take up the camaraderie in which they had all parted a year ago. Poor Edwin! He saw that all around him there were economic notice boards warning all and sundry that as a social factor, either in marriage possibilities or entertaining probabilities—except with an occasional bunch of swizzles—his class was out of it.

Soon his thoughts wandered to matrimony and he wondered how, even were his financial prospects changed, could he think of attempting to transplant one or any of those " foreign species " to his own atmosphere. He concluded that it would be cruelty to the " foreign species," as well as to himself. Inevitably at this stage, his train of thought led him to Bibi. How vastly different, in every particular, to the " species " he had just run from. Against the bold costumes of the dancers, as shown in every phase that night, he thought of the graceful simple folds of the East Indian's: so scanty, yet modestly covering her literally from her head to her heels. He thought of the artificial grins and high-pitched voices of the ball-room, and compared them with the frank and heart-to-heart laugh of the fair Afridi, and her musical lisping of " the Sahib Hamilton." " In the name of God," he gasped aloud, " Why cannot one do as he likes." Certainly he had again rejected the suggestion which had returned to him with a definite insistence; but he did so now less contemptuously than he had ever done before. Indeed it may be questioned whether he had, on this occasion, rejected the suggestion, or merely dismissed the subject. It so fell out that, about the time when he rejected the suggestion, or dismissed the subject, as the reader wills, he had reached the confines of the Estate and was heading it straight for his quarters, when he noticed that some of the labourers' ranges seemed to be keeping rather late hours, as evidenced by the moving lights. Intent however on picking his way along the road, ill lit and shaded by overhanging trees, he gave not another thought to the subject but dismissed it without even mental comment.

On reaching the verandah of his own quarters, however, he made more than mental comment; for there did he see the living embodiment of his own most recent thoughts: the grave faced old Afridi and his fair skinned daughter! Accustomed to many things, and to rumours of yet more, this " took some beating " : he nevertheless cloaked his surprise in a cheerful " good-night," and asked them to be seated. He thereupon hunted from its place a pitcher of milk and drew himself a glass. A supply of milk he always kept handy, but this glass he drew and proceeded to drink as much because he was thirsty as to gain time for thought. Had the old man gone daft with his troubles, or—unthinkable—had he fallen so low that he would imitate the custom of many, and had brought his daughter to traffic for some concession, privilege or favour. The fear was bitter and gave him a sensation of nausea. Could she have consented, or had the object of the mission, if such it were, been disguised from her. Could he under any circumstances turn them loose and drive them, perhaps, to some less scrupulous trafficker. "My God," he commented under his breath, " what a night of horrors " and then he turned to face his visitors.

"Well, old man, " he began, " you are out late tonight. What has gone wrong? Driver giving your house to somebody else? or what?"

"Sahib," replied the old man, "I have waited for your return for many hours." His voice was musical and he spoke with a correctness of diction that was remarkable. "The driver will indeed give my house to another man, for the "big Crosby" has spoken, and the paper has arrived which drives me away. The Sahib, my friend, will know how bitter it is that I leave everything. My cow and kine can walk the journey with me, but my rice field that I worked long and patiently upon, when the rains came not, must I leave; and my provision bed must I also forsake. I have done nothing, oh Sahib, my friend, yet when I ask why am I driven away to whither I may not choose,

I am told merely it is the "big Crosby's" will, against which nothing can prevail."

Edwin listened patiently to the old man's tale of woe, then he answered with his heart yearning in two opposite directions: "But old man, perhaps all will be for the best. You will make new friends, and perhaps better ones, at the new place. And then what can I do? As you rightly say, against the will of the Big Crosby who can prevail?" Then answered the wily old Afridi: "Against the will of the big Crosby nought can prevail. But the big Crosby: he the Lord of all, can be influenced. The very big Sahib is in favour with the big Crosby and a word spoken is a word of weight: you Sahib, my friend, are in favour much with the very big Sahib, for she of your blood comforts him, and is the light of his household, therefore a good word from you turneth away wrath. For this have I waited these many hours, until my daughter, weary of waiting came to seek me."

"Old man," gently urged Edwin, "Blood relations are not always in friendship, and neither are those whose ties are marriage. I fear thatI could help you little in the direction you desire. I will however see to it that you suffer very little, if at all, for your rice and provision beds."

Then the old Afridi spake again: "Sahib," he said, "All the treasure I have is my daughter. Cows can I buy again with the silver of my labour. Rice fields can I plant again with the sinews of my arms, but she is the jewel of my eye, and the apple of my heart. She is the moon of my delight, and the star of my morning. She speaks to me with the voice of her mother, and in her eye there dances the love light of my youth. Yet with all this my heart is heavy within me, for I have heard evil of the new Estate. The head overseer and the head driver are men of evil minds, and those under them readily do their bidding and follow their example: the little Crosby also dwells within their doors and finds no evil in them. Twice have I fled from mine enemies, and I would do so again but I am a 'bound coolie' and may not depart. Oh Sahib, if I am tempted to strike and take vengeance, for any evil to me or mine, the law is against me and will punish heavily."

At that moment Edwin Hamilton felt his heart leap from its socket, and his hands grow cold: then the truth dawned upon him; for he was suddenly seized with the fierce, savage jealousy of the male animal: his instinct primeval and unbidden, was to kill—whom he knew not, but anyone, from the big Crosby himself, down, who dared to suborn the graceful young woman sitting in his presence, into an unwelcome or repulsive embrace. Violently, the hitherto unnoticed and along subdued passion, blazed in his heart and challenged his reason. Then came the question to him: Could he love a " bare-toed " immigrant? Gradually he felt every bulwark of convention, and every ligament of tradition, crumbling and rending away from him. Generations of thought and prejudice: his sister's alarm, and his patrons' sneers, all he felt idle and futile. Thus, alone he stood, as it were, naked and empty handed before the altar of his great love for the truly beautiful Asiatic, who sat at his table shading her eyes from the rays of the rude lamp which was all the ornament boasted by Edwin's room, and the decision came, final and overwhelming.

CHAPTER FOURTH.

Edwin had made a stupendous leap in yielding his heart to the attractions of the Afridi's daughter. Other men of his class had indeed married East Indian immigrants before, but, either as a matter of convenience or expediency, and mostly in the evening of their days. Some, as the result of irregular association with these women, had grown up daughters, born of these unions, to whom, having reared them with every culture and refinement expensive schools and pensions could give, they found it pleasing and advisable to give the additional cachet of legitimacy, by marrying their mothers. Some others, again, threatened with some far-reaching Immigration Department circular on the subject of immoral relations with female immigrants, had found it advisable to seek defence or refuge in matrimony, usually long after every social avenue had been closed to them. But here was a young man—an Englishman by traditions and upbringing, and, even to the accident of his birth, which happened to synchronise with one of his mother's visits to the old country—white to all intents and purposes; on the threshold of his career; with the entree to the most exclusive circles; and, a future with scarce any limitations, taking a step that he knew would alienate his relatives and astound his friends, without even the excuse of a circular or the defence of old age. How his sister would take an affair of this sort: how he was to face her husband—his patron and benefactor—he gave himself no time to think. Obsessed by the occurrences at his sister's ball: depressed by the social and economic conditions of his calling, he felt only the freedom and the liberty of an outcast. All his innate chivalry roused by Abdullah Singh's tale of woe: his sense of beauty of form and feature, and his animal passion, long held in leash, intoxicated by the graceful pose of the woman whom he now knew that he loved to distraction—all drove Edwin to the leap. Throwing discretion to the winds, he vowed his future to a life of sacrifice in the protection of the now cheerless and unhappy girl; for, he knew only too well, that with such a step his own life would be infinitely rougher and harder to bear than even hers might have been did he leave events to take their course. Nor would she necessarily have to share any of the hardships or annoyances with which he may be beset. As his wife she would know none of his friends, therefore would suffer from none of their adverse opinions or prejudices. In his own case he knew well enough what he would have to face if he ventured into any social circles: but here the life of an overseer stood him in good stead. There were neither social amenities, nor social leaders in overseer life, so at least he would have peace in that direction.

Seemingly justified by these thoughts and ennobled by the sense of martyrdom, Edwin laid his hand upon Abdullah's shoulder, and calling him by his familiar form of address, said:

"Old man, have no fear. Your daughter shall be safe from harm. I pledge myself to you that she will not leave 'Never Out': and, perhaps, I might also be able to save your transfer."

"You, the Sahib my friend, are wise," replied Singh, "but how will you bring these things to pass, since you cannot influence ' the big Sahib ' ? "

"Well," said Edwin, " I propose to make it easy for her to stay, and impossible for them to remove her; for I purpose to make her my wife, if she will consent—that's all." Then he whispered to her, "Come close to me."

Bibi was not long in the coming; but Abdullah did not readily acquiesce in this startling proposal, for his worldly wise old heart felt many difficulties in the way: and, he feared the ultimate result of such an ill-sorted union. In a few moments, however, the girl, unaffected by any artificial coyness, was soon established leaning against Edwin's knee whither he had drawn her; for she had long secretly loved "the Sahib Hamilton," her father's frequent guest: although, and, as much perhaps, because, he had always treated her with grave and distant courtesy. She had never worked in his "gang," and therefore had never met him more frequently than during his visits to her father's hut; or occasionally on some part of the Estate going to or from their respective scenes of labour. On such occasions as the latter she had given little more than a coy "Salaam," and he had been sometimes moved to greet her in the European mode of lifting his hat; but, apart from looking ludicrous, he had felt that it would be little understood, and only be the means of subjecting himself to endless chaff from his brother overseers, so contented himself with a grave-toned "Good morning."

In view of the old man's fear and doubts many were the details that had to be settled and the plans to be made. Long and earnest was the confabulation that ensued. Bibi was bold and shy by turns. At times her full luminous eyes would look straight into Edwin's; at others they would be veiled and swept by their long lashes, and Edwin's heart would race the blood through his veins. Her scant yet modest clothing brought every charm of her supple form into bold relief: the contour and graceful curves of her bosom, as he occasionally drew her closer to him, would send Edwin's blood tingling to his finger tips, and the blood of his heart would cry that she was good to mate with.

Before finally closing the interview with his consent the old man said:

"Sahib, my friend, it is wise that you know more of her whom you would take as your wife; and it is meet that I, her father, should give you knowledge of all concerning her."

Edwin begged that he would defer the matter as it was drawing near to a day that would be pregnant with events; for the older man had fully informed Edwin of the cause of the midnight lights, which he had observed on coming in; and therefore their interview should be brought to a close for some much needed rest; but Abdullah insisted that what was there to tell should be known at once before he would agree to Edwin's proposal.

Abdullah's story in a few words was that his present wife was not his daughter's mother. His own father had been a wealthy land owner and had sent him early to Mission School: there he had shown great aptitude and his father had destined him to a University career. The god Cupid had however, once again, upset all parental plans, and Abdullah had fallen in love with a Hill Chief's daughter, and she had freely reciprocated. The old chief, who looked to his genealogy with as much punctiliousness as ever they did at Versailles, was mad and for some time the life of Abdullah Singh had not been worth the purchase. "That Sahib, had been the beginning," said Abdullah, "of all my troubles; and I would pray you watch carefully the temptations of an impulsive heart."

Edwin waved the suggestion aside and asked him to proceed.

Proceeding, Abdullah continued to relate how nothing but the fear of the English Raj had saved his life from the fierce resentment of the Chief: yet had the Chieftain followed him with persecutions wherever his purse could reach. He, Abdullah, had fled with his young wife from district to district, but ever the sinister influence had followed. At last the carefully nurtured girl, after having given birth to a daughter, had succumbed to her cares and hardships, and the constant anxiety concerning the danger to her husband.

That child had he named Ursula, in memory of his Mission school days; and that child was she whom he now saw a "bound coolie" in Demerara; and she whom all persons called Bibi. One serving woman who had fled with her mother and been faithful through it all, he had married after the death of her mistress, to secure her services for the careful nurturing of the child to whom she was much attached. The persecution of the old Chief had redoubled year by year, after the death of his daughter, and Abdullah in the hope to finally escape had crossed the "great black pawnee." (The Atlantic and Indian Oceans.)

"But," he naively added, "it would seem that I have escaped one persecution, only to be greeted with some other."

Edwin was now in better grace with himself and more fully determined than ever to wed the girl, whom he chaffingly referred to, with more or less truth, as a Ranee and a Princess.

It was now well into the early hours of the morning, and Abdullah made ready to depart and take his daughter home; but Edwin would not hear of his new found love being taken from him. Common though such practices were on all Sugar Estates this proposal nearly led to a rupture of friendly relations, for Abdullah was punctilious regarding his daughter's honour. Edwin however was obdurate though conciliatory. He claimed to have taken Bibi to wife what time the old man consented. Of what avail he asked were outward forms and ceremonies where true men and faithful hearts were concerned. Moreover, on a troublesome day like the coming one promised to be, what more fitting sanctuary could his wife find than his own quarters: for assuredly he would not have her run any risks. At last Edwin set the old man's fears at rest, as neither was bound by convention and each had the utmost trust in the other. Thus was the pact agreed upon, and Abdullah took his departure alone. It may be said that doubtful as Abdullah had been regarding Edwin's unconventional determinaton he had not near so much doubt as he would have experienced with many another European. For as has been earlier shown, Edwin was European even to the accident of his brith; and, in his veins there ran an admixture of French blood, which his father claimed could be traced back, through a bar sinister, to the Great Napoleon. This was a truth, and might indeed have accounted for some of Edwin's rude republican theories: even the treatment of his betrothed, or bride as he thought her, was no different from that meted out to an Imperial Princess of the house of Austria by his great forebear at Compiegne, while she was on her way to the Royal nuptials at St. Cloud.

Through many a night, as Abdullah had read with Edwin of the species and talked of allied subjects, he had formed the opinion that Edwin was a man to be bound by no conventions; but that his word could be taken at a higher premium than the bond of many another man. So he left his daughter and thought no evil.

The morning dawned in its full tropical loveliness. It was one of those mornings which seem to pronounce a benediction of peace on all the world: yet was there more of the curse of war on " Never Out." The Immigrants had been worked up to resistance point by the machinations of Abdool Karim: and when it was noised abroad that Bibi had slept in the quarters of the Sahib Hamilton on the night before, many and varied were the comments and deductions. Some confidently asserted that she had gone to buy the Sahib's favour, for it was well known that he claimed close relationship to the " big Sahib," as they called Walton. Some alleged that she was only in hiding and some others that the old man had sold her along with his other goods and chattels.

Nothing however tended to lessen the determination to resist the police when they came to effect the transfers of Abdullah and his family; for " transfers " are accorded the distinction of police escort. Whether Abdullah or his daughter had made virtue of a necessity, or otherwise, had ceased to trouble the immigrants as a body, as it was now regarded as a matter of high policy, although it may not have so recommended itself to them by name, to challenge the transfers, in the interest of their common good, irrespective of the old man and what course he had been forced to adopt; consequently there were many absentees from the cane fields on that day.

Edwin also with much to do that day absented himself from " orders " in the morning, to the great surprise of old Rapfuller. 'Old Raps' knew that Edwin had been to the great function the night before, but then he had never known Edwin to absent himself under similar circumstances before: he secretly hoped nevertheless that Edwin *had* registered his first drunk, despite the evil prognostications of the Boss on the subject. When some very little while after, the report reached him of Edwin's seeming moral lache with the Afridi's daughter, Rapfuller was dumbfounded. Could he have been wrong this once, when he told the Boss that ' the boy ' would run straight: or had " the first drunk " such disastrous results? Events however moved too rapidly to leave him any time to philosophise.

Immediately after " orders " Edwin set out to take the steps which he believed would effectually prevent the removal from the estate of Ursula, to give her rightful name, whom he now regarded as his wife *de facto*, and merely sought the necessary formalities to claim her *de jure*: and in this cause the motor bicycle which he had commandeered the night before, stood him in good stead. Riding from his quarters, he left word that he had gone to the " doctor," but the " doctor " was none other than the Revd. Dr. Talbot, a divine in residence on the outskirts of " Never Out," who was celebrated for his large-mindedness and eminent piety. He was a man who saw evil in nothing save uncharitableness in deed, word or thought; but when Edwin, arriving in the early morning, stated his business he quietly pointed out the impracticability of carrying through the ceremony that day. No banns having been published, it would be necessary to obtain the Governor's Licence before the ceremony could be performed; and he doubted if the necessary formalities could be got through to obtain the latter at such short notice.

Here was a set back Edwin in his utter ignorance of these matters had not expected. The result, however, of a hurried conference and search among the papers of the reverend gentleman was the discovery of a copy of the form necessary to obtain the Governor's fiat. Doctor Talbot in the meantime counselled further consideration of such an important step; particularly in deference to the great disparity in social standing, in colour, etc. Edwin however reminded the Reverend gentleman that " only those who knew all the circumstance could judge of the circumstance," meaning thereby that there was really not so much disparity in their social positions, if Ursula could take up her rightful place at the court of her grandfather. But Dr. Talbot, thinking it merely a veiled hint of the usual details in estate life discreetly held his peace for reasons of delicacy. In a little while, however, the necessary signatures had been obtained, with the Rev. Dr. Talbot as sponsor for the good faith of all; and Edwin raced to Georgetown, bearing the, to him, precious document that was to seal his hopes and dispel his fears. On reaching the city, he paid the necessary fees and bearded the officials at the Government Secretariat. Here he was met by the uncompromising attitude that it had been laid down that these documents must be filed at least forty-eight hours before they were actually required; therefore it would be impossible for the licence to be issued that day. In the midst of a rather heated discussion the Lieut.-Governor and head of the department — who was temporarily discharging the office of Governor, during one of the periodic absences of the substantive occupant from the seat of Government—arrived on the scene and quickly learning the essentials of the argument decided there and then to sign the document if all proved in order.

Sir Ralph Chisholm was long known throughout all circles as a regular 'Jack Blunt' for speeding up processes and his readiness to oblige; so the now thoroughly disconcerted officials of his department had nothing to do but prepare the document and get through the necessary formalities; for, as so far as legality was concerned, all was in order with Edwin's application. Meanwhile, Sir Ralph, leaning on the edge of his chief clerk's desk, chatted freely with the applicant. Half a Fabian, he was ever ready to practise, if not to preach, many of its doctrines, so he saw no sin in the marriage of Edwin Hamilton to Ursula Singh,—who ever she may be—though evidently East Indian. The document being shortly presented Sir Ralph affixed his signature, and with a cheery wish of good luck handed it to Edwin and passed out.

Meanwhile, events at "Never Out" were at no standstill. The arrival of the police sent to effect the transfers was the signal for an immediate and hostile demonstration on the part of the immigrants. There was no mistaking its tenor: the transfers were not to be permitted, and force was to be met by force. Abdullah was allowed very little say in the matter. The solitary posse of policemen deemed discretion the better part of valour and forthwith retired to the village station to report the state of affairs. The native non-commissioned officer of the semi-military police, who sat in authority at the station, affected to be astounded at the report:

"These coolies," he declared, " are 'forgetting themselves every day, and something will have to be done."

Suiting his action to his word, he proceeded to act as becomes one in authority; he wired his divisional officer:

" Unruly element at Never Out obstructing
" transfers. Am proceeding to effect arrests."

And with this mission in view he detailed half a dozen men, under his own command, " to make arrests," and then clothed his next in seniority with the necessary authority to act in command during his absence. Poor feeble man, yet a good example, and typical police officer, of the best native police force in the world.

Rapfuller had also promptly wired to Walton and the divisional officer of Police, and each had in turn communicated with the 'big Crosby' and the Inspector General of Police ; for the temper of the immgrants had been well described by Rapfuller as "ugly." As a result of these steps the divisional chief of police was directed to converge with armed force on the nearest station, and an additional force of the same nature was ordered to converge in support of the division. All things were ordered to the scale of a small war, as some recent experience—experience, that was, alas, to become only too frequent—had proved that in dealing with immigrants the most dire consequences have to be feared and provided against. In due course His Excellency the Governor was notified, and it may be said that the whole executive and administrative force of the Government of British Guiana was called into action, and issues moved into being which few could determine: and why? Because one heart had cooed to its mate, and that mate was bare-toed: her skin was not ivory, and she bound up the sheaves of the field.

CHAPTER FIFTH.

In Edwin's ride back to Dr. Talbot's nothing can be found to record: he indeed had time to think, but his hand was already to the plough and there could be no turning back. On reaching the reverend gentleman's house he succeeded in inducing that worthy cleric to accompany him back to " Never Out," and there perform the ceremony.

Edwin and Dr. Talbot arrived at " Never Out " about the same time as the plucky native non-commissioned officer and his half a dozen men. With the approach of this second posse of Police the people had worked themselves into a fine frenzy, and Edwin therefore deemed it advisable to put in an appearance and see what he could do, by good counsel and the explaining of the steps he proposed to take, towards reconciling them to what they were taught to regard as the will of the 'big Crosby'; or at least to keep them from violence meanwhile he effected the, to him, great coup. His appearance however on the scene was the signal for a more hostile demonstration yet. His feeble knowledge of their language, and his failure to secure immediately an interpreter who would be listened to by the people, strangled all his efforts at their birth.

Abdool Karim, seeing the superiority of numbers over the police and the absence of rifles or other arms, felt now that he had his rival in his grasp and openly incited the immigrants to drive the " black dogs " off the estate. Edwin, he pointed out, as the cause of all their undoing, and frantically urged them to make short work of him: but Edwin had been hitherto a general favourite and the people hesitated to carry, at least, that portion of Karim's directions into effect. Karim, maddened by this hesitancy, openly threatened Edwin, and, armed with a villainous double-handed stick, made for him: by good fortune however, and the feeling aforesaid, Edwin made good his escape; the police thereupon decided to effect the arrest of Karim for his violence and threats.

Edwin had no sooner effected his escape than he decided that the deferred ceremony must be forthwith performed, if it was to be of any effect in preventing bloodshed and staying the process of the law.

The police in the meantime proceeded to carry out their determination to arrest Karim. He, however, was a man strong of will and withers, and laid low the unlucky policeman who approached him for that purpose: immediately the entire force stormed the East Indian, and after a brief, furious struggle he was manacled and handcuffed. The immigrants, in doubt for the moment, had watched the struggle without interference. Bereft of their intellectual leader, they stood undecided and uncertain how to act until a young fellow, forcing himself to the front called upon them, loudly and with enthusiasm, to " rescue the driver." This sudden seizing of the vacant leadership, together with the enthusiasm of the speaker, acted like magic on the throng: in an instant the air was thick with flying missiles of every description; burnt earth and broken bottles; decaying vegetables and discarded bits of agricultural implements: all came hurtling through the air. There could be no question as to what course the police had to take, and they retired slowly on the manager's house. This movement being interpreted by the immigrants as a sign of weakness, and an abandonment of policy, further electrified them and the missile throwing was converted into an ugly rush, in which the handful of police, encumbered with a resisting prisoner, found itself hopelessly enmeshed. The work of rescue was thereupon easily effected and the mishandled police, offering an occasional effective resistance, for they are a crowd of stalwarts, standing well in their socks, soon reached their objective of cover. Here were now gathered some of the staff fully armed with repeating rifles and revolvers, and a show of these brought the now thoroughly excited immigrants to a halt; and, though some wild spirits among them clamoured and gesticulated for more aggressive tactics, the mob sullenly retired, bearing in triumph the rescued " driver." Karim, the half budding socialist, now urged upon the crowd the demolishing of the telephone and telegraph wires, and, nothing suiting the temper of his audience better than counsels of destruction, " Never Out " was soon in complete isolation from the outside world.

All was now excitement. Reinforcements were being momently looked for. The remainder of the staff made their way by various paths to the manager's house, and loyal local natives were being urged, from the factory and fields and surrounding domestic quarters, to concentrate at the point of defence. Futile efforts were then made to telegraph to the Inspector General of Police, but the silver wires were silent: nevertheless that good man had made his dispositions, and the tramp of armed men was moving steadily in every direction in obedience to his command: for, even as he had deployed men from his central station to support the threatened division, so had he also to call in, from other directions, supports to re-create reserves at his head-quarters.

In the meantime, amidst all these alarms, within the four bleak walls of his cabin Edwin was being indissolubly joined in Holy matrimony to the Afridi's daughter, around whom raged all this clash of arms. The completion of the ceremony was about co-incident with the arrival of Walton, the district Immigration Agent (" Little Crosby ") the Immigration Agent General (" Big Crosby ") and the armed posse of Police, twenty strong, under their European divisional officer; all of the latter in service kit and marching order, with twenty rounds of ball ammunition per man. The military force even included its Army Service Corps, for with it came arms and ammunition for the non-commissioned officer and his men who had come, as it were, in a civil matter.

As Edwin bade adieu to Dr. Talbot, he saw the armed men, and laughingly remarked that his was a military wedding, though he had no Cathedral Church for them to line the aisle.

" Aye, my son," answered the venerable prelate. " But, never forget that you have a Cathedral Church in the sanctity of your new made home. And, see to it accordingly."

Saying which, he took his departure, and Edwin concluded that the time had now come for him to make his great master move on Walton and the assembled officials.

Edwin's absence all this while, and now his sudden appearance at headquarters, was the subject for much comment. His compromising conduct with a female immigrant had been promptly advised, and guardedly discussed.

The " Well, Sir!" of Walton gave fitting expression to the feeling of all.

Edwin immediately asked for a private interview with his patron, and this was reluctantly, though promptly, given.

As soon as they had withdrawn into an inner room, Walton repeated his former " Well, Sir!" adding on this occasion, " I have had very disconcerting reports about your recent conduct and hope you can now give a thorough explanation: for you must surely know what conduct of that nature means."

Truth to tell Walton had not shared the general opinion of Edwin, but rather secretly hoped, and even believed, that there must be some foolish quixotic excuse which he would readily be able to get accepted by the " big Crosby," when once the family had been successfully removed.

" I will beg of you, sir," replied Edwin " that you forget any conduct of mine, and instead consider the request I am making bold to put forward,"

"Well, Sir," again, was all "Honest John" could find himself uttering.

"I have come to ask you, Sir, to reconsider your decision to have the Singh family removed from the Estate, and to get the police to desist from further action in the matter, so that bloodshed may be averted."

"Your request," Walton replied, "is, I consider, the most brazen piece of impertinence it has been my misfortune to hear. I think inded," he continued, "you presume far too much on the ties and connections between us. You forget, the relationship that must exist, within the confines of "Never Out," between you and me, is that of overseer and attorney. Apart from the question to which you refer." he proceeded, "any communications from you to me must be through your manager; and I am surprised at your whole conduct in this matter."

Edwin stomached his resentment, for he felt keenly references at any time to his home ties, as influencing his conduct, and replied as calmly as he could.

"Again, Sir, please forget my relationship to you, or even the position I occupy on this Estate, and think me merely a well wisher of the Sugar industry and of Immigration. I cannot therefore view lightly the prospects, and even the ultimate effect, of the coming conflict between the police and the people: and I see no way out of it but the cancelment of the transfers."

Walton now fairly fumed with rage. "The idea," he almost shouted, "of your daring to tell me of your 'views' and 'opinions' and 'well wishes.' To the devil with them all. Your conduct, and yours alone, Sir, is the cause of all this trouble to-day. I will, moreover, be damned, Sir, if I am going to be ruled by any puling preachers or truculent immigrants. The police have their duty to perform, and if conflict there must be, then, damn it all, let conflict be: and their blood be upon their own heads."

Edwin was surprised at the vehemence, though he had somewhat expected this tornado. But the visible twitching of Walton's lip gave warning to neither.

"I had hoped, Sir," Edwin proceeded, "to have made this communication under different circumstances, but I now have to state, simply,—and I hope that time will soften your disapproval—that I married Singh's daughter an hour ago this morning."

"Honest John" was not sure he heard aright: or was the word ' marriage ' used only in its courtesy sense to cover what already had been told to him. Drawing closer to ' the boy,' his whole manner changing, he laid a hand on his shoulder, and asked simply and gently:

"You have done what?"

"I have got married, Sir. Really married: an hour ago: by special licence, to Singh's daughter.

Walton's hand fell from Edwin's shoulder and he turned to go: flaccid in re-action: a defeated and disappointed man. An unsteadiness of gait attracted Edwin's attention but before he could reach his patron "the big man" had crumbled heavily to the ground with a gurgling guttural sound. The intense excitement, overwrought blood pressure, and sudden reaction had done their work, and Walton was out of action. Thoroughly alarmed Edwin hastily summoned assistance, and the throng in the adjoining room rushed in to find Walton, who a few minutes before stood among them, the man of power, now lying prone in a seizure of some sort. Hurried messengers were despatched in every direction, and these went unmolested, for the immigrants with the approach of the armed men had withdrawn within their lines to await the now expected attack of the Police.

Edwin, on being asked, proceeded to give his explanation of all that had taken place; and, at the conclusion, turning to the Immigration Agent General said:

"And I trust, Sir, you will now see the necessity of cancelling the transfers: at least as far as Singh's daughter —my wife—is concerned."

"Necessity of cancelling," echoed the I.A.G., "I don't see it. You are a free agent and can follow her if you choose. With your marriage I have no concern, save to remark that I do not know how it came to be performed without my consent in writing. However, that will form the subject of a separate enquiry. I shall, however, certainly not cancel the transfers. What I have ordered I have ordered." Saying which the great bureaucrat turned on his heels.

Edwin followed him protesting. "But Sir," he said, "she is my wife and the law gives me control over her actions, and the right, if needs be, of defending her by force."

"That may be," replied the 'big Crosby,' "but if you feel inclined to marry a woman under obligations to a third party, such a marriage obviously cannot cancel that obligation; and, so far as the third party is concerned, his rights remain intact. In a word, Sir, your wife is under bond to her indentures."

Edwin was dumbfounded. Not that he regretted the step: but his effort to stop bloodshed seemed now futile, and for his wife to be the bond servant of some coarse task-master was unthinkable. There was but one man to whom he could turn for counsel and that was Murray, a fellow overseer, and a character unto himself, of mixed colour; though not enough of white to pass, like Edwin, Eloise Funston, etc., for the original. He was unmistakably coloured. And it is fitting to here divert on the use of the word "coloured." In the United States the word coloured is used to designate everything that is not white—a demonstrably indefensible description for a man that is purely and simply black. On the other hand in old plantation circles in British Guiana and the West Indies a black man is called a 'black man,' and only is a person of pronouncedly mixed colouring of both races—black and white—referred to as "coloured," more particularly when the latter preponderates. This seems an utterly more sensible use of the word coloured: for if a 'black' man may be called coloured, then it would also be correct etymologically to call a 'white 'man coloured: white, as a colour, being created by a combination of the cardinal tints. But since it would be absurd to call a white or a black dress "coloured" so is it also absurd to designate single hued men, of either tint, in that manner. On the other hand a man or a dress showing a clear blending of colours can accurately be described as coloured. Therefore in the correct respect will the word always be used in this work.*

Murray was versed in the Immigration Law: he spoke Hindi like a native and what he did not know about cane planting, Sugar manufacture and Rum distillation it would be difficult to discover. Unhappily he also knew a good deal about the decanting of Rum and other kindred spirits; nevertheless he was of companions and fellows the best. Yet Murray had never risen to a Management: which was another story, and one of the cankerworms of the Sugar industry. For it is writ large in the ethics of those that control the destinies of the industry that no coloured creole may be appointed to a management. They may have every qualification under the sun: they may be as able as Attila: but they may not aspire to such appointments. Attorneys in authority can urge many reasons, and the consequent necessity for importing young, raw and untrained Europeans to train up for these posts, held in trust for them: but chief and truest of all is that the intelligent creole does not turn to a planter's calling until practically every other door is closed to him; consequently only the failures and those least fitted to govern may be found among the rank and file of under overseers. Manifestly therefore these are ineligible for the higher and better paid offices. There is undoubtedly great truth in these contentions, yet few seem to

---

* N.B.—Since writing the above, the matter has been made the subject of a judicial pronouncement by the Chief Justice of British Guiana.

stop to analyze the why and the wherefore of this boycott by an intelligent class of men who have left their stamp of worth, and impress of ability, on every other walk of life. In the Civil Service they rise with honour to themselves, and without the aid of nepotism, to the highest posts available. They exercise the very highest functions of the judiciary: in the other learned professions they are to be found in the very front rank: as great captains of industry and commerce they wield vast power and influence. Yet is their ability to manage a Sugar estate questioned; and it does not seem to occur to anyone that this boycott of and by them is due to the rotten economic conditions which ¡react on the social position, even such as it is, of the aspirant to Planting honours. Thus, none but those alien to the soil and to the social amenities of the country, and those who find other doors closed in their faces, are to be found among planting recruits.

It is no exaggeration to say that the man who elects a planting career sunders all aspiration to his own vine and fig tree, because of a system which is indefensible from every possible standpoint; save as an addition to the perquisites of the manager. Yet these managers cannot be considered as ill-paid. Estates can be "cropped," abandoned and sent to grass: owners may face the protection and obloquy of the debtor's court; but sugar estate managers and attorneys continue to retire with fat fortunes to spend the afternoon of their days in the sublime atmosphere of temperate climates. The young indentured European regularly imported to fill the constant demand, through failing of raw material, only half understands the conditions to which he is being drafted; and, did he thoroughly understand them the spirit of adventure would probably overweigh every other: for the secret hope of amassing wealth, and returning to his own social circle a bigger man than he left it, is as strong a factor to-day as it ever was. That the best material is not always obtained is only too apparent in the wastrels so frequently met with in the colony's industrial life.

Murray belonged to a class who, having made an early failure, are the better for it ever after. He knew he was now enmeshed in the calling in which he found himself: he could not go back, because that would mean starting life afresh from the bottom of the ladder: he could not go forward because of the well known bar to further progress. What wonder then that, cut off from all social intercourse, with the four bare walls of his cabin staring him in the face from 5 p.m., when he left his work, to 5 a.m., when he took it up again—save only for the break of dinner at the straight laced manager's table—that he found relief in a cheerful though dangerous occupation; he " took his grog"; the fate of so many of his calling, the only wonder being that there is not more wreckage from this cause. Yet nothing soured Murray: quick of wit and ready of counsel, he was a general favourite.

When interrogated by Edwin, in the corner of the verandah, where most of the staff had foregathered, Murray's reply was brief and emphatic.

"Boy," he said, "you can't do a damn thing, except buy their indentures."

As soon as Edwin had left the Immigration Agent General's party, a hurried confabulation had been held. Walton was now an invalid and receiving such attention as his precarious condition would allow, until the hurrying messengers brought medical aid, wife and nurses to his bedside. From the discussion, therefore, of necessity, he was eliminated. The council of war consisted of the Immigration Agent General, his district agent, old Rapfuller, and the Military member of Council, *i.e.*, Police Officer.

Old Rapfuller, clothed as it were in the authority of 'the boss,' was invited to speak first: and he spoke as one who knows the immigrant at first hand.

"You cannot do anything," he said, "but press forward. No management on the coast will be free from disaffection unless this thing is smashed here and now. 'Forward' is old Rapfuller's word, and 'the boss' would have said the same."

As a result of further consultation and argument it was decided that the armed police should move forward to secure what was now the virtual arrest of the 'transfers' and, of course, also the retaking of Abdool Karim. Thereupon the 'Military Member of Council' set out to take personal command in the field.

No sooner did the police reach the public road than a most unearthly din was set up from the immigrants' lines. The blowing of conch shells and the beating of drums seemed all resorted to for the purpose of exciting the enthusiasm and recalling the flagging recklessness of the immigrants.

The scene in Edwin's corner of the verandah had not been pregnant with less interest than the council of war previously described. On receiving the terse bald reply from Murray, Edwin echoed.

"Buy their indentures? Why! are these poor people just human cattle to be bought and sold?"

"Well," replied Murray, "that is not a nice way of putting it. People make a contract and have to stick to it; except when they can give some consideration for its cancelment. In this case the price of indentures is fixed somewhere about the cost of bringing the immigrants here, less what proportion of the indenture has been discharged. In Singh's case it must work out somewhere in the region of $50 each. If you have $150 just you pay over the money, and bring everything to a standstill."

But Murray had completed his sentence to the empty air, for Edwin was half way down the stairs, and soon racing for life to the scene of action; and not one moment too soon.

Before Edwin could get to the spot old Abdullah had been active in his efforts to avert bloodshed. His venerable form could be seen moving to and fro among the excited immigrants. With his hands uplifted he was vainly trying to make himself heard above the din.

"My brethren," he said, "of what avail are your passions against pistols? If it be the will of Allah I go hence, I beg that you will not endanger your lives in opposing my destiny."

Abdool Karim however shrieked that the old man had been bought; and no one knew whose turn would be next: to this the mob shrieked in unison, and shrieked defiance to the police.

At this stage Edwin arrived, and, after a hurried conference with the police officer, time was secured in which the preliminaries could be arranged by Singh, with Edwin's money for the cancelment of the indentures and transfers of his family. The police bivouacked on their ground and awaited further orders: the 'military member' stipulating that nothing could now affect the arest of Karim; but that he would await directions in the other matter.

In a short while preliminaries were satisfactorily settled and the Immigration Agent Geneal gave directions for the suspension of the order of transfers.

The re-arrest of Karim however was another matter, though the 'big Crosby' came on the ground himself. After some considerable time, and the display of exhaustive tact, all hope seemed lost and nothing left but an appeal to arms. At the moment however when final dispositions were being made, Karim surrendered.

CHAPTER SIXTH.

The thread of this tale will be preserved if it is briefly recorded that the indentures of Abdullah Singh and his family were duly cancelled and they stood once more free to reside where they chose. Abdool Karim was in due course brought to trial. The Police pressed three charges against him; one for inciting the people to violence: one for assaulting them in the execution of their duty, and one for using threatening language to Edwin. After many postponements convictions were eventually obtained in all three instances; and the Stipendiary, in view of the growing unrest on Sugar Estates, imposed the salutary penalty of three months' imprisonment under each charge—the sentences to run consecutively: which, being interpreted, meant that Karim had to serve nine calendar months in prison for his dangerous agitatings and escapades.

The case of Walton resolved itself into one of those not infrequently met with in medical practice; and on their arrival the doctors pronounced it to be an almost hopeless case; if his heart failed, as was most likely, he would die without regaining consciousness; at the most, the best that could be hoped for, at his age, was a long period as an invalid; but never again could he hope to resume the control of his extensive charges. All the speed that wealth could devise was set in motion to bring the now distracted

Marion to her husband's bedside, and she came supported by a retinue of trained nurses, and everything wealth or skill could design to prolong life. Eventually, however, the best aid was his constitution, which, nurtured by the strenuous life he once lived, now stood him in good stead and steadily and hourly drew him from the Valley of the Shadow. Walton gradually regained consciousness; but it was clear that his will and intellect had suffered. As soon as he could stand removal loving hands encompassed his transfer to his palatial Georgetown residence, and there the good Marion waited on and watched over him. The double shock she had suffered, and, now the grief and pain at her lord's condition, threw her more and more on the consolations offered by the Church to the stricken; and she served and worshipped daily in the beautiful Cathedral Church, erected by loyal Catholics in the city of Georgetown to the greater Glory of God. And such a cathedral, as rearing its magnificent and spired tower high into the heavens above all others, would seem like a beacon pointing to higher things above.

Although Walton failed to recover altogether his reason, as the days went by, it was pathetic to see how the once strong man sought something to cling to. Though he seemed unable to connect anything coherently, running all through his touching loyalty to his wife was a sort of befogged tenderness for Edwin. His own little son he scarcely seemed to notice. Old Rapfuller's best efforts and cleverest witticisms roused but the dimmest interest; but with the entry of Edwin into the sick chamber, Walton's whole face would brighten, and he would have " the boy " sit for hours at his bedside; not infrequently Edwin would have to wait the silent approach of slumber before he could steal away. In his absence Walton would complainingly ask for him, and consequently the latter found it necessary to be in almost constant attendance on the invalid's couch. Although Walton never seemed to distinctly remember, and certainly never referred to the cause of his almost fatal displeasure with Edwin, it was clear that he sought to draw "the boy's" affection to him by every means in his power. He would stroke Edwin's hand and tell him not to fret, because soon they all would be in England. Then his mind would wander and lead to disjointed remarks about youth, and folly to be forgiven.

Mrs. Walton, saddened and absorbed by her own troubles, had little time to give to her brother's reckless matrimonial venture: as his friends described his marriage. When she did have time to call it up in review her new practice, under affliction, of her old faith led her to take a different view point to that which she would have formerly taken as one of the leaders of Georgetown society. Now she was disposed to class all such considerations with the vanities of King Solomon; and, while she never ceased to deprecate the union, she, nevertheless, brought a more charitable mind to bear on Edwin's rehearsal of the causes and excuses which led him to take an Indian wife.

At Edwin's little home on the outskirts of "Never Out," things ran smoothly. Though Bibi showed wonderful aptitude for Western ideas, Edwin, however, resolutely set his face against any westernising of her dress; his chief aim being to order her surroundings in a somewhat similar manner to those which would have been hers had her fiery old grandfather not disinherited his daughter; and in this aim he was as successful as circumstances and his means would allow. Thus was ensured unto him his wife as a never-ending source of delight; never once had he felt that indescribable feeling of disappointment in seeing anything like *gaucherie* in any effort to ape the manners and customs of her Western sisters. Freed from the obligations of an agricultural labourer, she shone in her immediate surroundings as an Indian lady of grace and refinement. Old Singh was established in the house as a sort of Major Domo and the woman, who had all through, followed their fortunes, took up her place in the household as one of the satellites revolving round the central figure.

To Edwin himself, dividing his time between his duties, his exacting attendance on his sister's husband and his romantic attachment to his wife, the months flew by rapidly. Abdool Karim had been released from prison and, as far as the general public was concerned, the threatened *emeute* at Pln. " Never Out " had passed into the limbo of things forgotten. Then one fine morning Bibi complained of extreme weariness and being " Sick unto death." She begged that her lord would remain with her that day, but Edwin set her fears at rest and, summoning the necessary assistance, went forth to his duties promising to be back much earlier than usual. When he did return, however, he found that everything had progressed without any untoward occurrence and his wife had presented him with the loveliest baby girl that the world had ever seen—such at least was its father's conviction, and that of all those who surrounded the fretting little stranger.

The coming of the little hostage to fortune chained Edwin to the immediate vicinity of his wife's bed chamber. He simply adored the rosy-tinted cherub, and nothing but a most importunate wire from his sister succeeded in getting him to agree to resume his service of love at her husband's bedside. Eventually, after many goodbyes, Edwin took himself away and set out for Georgetown. On his arrival Marion slated him soundly for leaving her alone in the trying task of keeping an invalid in good humour: and one whom the doctors declared would be in grave danger if greatly upset. Then Edwin told his tale of the little jet-eyed stranger who looked at him with its mother's eyes, and yet with his sister's wistfulness. Whereupon, Marion, true to the contrariness of all her sex, proceeded to rate him again for not having advised her by wire: indeed, she claimed that she would be satisfied with nothing less than the removal, as soon as it could be effected, of mother and daughter to her own roof and care. For she vowed that the child must be brought up in Western, and not Eastern culture; no matter however excellent the latter may seem in Edwin's doting

IN BONDAGE. 61

eyes. Edwin, who was wise in his generation, saw at once that it would never do to remove his girl wife from her own surroundings, to be transplanted to the city where there would be nothing but false judgments of her standards, and unnecessary wounds to be borne by both. However, only too well pleased with his sister's loyalty and love, he procrastinated; and Marion, content that her brother's reluctance was due to an always evident delicacy about receiving too much at her hands, allowed the matter to rest there for the present. As though called by an unseen hand, Edwin could scarcely bide his usual time and in a very little while he was once more speeding homewards.

When he reached his wife's bed chamber he stood for an instant rivetted to the threshold, for he saw simultaneously entering, from the door opening on the Eastern verandah, a man armed with a villainous looking cutlass which glistened in the soft evening light with the keenness of its blade. Edwin's hesitation was momentary: in another instant he had thrown himself bodily on the stranger and pinioned his arms to his side. Then issued a struggle such as few would care to witness. Karim, for indeed it was he, strong and wiry, with his determination fed by a fierce intention, scarce met an equal in Edwin, whose horror and frantic effort to save those whom he loved so dearly, almost unnerved him: yet his sturdier physique stood him in good stead, and allowed him to gather himself together: moreover his was a rising energy while Karim's would soon be at its ebb. All Edwin's efforts were now directed towards disarming the man; but this was no easy task. Chance, rather than resolve, directed their struggles to the half-open door, and good luck gave Edwin the opportunity to get the blade of the murderous weapon right through the chink made thereby as it stood ajar, immediately throwing the whole of his weight on Karim, who yet clung to the weapon tenaciously, the poor-tempered blade snapped midway and left a useless stump in Karim's hand. Roused by the struggle, Bibi sat np in bed and beheld her husband in mortal struggle with him whom she at once recognised as the sworn enemy of both. Horror had her spell bound and she could neither move nor speak. Karim, now mad with baffled rage, espied Edwin's revolver on the little table ,just where it had been laid on its master's return from the fields aback of the plantation, for prudence had taught all overseers to go thus armed, and thither forced the struggle. Edwin, thinking little of the revolver, cared less whence the struggle swayed so he could retain overmastership and eventually force his antagonist to the ground. As Bibi recovered from her horror she recovered her speech, and gave out resounding shrieks: hurried footsteps heralded the approach of helping hands, but they arrived when a flash and crack announced that one chapter of tragedy had been closed. As the struggling men reached the table, it had been the work of an instant for Karim to snatch up the revolver; too late had Bibi thrown herself out of bed: the barrel had been pressed against Edwin's bosom and the trigger drawn. A crashing fall: struggling men—everything inextricably mixed; until at last the living and the dead were separated, and the intruder secured and pinioned. Edwin lay prone where he had fallen, and hurriedly summoned medical aid soon pronounced the fatal word. Edwin Hamilton had paid the dread penalty. He had crossed the bourne, and had been called upon to plough another furrow, and fill another cycle of his existence.

The widowed girl now provided a serious subject for attention. The excitement of the struggle; the murder of her husband, in her very presence, produced complications that few constitutions could have withstood, at that juncture, and in a few days she was gathered to the garden of her forefathers.

Thus did the fates call upon Marion Walton to put her plan into immediate action for the taking of her brother's wee little infant into her own home; there to be brought up with the love and care which characterised all her actions.

IN BONDAGE.   63

Karim was in due course charged in the lower Courts with the wilful murder of Edwin Hamilton. To the charge and proceedings he opposed a stolid indifference: not asked to plead, he made no comments; invited to cross-examine the witnesses brought forward by the police, he did not avail himself of the opportunity. And, at the end of the investigation, when the statutory caution was read to him and he was informed that he had been referred to the ensuing Criminal Session for " that he did feloniously kill and murder the deceased, Edwin Hamilton," his sole comment was that it was " the pleasure of the Sahib "and that to him " had power been given."

The day duly came on which Karim was to stand his memorable trial for the capital offence with which he stood charged. From early morning crowds of East Indians could be seen wending their way to the place of trial. Many a time had there been conflict of arms between immigrants and authorities, but always had the former only paid the sacrifice of life. Here had an immigrant been shot dead by an overseer, in more or less defence of his person: sometimes had it even been hinted that the immigrant had paid the penalty because, like Uriah the Hittite, his wife had been comely, and not averse to the advances of an over lord. At another place had besieged parties, stormed at by infuriated immigrants, had recourse to the deadly argument of fire-arms. Again and again had the police to apply " Lee-Enfield methods " to quell strikes and disturbances. After each and all of these had the slain to be numbered among the immigrants, and confidential reports sent to the Government of India on the slaying of some one or several of its wards. But never yet had one of the Governing class paid the extreme penalty of conflict. The one payment had consequently elicited intense interest all over the colony. Planters came in from every side, and immigrants swarmed to the venue of trial. Rumours many and absurd had travelled in every direction, and villagers of every hue had gathered to hear such spicy details as had grown in the telling. When the appointed hour arrived the scene was one that takes some telling. To the East of the great Victoria Law Court the quadrangle, used occasionally by peaceful citizens for tennis, and by nursing maids for a romp with their charges, was filled to its uttermost with a dense surging mass of every hue. Here was a beturbanned " Maraj " with his bare legs and Eastern shoes: there was a Hindoo with his tight-fitting skull cap; cheek by jowl with both was a negro in an Early Victorian coat and superannuated billy cock hat; all bent on being present even though they could hear nought of the proceedings. And not the least among them were their women; clothed in bright-coloured raiment, gaudy " Julahs," sparkling nose rings, and expensive armlets. Many even with foot rings; but each in her best, as though decked for some festival. On the western side of the grim structure the scene was but a repetition of the foregoing, with the Eastern always predominating. Here stood a huge marble statue of Victoria, she whom the great Disraeli, with a stroke of his master pen, had made the first alien Empress of India, looking down benign and calm on the struggling mass. Well indeed may that statue have been looking down from some pedestal in Western India rather than in one of the garden cities of South America and the Western Atlantic, so Eastern-like was the throng which surrounded it.

Nor was the crowd within the precincts of the Court itself disappointed with the forensic display provided in the course of the trial. Counsel for the defence was a young East Indian Barrister whose forebears had themselves been immigrants, in the long ago. He had been but recently called to the bar, and was credited with a good deal of " Nationalist " sentiment. The line of his defence was apparently taking a peculiar turn: he practcially took no notice of questions of fact, but was at great pains to bring out that Edwin had moved in the most exclusive circles, and could easily have chosen a wife from among the very highest in the land. On the other hand he gathered from the official witnesses that female immigrants were in painful minority; and he further elicited that Karim would have found it extremely difficult to find a wife outside of his race, even among the better class of negroes; for these regard the East Indian with considerable prejudice, even though they accept menial service for hire from him.

At the end of the case for the Crown the accused was put into the witness box in his own defence. It was clear that his own native intelligence had been well primed by Counsel, and that the latter was "getting at" the jury from two directions. Karim set forth his great love, in the early days, for the wife of the Sahib Hamilton: he claimed that he had been led to hope until the latter came on the scene; and then he proceeded to give his account of the incidents of the fatal night. Leaving his compound, he stated that he went to sharpen his cutlass for the work in hand on the following day; he had passed the Sahib and had he intended evil could have then accomplished it with less risk. On his way back to his compound however his "mind had given him" to pass the house where the woman he so greatly loved now lived. When he arrived in the vicinity, he said, he was seized with the overwhelming desire to gaze upon her; for he had heard that she was ill, and knowing that the Sahib was away he had felt that he could creep into the house without observation, and get away again after he had looked upon her and perhaps even kissed the bed clothes on which she lay. He had no sooner clambered up the verandah and entered the room than he found himself pounced upon, and forced into a deadly struggle. He had retained possesion of his cutlass to prevent his assailaint murdering him with it, and had caught up the revolver with the same end in view. In the scuffle for its possession the Sahib had got shot. He had not visited the house to do murder, least of all to the Sahib, for he knew that the Sahib had gone into the city.

The address for the defence was no less clever, and it resolved itself into a vigorous declamation in the general cause of the East Indian immigrant. Counsel urged the grievous wrong that was frequently done to these immigrants who were brought across two oceans to be shot down, or hanged; their liberty impaired and their wives stolen, or suborned. He played with great effort on the lot of an immigrant exile thousands of miles from home, in practically an alien country, where he was not being tried by twelve of his peers. He implored the jury to divest themselves of all Western ideas of ways of thought, and codes of etiquette or honour. "Do not consider for a moment," he said "what either of you may have done under similar circumstances, if the unfortunate deceased, whose family has my utmost sympathy, had won his wife over the head of one of you, and you had not the entree of his home. I would remind you, gentlemen," he proceeded, "that although Kipling has sung immortally that 'East is East and West is West' and claimed that 'never the twain shall meet,' we have here the meeting of the two in a most singular manner. Here we find the gorgeous East, with its riot of colour and extremes, its patriarchal standard of honour, and its restrictions and privileges of caste, all exemplified and stamped on the brain of the accused, facing practically what is a Western Court of Honour, steeped in a rigid sense of law and Justice, drawing its ideals from Mayfair, and saturated with centuries of a different standard of right and wrong."

"Gentlemen of the jury," he concluded in a brilliant peroration, "You must not think of the accused on that fatal night as seeking to outrage the sanctity of a Western home; but rather of a man despoiled, stealing to the scene of alien captivity of the woman whom he loved above rubies." He then dilated on the ease with which Edwin could have found a wife among the highest and handsomest in the land, and contrasted with that freedom of choice the frightfully restricted number from whom the accuseed could choose; and, at last, dramatically contended that "Hamilton was morally responsible for his own death." Lastly he dealt with the evidence of the accused, urged its coherency, declaimed on its extreme probability, and contended on its utter lack of malice. He charged the jury not to be responsible for " launching this man into eternity for having tried to steal a glance at her whom he had loved and lost."

The Crown's learned Attorney General for British Guiana rose to reply amid an intense hush. He was brief and direct. He claimed that much that learned counsel for the defence had urged was irrelevant; he asked for a verdict on the issues. The learned judge, he pointed out, would set out the law to them that every man was liable for his own unlawful acts. He moreover submitted that the accused had armed himself with a deadly weapon and had entered the house of the deceased in his absence. It had been laid down, he said, that where a man broke to enter———

This brought counsel for the defence to his feet, and a long wrangle ensued as to what had been proved. Had the door through which the accused entered been latched or hooked, or had it stood ajar? Each argued as suited him best.

Eventually the Attorney General resumed: he scouted the idea that the revolver had been seized as an act of self defence, or that the accused had gone to the house on a mission of peace. He rather saw malice and intent in that when the accused became temporarily disarmed he forthwith seized the opportunity of securing a more deadly weapon. And, lastly, he reminded the jury that they were not responsible for the penalty attached to any verdict of theirs; their duty being merely to say if the accused was guilty or not guilty of the offence of which he stood charged.

The judge summed up and delivered his charge to the jury, much after the text of the Attorney General and the jury retired to consider their verdict.

After four hours' deliberation the jury elected the lesser count and brought in a verdict of manslaughter against the **accused.**

His Honour the Judge, before passing sentence, enlarged upon the enormity of the offence, and claimed that he could not blind himself to the fact that prisoner at the bar had been responsible for the death of two persons; he therefore did not think that justice would be met with a less sentence than one of penal servitude for life.

In far away Jamaica a brilliant ornament of society read with feverish anxiety every detail of this memorable trial. Then her wide circle of friends wondered why she had at last accepted the thrice previously refused offer of marriage from Major Dodds of the island garrison; but who can judge of the part played in her heart by one of pensive brow, who had stood a stranger within the gates of a brilliant throng; and, then had passed beyond recall in the cloud of a ghastly tragedy.

CHAPTER SEVENTH.

Such then in brief were the antecedents and birth-history of the girl we now see on a September morning in the lovely island of Tobago, which, as every one knows, is one of the British West Indian islands set in the beautiful sun-lit Caribbean sea.

Seated on the gnarled roots of an old tree at St. Seriols on the sea side and the outskirts of Scarborough, the capital town, Marjorie Hamilton, who had now reached her fourteenth year, was indeed comely to look at.

Readers will remember the little infant girl who saw with unrecording eyes the grim tragedy fought out fourteen years before in her natal chamber, which robbed her at one fell blow of both father and mother. Marion Walton, true to her word, had seized upon the infant child and borne it home, brushing aside, with due conciliatives, the stately protests of the infant's maternal grandfather. No sooner had the memorable trial come to an end than Marion decided to remove from British Guiana altogether and seek a less strenuous atmosphere.

Counsels had been freely pressed upon her to retire to Europe with her son, infant ward, and invalid husband, but many were the reasons which eventually prompted her to make her home in the nearby island of Tobago. St. Seriols, originally selected for a brief sojourn, as much for reasons of economy, and the course of sea baths she had been advised to try for her invalided husband, as for its solitude and rest for herself, had thoroughly charmed her by its old-world life and peacefulness. Its chatelaine, an Early Victorian lady, who may easily have stepped out of Dickens, charmed her no less, with the result that mutually satisfactory relations were established for a prolonged residence on a sort of open lease and general freedom of terms. To all intents and purposes the house and grounds became Mrs. Walton's and the former owners merely life tenants of some of the buildings comprising the compound at "St. Seriols."

As Mrs. Walton's young son, Harold grew beyond his petticoats, she had sent him to the College of the Immaculate Conception in the neighbouring island of Trinidad whence he could return to St. Seriols for his vacations at little expense; and, as she had openly expressed the intention of devoting his life to the service of the church, his studies were directed accordingly.

Marjorie, on the other hand, Mrs. Walton kept by her perpetually. Aided by little private tuition, she battled with her education herself, from Marjorie's toddling days, and divided her service between a loving tyrant child and an invalid husband with heroic determination. What support she derived from that close communion with the church which she had never relaxed, it would be difficult to admeasure, but she nevertheless served uncomplainingly and with all her heart.

Under the influence of the constant sea air and daily baths her husband, the once cheerful Jim, had been gradually recovering. The daily pastime of Harold and the toddling Marjorie was to help work the hand pump which played the salt sea water on poor old Jim as he sat on the beach enjoying his bath as much as he could. Such generous treatment from Nature's own laboratory gradually began to create nerve centres in Walton, and as he commenced to hop around, his enquiries for Edwin had become more insistent. He had long since been told that Marjorie was Edwin's daughter—in which he saw no crime—but the dark details had been carefully kept from him, from fear of shock. Various excuses had been invented to excuse Edwin's absence in the early days. Eventually, however, his yearning love for " the boy " had taken another turn, and in his befogged brain he began to regard him as an ingrate who had neglected an unfortunate invalid.

It turned out, however, Walton's recovery had been his undoing. As he grew stronger he had been allowed to wander from room to room, and one fine day he stumbled upon a bundle of old Demerara papers which he forthwith commenced to digest. He had not run through many before he came across the ghastly fate of the " wayward Edwin," as he now sometimes called him. The reaction had been immediate, and when his faithful wife had come to seek her invalid lord she had found him prone on the floor, gripping tight in his outstretched hand the offending paper. He had evidently risen to confront her with the printed evidence of her dissimulation, but the shock had been too much for him after such a vivid recalling of every incident of the long befogged day when Edwin had bearded him at " Never Out ": for the newspapers, as customary, had rehashed all the particulars antecedent to the great trial. Poor " Big Jim " was now beyond all range of medical skill or assistance; nevertheless hurried messengers summoned to his bedside what little skill the tight little island could boast, but skill was of no avail; that night John James Walton passed from the here to the hereafter, and left his wife a widow indeed, as she had in truth long been in fact. Mrs. Walton had been but a brief three years at St. Seriols when she had been called upon to face this second bereavement from the one great cause—least understood.

More than ever after had Marion devoted herself to the habits and practices of a religious recluse; and in consequence had Marjorie grown up as much a child of nature as she was indeed a child of love. Had Mrs. Walton's habits been otherwise she perhaps would have exercised her *de facto* parental authority and put some restraint on the wanderings of her ward. As it was, she saw no hurt in the queer friendships of Marjorie, who found her companions for the most part among the humbler folk residing along the public road running to the East and West of St. Seriols. The younger generation, however, had no interest for her, whether of her own sex or not: it was among the old cronies, beldames and characters that she spent her days and lived her hours.

It was not alone among the living that Marjorie moved in a previous generation. Inheriting the taste of an omnivorous reader, she dived deep into the book shelves at St. Seriols.

It may have been her readings which threw her into the arms of the old people; or it may have been their garbled and romantic tales of the Eighteenth century and its by-gone glories and wickednesses which first sent her on the hunt for more. Certainly she lived now as completely in that age as though she were curtseying through the immodest courts of the Georges, or the Tuilleries. Even her games were Georgian; and in one she was taught the complet:

> The grass is green, the rose is red,
> God bless King George's noble head.

Yet Marjorie's readings developed none of the pensiveness of the scholar or the recluse: on the contrary, occasionally, she would feel the, to her, unmeaning leap in her bosom as men mated with Royal women, or fought for the splendour of their caresses; and she would return from each excursion into the realms of literature clothed with more romance and waywardness of heart than ever she went in.

At fourteen Marjorie had developed with all the precocity of the tropics and her Indian blood; her bosom and her form were as assuredly beyond most English girls of eighteen, as her intellect was beyond those of twenty.

Nor must it be thought that Marjorie was kept in ignorance of her birth and antecedents: Edwin, her father, had told his sister all he knew of his wife, and little by little Mrs. Walton had imparted to Mrs. Keith, the owner of St. Seriols, the details of that story. Marjorie had herself been given its outlines what time she had grown to an age of reason, but Mrs. Walton had stilled her prancing heart when she had pressed for more particulars. These, however, had been gradually wormed out of the graceful old chatelaine of St. Seriols; for that old lady had been thoroughly captivated by the charming and wayward ward of her tenant, and she could say her nay to nothing. Marjorie never forgot the red-letter day on which she learnt that she united in her own veins the blood of the old Indian chief and that of the mighty Genius who had stood astride the world, and rattled his scabbarded sabre in the presence of the Earth's greatest.

Mrs. Keith herself could trace her own ancestry back to the days of romance and sailing ships. Her own mother who had been a child of one of those "slave unions" so common in the Eighteenth Century, had in turn been elevated to the caresses of a Chief Justice; and His Honour had seen no evil in it. Then, unknown tropical diseases and the uncertainty of travel kept white women out of the tropics, and consequently white men, under indenture as Soldiers, Civil Servants, Merchants or Planters, found mistresses among the cane and cotton fields of the plantations. In those days there were no Immigration Departments to keep watch and ward over such subjects: women were the goods and chattels of their owners, to be elevated to their beds, sold into further bondage, or left to die from the illusages of underlings; as pleased the humour or the pockets of their owners.

Mrs. Keith's father had left her well provided with this world's goods; in his life time she had been sent to England for the polish of a European education, and some time after her return she had married an officer of the

English garrison then stationed in Tobago. He, though following the tramp of the army, had been a studious Scotsman; and had left the old Judge's library much richer than he found it.

Poor Mrs. Keith had had her share of sorrows; her only daughter had died from hydrophobia: that almost forgotten scourge of the early nineteenth century. Her eldest son, caught early by the romance of the sea and waves which almost surrounded his home, and driven by the fast changing economic situation in Tobago which heralded the decline of the Cane Sugar Industry, took to the sea, and after many years was lost in a gale, together with his gallant ship, off the coast of Chili. Her other son, after accumulating a fortune in the gold and forest industries of British Guiana, had retired to Tobago to spend it in peace and comfort; but fate had decreed otherwise, and he had disappeared while on a boating excursion to the lion-shaped "Red Rock" which keeps watch and ward over the roadstead of Rockly Bay.

Thus the lone warm heart of the elder woman found something to love and cleave to in the tender but capricious Marjorie. Mrs. Keith had seen Marjorie grow up from day to day, from her infant days; and as the child developed she was gradually admitted more and more into the elder lady's confidence.

It was in the course of these confidences that Marjorie had secured every thing of her own romantic history. What Mrs. Keith had not heard from Mrs. Walton she had gathered from the files of Demerara papers which she had constantly received from the days when her son lived and struggled in the Magnificent Province.

Mrs. Keith, while she cuddled the little stranger, would tell of her days of anxiety when her own little girl had been held in the grip of the scourge: how the little child would be nursed by no one but herself: how she had to carry it hourly on her shoulder to soothe its cries: how her husband would warn her that the child would bite; and

IN BONDAGE.

how she would ask it, "Baby daughter will you bite your mother?" and the little one would answer with baby pathos, "Me no bite Mother: only bad dog bite," the "bad dog" that was numbering her fast ebbing life by hours. Eventually the little girl had been laid to rest in the nearby woods, and through the years her resting place remains, and may be seen to this day, marked with a heap of smooth sea shore pebbles carried thither by the hands of her two loving brothers; two trees taller than all the others also mark the head and foot of the little cubicle.

Many a tale would Mrs. Keith also tell of the several home-comings of her sailor boy, and many were the treasures she could show; all marks of his own warm heart and the warmer and unforgetting affection of his mother. Then, alas, came the blow on one heavy rainy day; when it seemed to Mrs. Keith that the rains came and the floods descended on her desolate heart, for her elder son was no more.

Of the tale of sorrow of her second son she never wearied. The "Red Rock" was ever to her "that horrid old rock." She would tell how she besought 'George' not to go on that particular day, for she had many forebodings; but "George" had waved them aside and told her of his hair-breadth escapes in the wilds of British Guiana: how he had looked at death, not a few times, in the treacherous rapids and falls of the magnificent rivers, which spread like a net work all over his one time home. The sea in the placid southern harbour of Tobago's capital town he had likened unto a mill pond; and he had eventually left her with a kiss on her brow and laughter on his handsome face —never to return.

The long ago days of slavery in the West Indies also caught Marjorie's imagination, and she would sit for hours questioning Mrs. Keith, or some old retainer, of the days when there was much money but little marriage or giving in marriage. Marjorie also loved to delve into every question affecting those East Indians under indenture, who contribute so completely to the material welfare of the colony of British Guiana. She loved to note and compare every fact and fancy of the olden days in some measure, with the latter day system of indenture which was responsible for her own being, and the linking so romantically of the East and West in her.

When Marjorie heard of Des Voeux' great work on his colonial days, and the system of indenture as he found it, she was fairly wild with excitement. That book she demanded and meant to have; but that book she had to bide a long time for, as Mrs. Walton claimed that Marjorie already delved too deep into works of doubtful utility.

At the time when we see Marjorie seated on the gnarled roots of that venerable tree, she was evidently on the tip toe of expectation. She would shade her eyes with her hand and look far down the bay to the West of where she sat. Seeing nothing, she would, like a hunted being, start at a run towards the public road and repeat the process, looking along the road as far to the west as the eye could reach. At length she rushed impatiently into the house and exclaimed to Mrs. Walton.

" Auntie Wally, I don't think Harold is on the steamer at all, at all."

At this outburst Mrs. Walton smiled benignantly, and then calmly said.

"My dear Marjorie, I have always told you that it is unbecoming in a young lady to be so impetuous. I think we made out Harold pretty plainly, or some one uncommonly like him, as the steamer went past to her anchorage. Whoever it was certainly waved us friendly greetings."

Marjorie, still breathless and none abashed just rattled on, so soon as her aunt stopped speaking, or to be more accurate, as soon as she could get a word in.

" But Auntie, I am not impetuous: I have not hugged you to death, nor upset your head gear, I was merely saying————"

IN BONDAGE. 77

"Marjorie," called Mrs. Walton with some effort at sternness, "I do beseech that you give up your extremely unladylike way of referrng to things. I do not mind your referring to my cap as my 'head dress,' though I do detest even that manner of speech; but at 'head gear' I must certainly draw the line. Whatever Harold will think of you I don't know."

At this Marjorie sighed and inwardly promised to be as sedate as a nun.

But all further lecture was brought to a sudden close, for Marjorie espied a straggling line of good folk appearing over the edge of the wooded cliff which marked the descent of the miniature plateau sheer down to the water's edge.

CHAPTER EIGHTH.

For the fraction of a second the resolution to be " as sedate as a nun" had held Marjorie in leash, but, as the straggling line came into fuller view, her warm animal spirits burst all bounds, and with the boisterous shout "Here he comes," she was off like a rocket.

Down the winding path she flew: had she the fabled silver winglets pinned to her ankles she could hardly have sped faster, and before Harold, for he it was, could recover himself he was folded in an embrace as uncontrolled as it was affectionate; bearers and boatmen meanwhile looking on with amused attention; one fellow summing up the feeling of all in a brief, " Eh! Eh! de Missy glad fo' true." And " glad fo' true " was she.

" Oh, Harold," she cried as soon as he had disentangled himself, " I thought you were never coming. We could not tell whether you would come by boat or road, and looking between both places I never saw the boat: and now you are here."

" Well, young lady," said Harold, " let that be a lesson to you in life. Choose one path and stick to it."

" Oh, but Harold," cried Marjorie, " how could I ever tell which way you would come by? I might have chosen the road and you might have come by the bay; if I had chosen the bay you might have come by the road."

"I don't know," answered Harold, "Anyway, old Father Hyacinth says the great successes in life are those who choose the right way and stick to it. The failures, those who choose the wrong: and, the great armies of nobodies those who try to look both ways; or, as Gaston de Garcia would whisper, those who put equal money on both horses, and hold up a kicker on the 'outsider'."

"Oh you are talking rubbish," airily replied Marjorie, "and Gaston de Garcia has more sense than you; so 'just walk into my parlour said the spider to the fly'."

By this time, however, Mrs. Walton had abandoned her reserve and self control, and had advanced from the "parlour" to the head of the path which the new comers had just negotiated; and she greeted her only son affectionately. She then led him into the morning room where they found Mrs. Keith; to whom Harold gave an almost filial greeting.

Meanwhile Marjorie busied herself with the housemaids, and bearers, and boatmen. Harold looked on with amused tolerance: both Mrs. Walton and Mrs. Keith having grown too accustomed to Marjorie in that role to notice that there was anything out of the ordinary in this girl of fourteen being practically in supreme command.

Mrs. Walton dutifully enquired of His Lordship the Bishop, and wordly wise old Father Hyacinth, and drew some trivial account from Harold of his last term at college and the few details of his trip across from Port-of-Spain to Scarborough.

Marjorie, through with the luggage, had turned her attention to the ordering of an early breakfast and now joined the trio, flushed with the joy of Harold's homecoming and the bustle and excitement of active service. Her eyes sparkled and the dull white of her complexion gave place to a radiance that was charming to behold.

The coming of Marjorie was like a recharge of fluid to a half-worn battery. Harold had to retell all that he had told before, but with Marjorie's quips and sallies he

semed to have caught some of her verve in the telling.
Then having got it all out in her way, she marshalled them
all to the breakfast room.

The breakfast, or forestalled luncheon as it really is,
was plain, homely and wholesome. The tail of a succulent young snapper—the salmon of the West Indies—lay
invitingly in its dish, all pink and white in its delicate covering, fresh Sea Whelks, picked from the nearby rocks
and crevices that very morning by Mrs. Keith's own maid-of-all-work, and stewed in goat's milk; mutton from home
grown sheep; avocado pears and cassava farine made into
tasty side-dishes; then the floury cassava " sticks " themselves
bitter-sweet and wholesome, flanked by simmering white
rice. Cocoa, from home baked beans, rich in all its natural richness, unmedicated and palatable. Pine apples, bananas, and sapodillas; all in their natural splendour and in
the setting given by that famous breakfast room at St. Seriols
which looks out from three sides on the sparkling Caribbean: veritably an array that would have tempted the most
chronic dyspeptic.

At Mrs. Walton's request, Mrs. Keith had consented
to join the board, and a merry party indeed they made,
with Marjorie as the life and soul thereof. Despite her
aunt's frowns, Marjorie threw more or less disrespectful
quips at His Lordship the Bishop: wondered if he preferred " stale-mate " old bacon and eggs to West Indian
fish; fancied his eating farine with rancid coconut oil, or
worse, that " pale taster " olive oil; imagined his preference
for oysters or Scotch Haggis, over whelks and Tobago mutton, and wound it all up by temporarily calling Harold
" His Lordship." Next she brought old Father Hyacinth
under the fire of her wit, and wondered whether he would,
" go," under his " direct policy " scheme, for the upper part
of the snapper or would want to peep first at (the under
side. Gaston de Garcia she fancied juggling with a whole
banana in his mouth, and putting equal money on the port
and sherry, while holding up a kicker on something stronger.

That day Marjorie dwelt in Olympia and the hours sped on silver wings. She would be denied nothing and planned and replanned excursions, and everything imaginable, for the month that Harold was to remain at home before departing for the seminary in Germany, whence he would return a full-fledged priest of the Church of Rome. Harold was like clay in the hands of the potter; he could say "nay" to nothing his impetuous cousin proposed; and Mrs. Walton was only too content to let them have their way, provided she was left alone. There were many places that Marjorie's compelling imagination made her long to see, while she listened to the tales of days when Tobago was peopled by the "giants of those days." Mrs. Keith's uncanny tale of her son's fate drew Marjorie to the grim "Red Rock." Folk lore invited her to the cave of Robinson Crusoe; for though Juan Fernandez may have lived and looked for succour on an island in the Pacific, the locale of DeFoe's masterpiece is certainly Tobago. Tales of the Napoleonic wars, in which she took a more than passing fancy, caught her fast, and for Fort St. George, which had seen so much of the ebb and flow of those wars, she wanted a whole day. The grandeur of her own immediate coast line whetted her appetite to see the entire coast of Tobago. Harold was soon enthused of her plans and proposals for the month ahead, and schedules were prepared accordingly.

After some days of preparaton and postponements, the morning of the first excursion duly dawned. It had been agreed between Mrs. Walton and "the children," as she continued to call them, that Mrs. Keith should not be told of the destination of the first day's venture, for she would grow frantic with her protestations against it; for it was no other than "Red Rock" that they had won Mrs. Walton's permission to visit.

Harold, up early, and dressed only in shirt and trousers, lay in an easy chair in the verandah awaiting the coming of Marjorie. As he sat and mused he was indeed comely to look at: his well-shaped legs stretched before him were just easily crossed at about the instep, one over the other: his head rested on one forearm and the other hung listlessly by his side. His shirt half-opened at the collar displayed a neck and throat that may well have been envied by some society beauties. This comeliness of throat he inherited from his mother, as well as the deep limpid eyes, now half-shaded by their sweeping lashes; his well-shaped head carried the stamp of intellect, and his brow stood high and open; but the physiognomical student would have seen in his lips and chin something to give pause and study, for there were lines of strength and lines of weakness most inextricably mixed. The soft, full, but shapely upper lip may have been owned by a Borgia or a Stuart, while the firm and finely chiselled chin and under lip may have belonged to a Torquemada or a Hampden.

As he lay with his eyes half-closed, fancy took hold of him, and time was not. The thought occurred and challenged him as to whether he was following the course of wisdom in yielding so entirely to his mother's wishes and devoting himself to such undivided service as the Church of Rome demanded from its clergy and religieux. It was quite true, he admitted, "that it is noble to devote oneself so unselfishly to Church and Poor." Father Hyacinth had told him of the ascetic joy in renouncing the world, the flesh and the devil: still, the world was a goodly place, as Gaston de Garcia had so often tried to show him; and the flesh was, as a rule, comely to look at—as Marjorie; and, as to the devil, why, he need never have any " truck " with that sulphuretted gentleman.

In the midst of this reverie, Marjorie literally blew into the verandah, talking as she came.

"Harold, the boatman says we must hurry on or it will be too late to go to the 'Red Rock' and come back with the morning sun: and that the sea might also grow rough."

And then Marjorie grew silent for she beheld Mrs. Keith standing at the far end of the verandah rooted to the spot as though that good lady had seen a ghost.

"Oh! Marjorie" was all Mrs. Keith could ejaculate. "How could you?"

"But Mrs. Keith, there is nothing wrong," answered Marjorie. "We shan't be gone a minute before we are back again."

"My child," said Mrs. Keith, "if I could forbid the excursion I certainly would, for I have a terrible horror of that old rock."

"Never mind, dear," replied Marjorie soothingly, "when I return you shall have such a hug as to leave no doubt that I am very much alive."

Saying which, and fearing some future trouble, she was off, tugging Harold in her wake, before poor Mrs. Keith had time to say another word. Left to herself, that dear old lady sank into a nearby chair with tears in her eyes, for she dearly loved the wayward Marjorie.

Meanwhile that young lady ran down the winding seawards path still dragging the now well-back-to-earth Harold in her wake. It was but the work of a few moments for them to clamber down the rough foot way, hewn in the cliff, leading from the path above to the seashore below. In another few seconds they were in the little cove in which rode the boat that was to take them to their destination. Carefully picking their way out on some jutting stones they were soon abreast the boat and on board. As soon as Harold and Marjorie were comfortably seated, the boatman cautiously poled the boat through the narrow passage which gave egress from the cove within to the wide sea without; this duly negotiated, the men bent to their oars and headed for the open sea which lay between St. Seriols and Red Rock. Immediately Marjorie wanted to learn all about the tiller and steering, and would not be content until Harold had put the steering gear into her own hands and imparted to her what little of the mysteries he knew. There was, however, little steering to be done: the early morning sea was as still as a pond of glass, and the little boat propelled by its two oars steadily held its way.

St. Seriols lay well to the East of the shipping, and "Red Rock" lay well to the West; so it proved a good long pull across the wide expanse of water. At first the rock, seeming to stand well out to sea, showed up a dull reddish brown and looked rather small: as, however, the distance shortened, the rock loomed larger and larger, and assumed a brighter red colour. Marjorie was charmed with its ever changing aspect and fain would have lengthened the journey of approach, were it in her power. The first pleasant surprise for Marjorie was, that as they drew nearer the rock the water changed colour from deep blue to light green, indicating a decreasing depth. yet she was loath to believe the assurances of the boatmen that it was not due to some unexplained phenomena; because the acute horror of Mrs. Keith had always seemed to indicate that the rock rose sheer from the depths of the unfathomable ocean, and nothing but sure death could be the fate of any one who fell from its side into the water below. However, as the boat drew nearer there was little room for doubt as Marjorie gradually commenced to see the bottom; and by the time they reached the base of the rock she could well imagine herself in one of the coves around St. Seriols so sloping was the shore and so friendly the little wavelets that licked the feet of the giant rock. Another illusion that vanished was the structural shape of the rock: from St. Serols it looked one huge mass of rock carved in the form of a lion couchant; now the nearer view disclosed that it took two rocks to form the illusion; the main rock forming the head and shoulders, while a growth of cactus made the royal beast's shaggy mane, and another smaller rock some stones' throw away, formed the hind part of the lion. Hundreds of sea birds greeted the coming of the trespassers. "Mass Ben," the pelican, serious with his own importance, silently hurried away in long, swooping flights. The noisome mag-pie coloured "booby," which preyed on the catchings of the bigger bird, shrieked its protest and followed suit. Some others barely glanced over their shoulders indifferent to the approach of man.

Marjorie was insistent that she be forthwith allowed to land and explore the little caves and grottoes of the great rock, and soon she had Harold on the trail. Pretty sea shells caught her eye, and she was not slow in their appropriation. On reaching the southern side of the rock, they came upon a lovely little nook and Marjorie cried:

"Oh Harold, let us have a bath. It would be such fun to tell Mrs. Keith, and see her shudder. She does so think that if there is one sure gate to the other world it is located right here."

"I do not think it will be quite safe," answered Harold, "and I am not taking any chances. Moreover, you have brought no bathing costume."

"Oh don't be a fright," petulantly exclaimed Marjorie, "you know very well we seldom bother with those horrible clothes here. Go and ask the men if there is any danger, and leave me in peace. You will have to undress round that rock and I will do the same here. When I am well in the water you can go in from your side and then swim around to me; and after all, whose business is it what we do? All the same I won't undress before you," she added sadly, and as an after thought.

"Very well, young lady, I will go and ask them, and see," answered Harold.

Getting round leisurely to the boatmen, Harold learnt there was no danger in bathing from the rock. "At least," cautiously added the older of the two, " not more than in bathing anywhere else."

"And Mass Harold," added the younger man —he was Mass Harold to nearly everyone,—" if yo' was 'fraid why yo' bring dis?"

Harold, on examination, found that the servant who had brought the light repast for the homeward journey had also put in his bathing towel and one of those atrocities known as bathing trousers, which really cover little but the loins.

"Not much to go on with," mentally commented Harold; aloud he made a laughing remark, and went off with the two scanty hostages to Mrs. Grundy.

Marjorie hailed his approach with delight, for the welcome towel in his arms gave the answer to her waiting impatience.

"Well," said Harold, "here are two garments; or at least one half garment, and one possible." Indicating the towel, "You can take your choice."

At this Marjorie laughed intemperately "Why, Harold," she said "they are as bad, or as good as nothing: anyway I shall lay hands on that 'half' of a bathing costume of yours, and you can make shift with the other. Now hurry." With which she gave him a parting push.

"Don't come until I call you," she screamed, as he disappeared round the projecting edge of the rock.

Marjorie quickly divested herself of her garments and soon stood in Harold's "half of a bathing suit"; her finely sculptured bosom guiltless of any covering save the sunlight. As she stood with the water barely ankle deep she was a magnificent picture for artist or sculptor; affected by the cool morning air she bent somewhat, and held her clasped hands between her knees; her wealth of raven hair stood poised high upon her head: and the colour of her skin radiantly heightened by the keenness of the air. Courageous as she was she stood hesitating to venture further into the lonely and unknown waters: perhaps half held by those tales of horror which she had imbibed from Mrs. Keith since baby land.

"Harold," she called, "I am not going in alone. Come over."

Harold immediately made his appearance, and a sorry picture did he cut, with his bathing towel improvised into a sort of cross breed between Roman toga and East Indian loin cloth.

"Coward at last, eh!" he called, but Marjorie heard him not. She was in convulsions of laughter at the spectacle he presented.

"If you go on like that Marjorie," sternly called Harold, "I will not bathe at all; but just go right back and dress."

This threat brought Marjorie back to her senses and they entered the sparkling water hand in hand.

CHAPTER NINTH.

Harold and Marjorie splashed in the sparkling sea to their heart's content. Marjorie was an intrepid swimmer; they swam races, had diving matches for sea shells thrown to a given point, and in general enjoyed themselves as unconsciously of each other as any sand boys. At length the fast climbing sun and the growing size of the waves warned them that it was time to depart. Hurrying to his shelter, Harold soon divested himself of his improvised bathing suit, and, wringing it dry, threw it as far as he could reach for Marjorie to pick up and make shift as best she could. His own pachyderm he dried by frantic motions in the sunlight. In a little while both had donned their garments and were once more presentable to civilized people; thus together they made their way to where their boat rode merrily at anchor, with the two boatmen sprawled over seats and gunwales, basking in the sun like two huge brown lizards.

The boat was soon hailed and all once more aboard: Marjore again took the tiller, while Harold hunted for the good things that had been stowed aboard; thin rusks of cassava bread toasted and buttered: home made sweet bread studded here and there with dainty sweet meats and currants: rich biting sorrel drink: soft sparkling maubee; and somethng stronger, much stronger for the boatmen. These went to make up a menu that all united in thinking the best that could be obtained in the world. At length when the viands had been despatched, and the journey through, the travellers found themselves once more back at St. Seriols.

Marjorie forthwith hastened to give to Mrs. Keith the famous hug which she had threatened, and then proceeded to tell of her royal bath in the shadow of the King of beasts, at which the old lady grew pallid.

"My child," she said, "you are too prone to take risks in life, irrespective of the possible consequences; but I trust that fortune will always favour you."

Marjorie once more threw her arms around Mrs. Keith's neck, and giving one of her bear hugs, declared:

"You are the dearest old lady in the world." Saying which she made off to join Harold and his mother.

Days melted into nights, and nights breathed again into mornings, and all was happiness at St. Seriols. Each day brought new plans, and each succeeding one brought the next nearer to realisation. Among the earliest executed was the proposed visit to Fort St. George on the top of the hill overlooking the town. Early one morning Marjorie packed her hamper and, with the ever-willing Harold in her wake, started on the journey. At once she decided that the roads through the town would consume too much time, therefore the ascent should be made by the rude footpaths formed by water courses, and foot beaten by herdsmen. Heading straight from St. Seriols, they climbed up and up the steep hill side: first by one rough track that semed to head them far to the right, then by another which crossed the first almost at right angles: each climb however bringing them appreciably nearer the top. At last they came to a grassy plain immediately below the turreted battlements of the old fort, and then these came into full view. Marjorie stood to draw breath, as indeed they had previously many an occasion to do, and looking up at the walled embrasure, exclaimed:

"Harold, this must have been the side the English advanced from, when they last took the fort from the French."

"What nonsense are you after now?" asked Harold.

"Nonsense!" replied Marjorie, "what do you know about nonsense? What ever do they teach you all at college, if you don't know that this place has changed and rechanged hands between the French and English many times?"

"I am afraid," humbly ventured Harold, "I must confess my ignorance. At college we always have too many things to learn without bothering about poor romantic Tobago."

"There you are! you see," triumphantly said Marjorie, "I learn more at home, talking with all my old friends, than you ever do at college. Hannah has many stories of the old days and when we get up there, I shall ram some of them down your throat."

Saying which she once again led the way, and in a little while they had reached the summit, and clambered into the precincts of the fort itself. But, oh what a desolation greeted their view in those empty roofless buildings. On every side of the rectangle rose high brick superstructures, representing the one time gallantry and life of a garrison; now shutterless, roofless and empty. On the Eastern side rose a wall escarpment with gun embrasures: on the Western side, and well overlooking what shipping there was in the harbour, were long series of earth mounds from between each of which obsolete cannon frowned down. As Marjorie led Harold from gun to gun, the picture of the defence of Gibraltar, and Elliot's red-hot balls raining on the decks of the shipping, rose before her eyes. Turning to Harold she said:

"This fort must be as strong as Gibraltar, if only it had the men and the guns, eh!"

Harold smiled at her enthusiasm, but said nothing; for he knew what he would get if he did. From the guns

IN BONDAGE.

they descended lower on the Western side, and came to what was known as the "French" garrison: probably because of some additional buildings erected there by the soldiers of France. On this side also stood an old "bell" tank which hugely amused Marjorie. It reproduced with faithfulness every sound entrusted to it. Discovering this, Marjorie shouted to it that Harold was a noodle, and Gaston de Garcia a scamp: the tank faithfully admitted the libels; agreed that Harold was without intellect, and Gaston de Garcia without integrity.

After an hour of roamings among the various historic sites, the cousins sat themselves down amid the ruins to partake of their frugal meal and Harold remarked:

"Marjorie, you have forgotten all about your tales of the Wars of the Roses you so graciously promised to tell."

Marjorie laughed.

"Oh, you mean old Hannah's tales. There is not so much to tell: you have to fill in the blanks yourself and people these buildings with soldiers; then you will know all about them. Hannah remembers very little herself and can only tell of the the piping times of peace. Otherwise it is her mother's stories that she retells. Her mother remembers well when the French drove the English garrison up to Concordia—we must go there, by the way—and then the English had to surrender. After that every citizen had to appear in the streets with the French Cockade, and her old mistress roped in many pounds by making and selling them at ten shillings each. Then she remembers hearing how there was great voting at one time and everybody shouted "Napoleon." Just fancy, Harold, this little speck had its voice in seating on his Throne our great grandfather, or whatever he was.

"But Marjorie, you believe that nonsense about our descent from Napoleon?" asked Harold, "all of the boys had it at college. I should be a little ashamed of it if it were true."

"Oh! don't be a crab, you," stormily replied Marjorie, "Auntie says it's true, and I believe her; and as to being ashamed—you go and ask the Bell tank and it will tell you what you are."

"Never mind, tell us about Hannah," cried Harold.

"No, I won't; go to Hannah yourself. Boys that are rude and foolish don't deserve anything."

But Marjorie could be nothing long, and soon Harold had her back in good humour and sailing full before the wind.

"Just fancy," she at length recommenced, "when the English returned, they landed secretly right at the back of the island and marched on the Fort. An old man who piloted them was long teased, and known to the day of his death, as "John Forty Gallons," because every brook they crossed he had to drink of, so as to guarantee them its wholesomeness: it must indeed have been a thirsty tramp. When the English got to the fort the poor French soldiers were all in the town, far from their arms, and the English captured 'the Rock' without firing a shot. Best of all, there was not a flag among them and an English soldier ran his red tunic up the flagstaff."

"Excellent, oh Marjorie," said Harold, "but better told than likely true."

Marjorie thereupon lapsed into ill humour and signified her intention to go home: Harold again expressed contrition and tried to coax her back into good humour, but was hardly as successful as on the previous occasion; sufficiently, however, to set them in good graces for the return journey, which was duly accomplished with both the travellers sound of wind and limb; though many a time Marjorie vowed that her ankles had gone at last, at some more than usually fierce stumble down the rugged pathway, that they had elected to make the return journey by.

Next on Marjorie's itinerary was the visit to Robinson Crusoe's cave, and the morning of the appointed day dawned to find her on the tip toe of expectation. Harold had been

IN BONDAGE.

duly wakened by her at an early hour to brush up the ponies, saddle them and generally get them ready for the long ride. Marjorie herself had to be rigged in her new riding habit, specially made for the occasion and right well did she fancy herself in it. At last everything was complete and both excursionists in the saddle. Waving a fond farewell to the two stay-at-homes, Harold and Marjorie set their ponies at a canter and were soon lost to view.

The road from St. Seriols to Scarborough lay for a mile or so along the foot of Fort St. George's Hill, at a good height from the sea shore. High enough to obtain a firm metalled road; low enough to keep the blue sea always in view. An ideal ride it makes. When Marjorie had cantered her pony for two or three hundred yards, she felt the blood leaping in her veins and mounting to her cheeks. She had ridden, and ridden at a faster pace many a time before: often had the salt sea air fanned her brow whilst galloping, but never yet had she felt that pulsing in her veins and that half-lifting and half-suffocating sense within. Still she uttered no word nor gave any sign. She would not have drawn rein for worlds, and as she glanced at the steady easy rein with which Harold rode she found pleasure in his being. The crisp morning air, the sheen of the sea, the easy motion of the ponies, all played tune to her feelings and kept her silent.

Harold, as yet unconscious of the dawning loveliness that rode beside him, thought more perhaps of the object of their journey than anything else, and his chief object was lest the guides should fail them, or the sea be not low enough to permit a thorough exploration.

As they drew level with the old fashioned Parish Church of St. Andrew's with its high mullioned windows and quiet church yard, "where the rude forefathers of the hamlet sleep," Harold almost unconsciously tightened his hold on his reins and called to his companion briefly and as with authority: " Slow down."

Whether it was the peaceful slumber of the dead he would not disturb, or the near approach of the busier part of the township which he would not startle, it would perhaps be impossible to say. Marjorie, however, for once, obeyed without comment and reined in her pony. As the sturdy little animal broke into a walk she just gave vent to one deep-drawn, " Oh that was delicious."

The travellers rode at a walk through the town, past the little straggling houses, down the weedy street, past the old jail, until the town proper was cleared and they emerged on the sandy sea beach which ran to the West of the town, curving and stretching as far as the eye could reach. Marjorie headed direct for the firm, white sand of the beach, alongside of which runs the public road which offers a safe retreat from the rising tide. The ride from St. Seriols was within sight of the sea; the ride from the town was now on the sea shore itself, with the sea waves occasionally rippling between the hoofs of the ponies, and the water sometimes splashing to their girths. As the ponies sniffed the rank sea air they tossed their heads and champed their bits as though eager for another gallop, and Marjorie, taking her own at his desire, gave him rein and called to Harold to follow. Once again, this time on the firm white sand, damp and dazzling in the morning light, did they let the little beasts go at a rousing canter, and once again did Marjorie feel the inward exhilaration and the mounting of the blood to her cheeks; again they drew rein, and after crossing a couple of rivulets took to the road.

Many tales had Marjorie heard of the Hope and Lambeau rivers, in time of torrential rains, carrying away foot passengers, who were foolhardy enough to venture the crossing, far out to sea and of their being heard of no more; and, now, she was coming to, at least, one of these unbridged death traps.

After following the high road for some while they came once again to a little bit of sand crossed by a stream and Harold called "Marjorie, here is your famous Lambeau river."

"Oh, no," airily answered Marjorie," this is a mere streak: it could not drown a good sized rabbit, even if poor bunny were half asleep.

"Therein you err." replied Harold, "when the rains come this 'mere streak' becomes a roaring torrent seeking whom it may devour. Doubtless that bridge engineer who came over thought like you, for the *foutee* bridge that he put up went to sea at the first asking and now is no more. Perhaps some other day they will put up another bridge that travellers will be able to find when it is most needed."

"Well, I never," laughed Marjorie as the water in the little rivulet barely reached to the ponies' fetlocks.

Mounting a little eminence, they rode on, between groves of coconut palms towering high over them, through little hamlets and past abandoned sugar Estates. Hamlets that lay "far from the crowd's ignoble strife," and sugar estates that once kept their owners in affluence in the old country, but which went to the wall in the stern economic struggle brought about by the unrelenting competition of Bountied beet.

Then Marjorie, looking to sea, espied the Red Rock bold and grim in its outlines in the morning light, and seen to much greater advantage from that point than from anywhere else.

"Now," she exclaimed, "I can nearly believe Hannah's old world tales."

"Well, what next?" asked Harold.

"Oh, nothing much, this time, only she declares that her mother remembered hearing of the time when cornfields lay well and far out between here and Red Rock—where is now this wide expanse of sea. She also declares that her mother claimed vehemently that the old time folks could walk to the rock."

"Well, and what makes you believe it more now?" further queried Harold.

"Nothing so very particular," answered Marjorie, "only it looks more true from here than from St. Seriols. And the earth down here is not unlike that at Red Rock and may well have been joined to it at one time."

Marjorie had stumbled on a sound geological proposition; and on another which had played its part in the cane sugar industry. That "red" earth had been the "rich red clay" which had been the boast of the planters of the bygone. A clay which had indeed yielded them wonderful crops, but which was also their undoing; for it had taught them to rely alone on the field, to the neglect of the factory, and when the *debacle* of prices came, it found them like the unwise virgins, unprepared; and they went under, never again to rise.

Harold laughed his laugh and said:

"I won't wonder at your writing a book about Tobago, one of these times when you grow up."

"Who knows," perkily replied Marjorie. "That at least will be better than burying myself for life as you are going to do."

"I am not going to bury myself for life, as you put it," seriously answered Harold, "I hope, and hope sincerely, to yet do a lot of good in the world."

Then both relapsed into silence and no sound broke the hush of the morning air, save the twittering of the nearby birds, and the rhythmic beat of the horses' hoofs on the metalled road.

CHAPTER TENTH.

Travelling at an easy rate, with an occasional canter when the beach or the road invited it, Harold and Marjorie came in view of Crown Point, where the fabled cave lay; but, as previously arranged, they turned their horses' heads to Pln. Felicitie where they were to breakfast with its owner, old Mrs. Warrington, and thereafter pick up their guide for the exploration.

On reaching Mrs. Warrington's, that grave faced old lady was overwhelmed with joy. Marjorie possessed the knack, in a superlative degree, of marching easily into the hearts of all and sundry, while Harold's quiet dignity endeared him to all. Mrs. Warrington welcomed them with all the old time courtesy of the Eighteenth Century. She lived in what was known as the Great House, great to-day in little but its memories; those fast-fading memories of the olden days when all that was great and gay in the by-gone days of Tobago's splendour used to congregate in its spacious halls to pass the time of day. To-day most of the Great Houses, as each principal residence on all the Estates used to be known, have fallen victims to the hand of Time. That at Pln. Felicite stands out however on the skyline as a sentinel on the sands of time. If its exterior showed the trace of the years, its interior bore the charm of its mistress. Lounge chairs, sofas, rocking chairs, all spread invitingly to the weary limbs of the travellers.

Mrs. Warrington, flanked by an army of retainers, had stood in the hall to receive her visitors.

"Welcome, my children," she cried, and then folded Marjorie to her bosom. Disengaging herself in a moment, she clasped Harold's outstretched hand in both her own and exclaimed:

"I am delighted to have you both."

"Well if you are delighted," replied Harold, "we are just overflowing with gratitude."

"Granny," chimed in Marjorie, "I have been longing and longing to see you, but could never get an escort to bring me down; and since that little riding business last year with "Marechal Neil," Auntie won't even hear of my going on any rides alone."

"Why didn't you let me know?" answered Mrs. Warrington, "then I would have sent two of the hands to escort you down. I quite agree that it is about time dear Mrs. Walton laid some hands on you; you trying little wild cat."

Then she gave Marjorie another hug, and calling to two of her retainers she bade them:

"Show Master Harold to the big room." Then adding mischievously, in a sort of *sotto voce*, "As if ever he wanted any showing." Then louder, "and you, Marjorie, come along with me. The balance of you people get along with you, and put breakfast on the table," saying which, she waved the remainder of her retainers out of sight.

So soon as they were all out of earshot Mrs. Warrington remarked to Marjorie.

"I am sure I don't know what to say to that stupid Harold, running away to bury himself in any old convent for."

Mrs. Warrington was a real old world Non-conformist, and she knew as little about the Church of Rome as of astronomy; it never seemed to bother her old Tobago mind that a convent was for ladies exclusively. Indeed there was no convent in Tobago and it may well be questioned if the dear old lady had ever seen one in her life. For years she had never read a newspaper, and she dwelt as completely among her sheep, and other live stock, as ever the children of Israel did in the wilderness.

Mrs. Warrington was much attached to both Mrs. Walton and Marjorie, and had consequently heard all about Harold and the plans for his future: but it was a constant source of regret to her that they all belonged to " that French Church," as so many people in the dear little island regarded the Church of Rome; out of delicacy her references to the subject had been rare, and of very few words. To-day her romantic old mind, regarding Harold and Marjorie such a ' good match," as she thought, revolted at the proposed barbarous wrecking of an engaging romance; but none of these thoughts did she give expression to, save in that whimsical remark above recorded.

' He is not going to a convent, granny," answered Marjorie with a smile, " but to a seminary."

" Seminary or convent is every bit the same," Mrs. Warrington declared. " All the same here is your room."

She then pushed open the door of the room in which Marjorie and Mrs. Walton had spent many a happy day at the invitation of this old time lady, who was now left lonely save only for her faithful retainers; every one of whom, and, in some instances, even their parents before them, had been born on " Felicite." Though Marjorie had visited Mrs. Warrington on many a previous occasion, on each of these they had come and gone by waggon through the main road, hence her unfamiliarity with the round about route taken that morning, and her discoveries in Geology and bridge building.

" You are a dear," cried Marjorie, " why you treat me like a Princess," she exclaimed as she looked in at the newly prepared room, " and as though I had come for a year," and drawing Mrs. Warrington into the room she added:

"But granny, you forgot that Harold will be back in about four years' time, so we shan't be losing him altogether."

"Four years' time!" scornfully echoed Mrs. Warrington, "And as what? A Priest, with his face as long as his gown. Thank goodness Charles Warrington never became any stupid old priest!"

Marjorie, missing entirely the last point, laughed immoderately at the pictured length of Harold's face, and declared it good enough for a book.

"Never mind, child," consolingly added Mrs. Warrington, "freshen up your face with that cold water, and then drink of this glass of milk," as a barefooted black girl appeared in the doorway with her face all wreathed in smiles, and bearing the life giving milk, fresh drawn, warm and refreshing, straight from the faithful old cow which stood in a nearby paddock.

Marjorie having complied, Mrs. Warrington took opportunity to look over her. Taking both her hands in her own the elder lady exclaimed:

"Why, child, I can scarcely believe my eyes." Scanning her from head to heel, she added: ' and you tell me that you are only just fourteen: you look every inch of eighteen."

"Well, I hope when I am eighteen I won't look eighty, that's all," saying which, Marjorie impetuously kissed the diminutive old lady.

"Harold must be ready for breakfast," at length declared Mrs. Warrington, and, Marjorie signifying agreement, they both sallied forth in search of Harold.

Harold was not long in the finding, and Mrs. Warrington greeted him with the unbending dictum that not another word was to be-spoken until they reached the breakfast table. At which, Marjorie, with a mock warning

IN BONDAGE.

"Harold!" put her index finger to her lips and led the way to the breakfast room.

Mrs. Warrington, linking her arms in Harold's, followed in her wake, declaring meantime, that "she did not know however dear Mrs. Keith or your Mamma, got on with that dreadful tease."

"Oh, Marjorie is all right," answered Harold, "she is not always that, and never anything long. Just now they are saved it all and I am the butt for everything."

On reaching the breakfast room they were met by a galaxy of servants. If Mrs. Warrington had few relatives she certainly had many servants; a feature, possibly, in all West Indian country houses. A separate servant drew a chair for each of the covers, and soon the charming meal was well on its way.

As Harold glanced round the old wainscotted room to which he had made many a boyhood visit, several were the thoughts that came crowding to him.

The room breathed of a bygone generation. Hand carved mahogany chairs ranged round the board. On the walls hung old time steel engravings in gilt frames. The old fashioned high backed mahogany side-board groaned under cut glass decanters, high class candle shades, and valuable china; and bore them all with a stately grandeur which gave promise to hold them for generations, if undisturbed by the bargain hunter or the indifferent.

Then Harold remembered the few years that had passed since he last visited Felicitie and remembered also the two sturdy boys, Bill and Jack: boys who to him had seemed to know everything. They had taught him how to set flying traps for "Mountain" doves; horse hair traps for "Ground" doves; and "lagley" for sugar-eaters and blue birds. They had taken him to the stream which they called a river, and shown their dexterity in groping for crayfish: there also had they taught him to swim, with the aid of an empty soap box turned upside down. They had initiated him into the mysteries of the "sling shot" or catapult, as they rightly called it; and soon his prowess had equalled their own. Many a day at college had he remembered the red-letter day on which they all three had decided to test the accuracy of their aim on a smart " billy cock " hat of one of the island's dudes, as he rode past. Taking post behind the low wall that divides the peaceful graveyard of St. Andrew's Anglican Church from the public road, Bill had claimed first shot and missed: Harold next in turn, and over anxious to take the hat, but miss the head, had missed also; when Jack, fiery and impetuous to " bring the game to earth." let fly a whizzling shot which missed the " beaver," as they called it, but tore the unhappy man's ear in two. Jack always maintained that it was the bumping and a swerve of the horse, which had thrown out his aim. That however, was poor solace to the rider, even if it were known to him, and he, throwing dignity to the winds, had wheeled his horse straight for the wall. The boys immediately took to heel, and the rider, dismounting, gave active chase. Over graves and gravestones ran the boys: over ditto, ditto chased the man; who, however, soon seeing himself outpaced and ridiculous, gave up the chase.

A stern letter to Mrs. Keith respecting the " strange boy who lived with her," gave Harold some pangs, for he bore his mother's landlady a chivalrous regard. A similar missive reached Mrs. Warrington and things for some time looked black for " Jack the shooter," as he was known ever after, for he had readily owned up; but his saving sense of humour in distinctly and grievantly blaming the horse, won him temporary consideration. At length, as none could bring themselves to discuss the incident with sufficient gravity to impart the needed severity to the lecture or castigation, the boys all got off scot free.

Clothing his thoughts with speech, Harold enquired of news of his erstwhile playfellows.

" I can't get Bill to give up the sea," answered Mrs. Warrington. " The last letter I got from him was dated from Shanghai. He says he hopes to get his ship next trip.

IN BONDAGE.

I have heard that so often; but even if he does 'get his ship,' as he calls it, what consolation will that be to a poor lone woman?"

"And 'Jack the shooter'?" queried Harold. At the old time appellation they all laughed heartily.

"Oh, Jack is in London," answered Mrs. Warrington, "and," she added petulantly, "grinning his face at stupid people from some rickety old stage."

Thus did poor good Mrs. Warrington describe one of London's most famous comedians. Jack acted in comedy or appeared at Music Halls as the moods took him. At the latter he had made much money and kept very many audiences in roars of laughter as he related the famous episode which had given him his name. The incident had been variously billed as "the Boys and the Beaver," "the Chaser and the Chased," "A test of marksmanship," etc. No matter how it was billed, when Jack got to the point when he, self-confident and impetuous, sprang from behind that wall and sent the pebble whizzing after the beaver, but caught instead the wide-hanging auricular organ of the rider, the house became uncontrollable. But when he described the chase over graves, and slippery grave stones, across drains and over carefully tended hedges, colouring it all here and there as suited his audience: when he mournfully described the effect of the gory drops which ran freely from the wounded member, all became frantic, and many of the audience could you see with the tears, bred of excessive laughter, coursing down their cheeks. But a prophet is not without honour save in his own country, and Jack's own mother described him as " grinning his face at stupid people from some rickety old stage."

"Poor Jack, I should like to see him," said Harold.

"Yes, you would like to see him," answered Mrs. Warrington, "but I am sure I would never like to see my own son making such a fool of himself."

"A fool of himself," echoed Marjorie, "oh, Mrs. Warrington, I should just love to go on the stage myself."

"I dare say you would," replied Mrs. Warrington, "I don't know of anything hair-brained you would not like to do."

"But that is not hair-brained," protested Marjorie, "Just think of being able to hold audiences spell-bound every night. Just think of being able to bring laughter and merriment to thousands of hearts every day. It's grand."

"That's very well," answered poor lonely Mrs. Warrington, "but I only wish somebody else's son was doing it, and I had my poor scattered-brain boy by me, in my old age, to bring laughter and merriment to my old heart."

Then Mrs. Warrington launched out on her pet subject.

"I don't know what is coming over poor Tobago," she said, "All her sons leave her, the brightest and the best, to make a home somewhere else. Old Mr. Gregory, my minister, says it is not to be wondered at, as there are no openings here. Even you, Harold," she continued, "whom we have come to regard as a Tobago boy, must needs be running away to become a stupid priest."

"Well, a priest I suppose I will become," answered Harold, "but a stupid one I hope to escape from being; if even I have to come to see you every now and again to keep my old head going."

Thus, as they chatted on everything imaginable, the breakfast came to a close and, shortly after, the travellers started for their objective.

The guide who had been engaged, answered readily to Harold's call, and the trio set out for Crown Point Bay; not however without a solemn warning from Mrs. Warrington not to run any undue risks, as "the cave," as she called it "was not as safe as it used to be." Marjorie laughed and declared to Harold "Another Red Rock story!"

On arrival at the open bay leading to the cave the first note sounded by Marjorie was one of disappointment.

"But Harold," she cried, "what sort of a thing is this?"

"What sort of a thing is what?" querulously asked Harold in reply.

"Why, the cave, of course"; Marjorie answered. "Where are the 'look outs,' and the galleries, and the terraces?"

"You seem to have expected a sort of Gothic Cathedral, and I regret the disappointment," ventured Harold, "but you seem to have forgotten the inroads of the sea. In dear old Crusoe's time—to go back to your dream land—the sea was miles out: this bluff of land was higher and further out; in short the whole frontage of your Cathedral has been smashed in. Just what you told me about Red Rock and old Hannah's cornfields is just what has happened here."

"Oh, then let us get in before more of it is washed away, that's all," impetuously urged Marjorie.

"Let us get in by all means," answered Harold, "but let us get out before the tide comes in."

Marjorie, unhearing and unheeding, simply marched right in. The cave was spacious at first, but as her companions followed and they went further and further in, the chamber shrank until no further progress could be made without stooping.

"Well, this is enough," called Harold, "and it is time we go back."

"Not me." cried Marjorie, 'I go on until I get to the far end and come out at Cove bay. What is the use of coming if I may not see all of it."

"Marjorie," soberly ventured Harold, "don't be so venturesome. You heard what Mrs. Warrington said. The cave is not quite safe. I don't want to stay in a minute longer than absolutely necessary. And, besides, by the time you got round to the Cove side the sea might be in, and any fall of earth behind us may cut off our retreat at any minute; with the sea advancing from both ends we stand a chance, with too much delay in here, of being drowned like rats in a hole. Come back," he cried imperiously, as Marjorie, scarce heeding his warning, was groping along almost on her hands and knees.

"Go back yourself," she called back, "who is making any delay but you, with your sermonizing. I can drown like a rat if I choose. You, I suppose, would like to drown like a Rajah; then keep out," she cried, and steadily advanced in the gloom, none of them having brought any lights of any description.

"Come along, old man," she called to the guide, "and don't let me drown like a rat in a hole."

The old man hobbled on to keep her company, though petulantly declaring that "de Missy was too hard ears." Harold reluctantly bringing up the rear, dutiful, if doubtful.

Marjorie suddenly called a halt.

"What in the name of goodness is this," she cried, and held up to view some bleached bones. "The balance of Crusoe's last dinner, I swear."

Old Cudjoe, the guide, fumbled for his flint and steel to coax a light in the gloom, but Harold found himself still the happy possessor of a box of lucifers which he had taken to the stable early that morning, and in their fitful gleam they discovered some more stray bones and the unmistakable skull of some small animal.

"Oh that is mine forever," Marjorie declared in a sort of stage whisper, as she pounced upon the gruesome find. "*Momento Mori* indeed, and of my death like a rat in a hole."

"Don't talk nonsense," called Harold, "do you know what you have there? Nothing but proof positive of what I told you. That animal probably came in to shelter from the weather and got caught by the tide, and he left his bones here. I have no desire to imitate his example, so let us return, I say."

"Oh no," Marjorie replied, "we are in already: let us get out by all means, but by this end," and thereupon she continued her scramble onwards.

Persevering in her determination for a little while, Marjorie at last cried out:

"Aha my boy, light ahead." And in truth there, at the far end of what was now little but a tunnel, a small speck of light showed itself. "At least," she added, "the sea is not yet in at this end."

Hurrying their paces the amateaur explorers emerged in the full light of day, and Harold breathed freely once more, meanwhile vowing that he would never more follow his cousin on any of her mad cap races.

"But see, you chump," triumphantly cried Marjorie, "Here is my skull. If I had not gone on, I would not have had this to show. What is it, anyway? she asked, turning to old Cudjoe.

The old man made a short but critical examination, and then cryptically announced: "Daady goat," which, being interpreted according to island parlance, meant the head of a he-goat, and Marjorie was as pleased as punch.

Soon after, Harold and Marjorie bade their guide adieu and set out on their pleasant ride back to St. Seriols, after once more calling on the good Mrs. Warrington and reporting due progress.

CHAPTER ELEVENTH.

Gradually the time drew near for Harold to make his long journey to Europe, there to develop into a full fledged member of St. Dominic's Order of Preachers. In the early days Mrs. Walton had set her heart on Harold taking the oaths of the Society of Jesus, but the close environment of the good fathers of St. Dominic, who ministered to the handful of Catholics in Tobago, had eventually turned her determination in favour of their Order; she moreover felt that in that Order which was created to bring back, by preaching and spiritual teaching, those alienated from the Church, lay greater chances of Harold's return as a Missionary to Tobago, when together they might devote their lives to bringing that once Catholic province back to the faith of its early settlers.

Accordingly, arrangements were made that he should go to one of the seminaries in Germany, and there complete the work so ably commenced by the College of the Immaculate Conception in Trinidad.

Marjorie watched the fleeting hours with an aching heart: she saw the disappearance of all those joy rides and excursions with which she had filled her days and peopled her dreams, since Harold's return from College. Her young heart traced its sorrow to no other cause than the loss of her companion. The inexperience of her young heart told her not that it was the budding womanhood in her which cleaved to the comeliness of the male, who was her constant companion, as tenderly as the ivy to the oak.

But yesterday they had made a homely little excursion, along the sea shore skirting St. Seriols, engaged in the diverting pastime of picking the luscious whelks as they cleaved to the rocks or made their way down the little crannies and crevices of the bays and coves.

Heading straight to the West, they had passed by the silent grave of the long dead little Helen, and striking the ravine which divided St. Seriols from the next property, had made their way down the dry water course of the " divide." That, to the imaginative Marjorie, was in itself a pleasure. Following the depression made in the hillside and clambering down the steep banks, here a big boulder to be slid down, there a deep pool of stagnant water to be negotiated, each and every one added to the joy of the excursion. Sometimes shrieking to Harold to help, sometimes perkily rejecting his kindly offices, until at length they reached the sea: then commenced their slow journey back East.

Marjorie with Mrs. Keith's wide-brimmed sun hat tied close about her ears, carried a basket over her arm; and Harold with an old felt hat battered close on his head, to defy the most persistent gust of wind, carried an old cutlass and an iron rod.

Many were the pleasures of that morning. Nothing pleased Marjorie more than to see Harold prone on his stomach, trying to reach some giant ,whelk or the other, overwhelmed in an instant and drenched from head to heel by some incoming breaker which he had neither heard nor noted. Marjorie inded sometimes got her share, but as she was more often than not on the look out, she frequently had time to get clear of each aggressive wave ere Harold could take advantage of her warning shout. As they potted from bay to bay and cove to cove, each of which exhibited its own characteristic beauty, Marjorie drank in every crag and line of the landscape beauty.

"You know, Harold," she said at last, "I wish I could paint."

"You do," answered he, full of the work in hand, 'Paint what?" he asked as he wearily straightened his back.

"Oh, paint right here," said Marjorie airily.

"What! with me in these togs, like a broken down fisherman? No, sirree!" laughed Harold.

"Oh, you can be left out," said Marjorie, "one speck of rock more and *you* won't be missed off the face of the earth. Just you look at this double bay with its back ground of cliff and wood"; and as she grew more enthusiastic she caught at Harold's arm. "Look again at that gallery of rock which separates what Mrs. Keith calls the 'gravel' bay from that which she calls the 'boat' bay; and then that bluff of land straight ahead, with the remains of the old target range right out to sea, and the waves breaking over it. It's fine. Oh, Harold!" she continued, 'I would like to do something great. Something not for the world to call great, but something I could feel was great. I feel the inward pressing to do; but there is no way I can see before me. I am ignorant and know nothing."

Harold was inclined to make a flippant reply, but as he looked into his cousin's face and saw its gravity, and the wistfulness that was there reflected he strangled the rising jest, and spoke seriously, with wisdom far beyond his years.

"Marjorie, if you feel that way, don't be in a hurry. Remember what your old Hannah says, 'hurry spoils the pot.' You will find your work one day. It might not be in the direction you would now choose: it might be merely the girding on of some soldier's armour and the steeling of his heart for battle, then you alone will measure how great has been your task; but, nevertheless, prepare yourself as best you can."

Saying which, he placed his left hand on the top of her head and tipping up her chin with his right, looked straight into the wistful face and added:

" You would never, with a look like that, ' bring down ' a house like ' Jack the shooter.' "

In a second Marjore's face was once again wreathed in smiles and their progress was resumed, for the tide continued to ebb and more tempting clusters of whelks to disclose themselves. Rounding the promontory on which stood the long discarded target range and the " copper " bay, and working through the rocks, they came to the big " sandy " bay which marked the limit of their journey for that day.

The great big " sandy " bay had alike been the charm and the terror of the two when they toddled together and helped old Jim Walton with his baths. The other bays were more or less divided into small ponds and, as they were also sheltered in a degree, their waves were diminutive accordingly: but at the sandy bay there was one wide expanse of sea, roaring on to the beach, unbroken by a single stone or boulder. On this beach could be found, high and dry, trunks of fallen trees, sea shells and hundreds of " sea gru-grus," swept thither from the mighty Orinoco.

Here, while walking along the beach in a sort of recreative promenade, Marjorie remarked that the next day would be the last of their excursions, and they would go for one last long ride right through the centre of the island; Harold, who could deny her nothing, readily agreed, and on reaching home, ordered the ponies accordingly.

Marjorie was awake early the next morning, on the tip toe of expectation for this last day's ride; and sat at her bedroom window watching for the ponies to come into sight along the high road leading out from Scarborough. No sooner did she espy them than she bounded out to waken Harold, who was still sleeping soundly in the adjoining room.

Marjorie, woman in her every sentiment, except awakening consciousness, when she entered Harold's room and saw him sleeping so soundly and peacefully, felt the unerring mother sentiment of love and protection surge in her breast. It was a feeling as free from sex as it was impersonal. The child-woman as she stood looking at the sleeper hardly understood it's meaning. All she knew, or was conscious of, was a desire not to waken, but to still the room and keep off intruders: then she murmured, scarcely above her breath:

"Poor fellow! he must be tired."

The sleeper lay with his face pillowed on his forearm, with an easy grace and litheness of limb that it was a pleasure to behold. At the muttered words Harold sighed and moved uneasily, and Marjorie felt the overwhelming desire to take him in her arms and hush him back to slumber. Acting on the impulse of the moment she knelt by the bedside and kissed him gently as she would a sleeping child. Harold was awake in an instant.

"Mother, that you?" he said, and then opened his eyes.

Marjorie, smiling sweetly, with the echo of the maternal still upon her, answered:

"Harold, it is I. You somehow slept late, but on my coming into the room to waken you, you looked so much like a sleeping baby that I actually kissed you for one."

Harold smiled and blushed visibly. Exchanged kisses between these two had been no rare thing, though growing consciousness, at least on Harold's part, had made them less frequent of late. Harold, to cover his confusion busily threw off the bed clothes and jumped out of bed.

In a little while the travellers were well on their journey. Harold, now fully conscious of the charms of his cousin; she, sublimely unconscious of every feeling save that his companionship was pleasurable.

The ride that morning, for the first part, lay along the level road, skirting the sea and at a fair elevation from it, which had been taken on the excursion to Robinson Crusoe's cave. As soon as Marjorie entered upon the fair stretch of road, with the sea spreading far to the East and West, her pulses tingled with the pleasurable remembrance of the gallop previously referred to, and, calling to Harold to follow, she gave rein to her little charger. Anon her blood began to mount to her cheeks, the old joy of *abandon* returned, and she for the first time wondered if the personality of her companion had any part or parcel in ministering to her joyousness. Swift as an arrow, new sent upon its errand, Marjorie substituted, in imagination, many of the men and maidens that she knew, in Harold's place; but in each and every instance there was the gaping blank of disappointment, and eventually it reacted on the present enjoyment of her gallop. Black despair seized upon her, why, she knew not; then, sudden like, and, almost unconsciously, she reined in her startled beast upon his haunches.

Harold, unwarned of her intentions, had shot past and she was alone with her thoughts. So peculiar is the female mind that in the instant Marjorie felt nothing but irritation and annoyance with him. It did not occur to her to warn Harold of her intention to slow down; and, if it did, it may be doubted if, in her moment of petulance with him, she would have done so; as a consequence Harold was yards in front of her before he could bring his mount to a halt.

"Hallo, Marjorie," Harold cried, "what's wrong?"
"Nothing," answered Marjorie, laconically.
"Then, why did you pull up?"
"Nothing," again answered Marjorie.
And Harold said nothing.

Then Marjorie's heart, prompted from she knew not where, suddenly asked itself:

"Suppose it were Gaston de Garcia?"

In an instant her face was one wreath of smiles and once more she gathered up her reins and called upon Harold to follow. The gay substitution however gave her no satisfaction: the illusion was imperfect and Marjorie once more reined in; in a much better temper, however, on this occasion with Harold, for she gave him due warning and they pulled up together.

The riders again cleared the Town and wheeled in a Northerly instead of a Westerly direction. In the place of the sanded beach they now rode along shaded lanes, past the famous King's Well, with its drinking trough fashioned after that King's coffin which was set in the market place as a drinking trough for horses; past Rocky Vale now but a name and a memory, through to Mile End, and then to the tragic "Governor Ross's Gully," down which that ill-fated representative of the pomp and panoply of Royalty fell, while driving home one night, and paid the forfeiture of his life. Climbing up by easy stages the hills which overlook the town of Scarborough, Marjorie and Harold soon reached Government House; and then on to Concordia, with its ghosts and its graves of a by-gone generation, whither that one time island garrison had withdrawn before surrender, in the days when Tobago was one of the pawns on the political chess board. Here overgrown with rank vegetation, with its tombstones indecipherable and crumbling to dust, stood an old grave yard which spoke of a by-gone day of learning and of culture. Here may be seen, if the riders had turned aside from the beaten track, tombstones and marble slabs all futilely seeking to indicate to an indifferent generation the virtues of the forgotten dead.

Looking back from this point the riders could see Scarborough bay—or Rockly bay, to give it its correct geographical name—in all its loveliness, with the irrepressible Red Rock, standing well under a bluff of land, cold, stern, and defiant of time and the sea.

Pausing for some while to drink in the glories of the scenery, Harold wondered how came it that such a fair garden of nature, where all was perpetual Spring, could thus lay neglected and desolate: its factories ivy-grown and silent; its best sons wanderers on the face of the earth—one

IN BONDAGE.

"grinning his face" at London audiences, another roaming the vast and measureless ocean; and hundreds of them God knows where. Harold knew of the days when Scotland sent its best to settle in Tobago, and he now wondered at the desolation. Simple youth. He could not trace the stupendous folly of a generation which took no thought of the morrow; nor the devastating effect of a hurricane which dated back to 1847.

Once more, the riders went on; past Adelphi, where stands a village church which was once the pride of the surrounding gentry, but now struggled gallantly, with the aid of a negro peasantry, to keep its timbers together: past the "gap," leading to the Alma, and thence on to Mason Hall where stands another edifice reared to the greater Glory of God, but, to-day, a mere mile stone in the road of degeneracy. Then through some of the most ravishing rustic scenery, past tall, graceful bamboos, curving under the weight of their fronds and shading lovely waterfalls, all of which create the most entrancing sylvan retreats; past Mount Dillon, Highlands, Moriah: each and every name calling up the gallant days when Cane Sugar was King, and West Indian Merchant Princes vied with the Blood Royal itself in the magnificence of their spendthrift caste. Always, always with the heads of the riders' horses pointing almost due North, until at last Marjorie caught a glimpse through the hills of the bright blue sea beyond.

Marjorie had read much of travel and adventure, and as the sea came into bolder view she pulled her horse to its haunches and exclaimed:

"Oh, Harold, look at the sea: We left it behind, and see! here it is again. I can feel almost some of the joy Cortez felt when 'silent upon a peak in Darien,' he saw the Pacific wide before him. It must have opened on him through the hills gradually as this has done. Somehow, although I knew the sea was on this side of the island also, I only half expected to see it."

Harold listened in silence, and then remarked:

Don't follow Keats. Balboa discovered the Pacific, not Cortez. But your romance will cover everything with imagery. There is nothing much in coming to the sea which we left behind: though I grant you that it is lovely. Will you ride down to it, or what?"

" No," answered Marjorie, " I won't go near enough to wreck the dream. We shall return from this point."

Harold then pointed out the hut of the guide who had taken them to Robinson Crusoe's cave, and who had begged of them to honour his little home with a call if ever they went in that direction, and suggested a visit.

Marjorie, ever on the lookout for novelty and romance, agreed, and forthwith they decided that old Cudjoe was to be visited.

If Angels had descended on the habitation of the old African, who had "come from Guinea," he could not have been more overwhelmed. His hospitality, though prescribed in kind, was as boundless as it was comprehensive. Calling for some rustic stools, he placed them in the shade of the big tamarind tree, which sheltered his rude hut, and bade the travellers be seated, while he got " a mouthful a' grass fo' de animals."

His visitors, however, were not to be neglected for his four-footed friends, for, as he hurried to serve the useful beasts, he called to one of his grandsons to pick some " water " coconuts; and by the time he got back, these were ready to be presented. Anyone who has ridden a long journey in the tropics will realise how refreshing it is to be thus regaled with the gentle sub-acid milk of a young coconot: for such indeed are those known as " water " coconuts. Evidently, the old man knew his business; he nevertheless ventured that the offering was little, but, he spoke as one of and for his guests, that " we will mek much of eet an' be tenkful," at which quaintness of humour Marjorie wes delighted. Soon the faithful old servitor was leading his visitors all over his little patch; dilating on this, and extolling that, as proudly as any Lord of the Manor expounding on his beeches or his game. In half an hour they had admired the old man's poultry, praised his heifer, and scanned the rude comforts of his retreat: having done all of which they signified their intention to depart. Ordering up the ever willing grandson with draughts of fresh drawn milk, for his visitors' further refreshment, the old man himself saw to the bringing up of the ponies. That to him was a service of the greatest importance which could be entrusted to no lesser mortal: there were bits and bridles to be carefully adjusted, girths to be tightened, and stirrups to be tested. All of these none but his practised hand and eye were to be trusted to examine and pronounce upon.

Harold, before leaving, thanked the old man and sought to press some largesse upon him: but this gentleman of nature would have none of it. Though he could not express himself very clearly, it was patent that he desired to convey that though he was not above labour and its due reward, he was above largesse. What time he had worked, *i.e.*, guided them to the cave, he had been paid; to-day they had done him great honour and that was enough. Harold, touched by the old man's rude dignity, offered him his hand instead, and Marjorie following suit, the old man brushed aside a tear, as his guests they rode away.

The journey back to St. Seriols was accomplished without event, save that Marjorie was sad of heart and silent because the hour of Harold's departure drew nigh.

That day of parting came, and with it Harold's departure from his family to the bosom of the Church. Mrs. Walton wept gently; Mrs. Keith shed a tear here and there, but Marjorie held a brave front until Harold was well away. Then, as she watched him ride through the gates and disappear, she felt the undeniable stifling clutch at her throat, and forthwith made for the retreat of her room. There she threw herself upon her pillows, and burying her face, burst into passionate weeping. The whole burden of her soul seemed, to her, to be the fact that the Church was stealing from her her own play-fellow, and that their rides and excursions were at an end. Beyond that, she knew not.

CHAPTER TWELVTH.

In the brief span of human endeavour years fly rapidly, and those that saw Harold absent and Marjorie watching for his return, were no exception to the rule. Never once had Marjorie forgotten the counsel which Harold had given, and then promptly forgot, that she should prepare herself: whether for her own achievement or for the better girding on of the armour of some Knight, she never paused to consider. Her half-neglected music lessons, under the joint care of her Aunt and Mrs. Keith, both of whom had had the benefit of first class teachers, she had taken up with avidity; and with her native ability and high emotional intensity she had developed into an executionist of some considerable ability.

Neither had Marjorie neglected her literary pursuits: the more she read the keener grew her appetite, and in the lonesomeness of St. Seriols she dwelt amid scenes of life and action that took her far away and appealed to her every sense and instinct.

In the library of that high colonial official, long gathered to his fathers, Marjorie found books illustrated by Cruickshank: bound volumes of pictures by Hogarth. Novels by Dumas and George Eliot. Poetry by Byron and by Pope. In the latter the Essay on Man held her spellbound: its strange witchery and deep mysticism: its flowing periods and beautiful rounded sentences, at once fired her imagination and soothed her sense of harmony. That most harmonious of all the passages to be found in the garden of the muse:

> Lo, the poor Indian! whose untutor'd mind
> Sees God in clouds, or hears him in the wind;
> His soul, proud Science never taught to stray;
> Far as the solar walk, or milky way;
> Yet simple Nature to his hope has giv'n,
> Behind the cloud-topt hill, an humbler heav'n;

touched her as poignantly as a weal. On many a morning she would hie her to the sea-shore and there ensconced upon her favourite boulder, which was shaped by nature's own hands into arm-chair shape, read and re-read pages and pages of her favourite authors. With Pope her selection would attune itself to the mood of waves and sky. Rough, rugged weather would find her racing through the pulsing lines of the Rape of the Lock; but when sun and sky would smile: when the sea would be as gentle as a crooning mother and the wavelets would lick the pebbles at her feet, she would turn her pages to the graceful periods of his great Essay, and comtemplate Man:

> Placed on this isthmus of a middle state
> A being darkly wise and rudely great,

or else lose herself in the reverence of the Universal Prayer. At a time when few girls of her age could tell even what Pope wrote, Marjorie could repeat almost letter perfect " The Essay on Man."

In this library it was that Marjorie had found old volumes of Temple Bar and Bentleys Miscellany. Here she found Rollin's Ancient History and Macaulay. Here she flirted with Marryatt's Naval Officers: hugged Chas. Kingsley's " Westward Ho " to her bosom, and gavotted through the pages of Thos. Hardy. She stepped a measure with Louis Quatorze at Fontainebleau; flitted through the

Tuilleries with La Marquise de Pompadour, and sang the Marseillaise with Mirabeau and Barere. She crossed the Ganges with the soldiers of Semiramis; stood with the captive women in the tents of Darius, the time Alexander made them his memorable visit; and felt the soft warm arms of Cleopatra as she tossed off the pearl in vinegar. She fought in the mountain fastnesses of Scotland with Wallace, and saw the faithful Marion cut down by Southron soldiers: she stood cheek by jowl with Potempkin at the barbarous Court of the great Catherine; and she went down to the shades with her great ancestor at St. Helena. Through it all, in fancy, she led Harold by the hand, and longed for his home coming.

At long last, news arrived that Harold had been ordered by his Superior to work in Trinidad. From time to time word had trickled through to the outside world that Harold had completed his studies: then, that he had duly taken Holy Orders and in the taking had assumed the name of Francis Dominic; for as the great Prototype of the Christian Religion had renamed Simon Barjona, so did this order of St. Dominic decree that at ordination each priest should be renamed in the service of the Church. Young Father Francis Dominic, youthful though he was, had already earned for himself the laurels of an effective preacher; which is no mean achievement in a great order of preachers: and thus had his fame preceded him, that when he did arrive in Port-of-Spain and it was announced that he would preach his first sermon, the church was filled to overflowing. Nor was the congregation disappointed.

Choosing a text beloved of young preachers, who, however so frequently fall short of the grandeur of their theme, Harold took the oft quoted words of the Christ when his enemies sought to overthrow him, on the payment of tribute to Caesar. He dealt with the subject lucidly and at length. He traced with a master hand the tense political feeling of the day when the

Jews, an imaginative and virile race, found themselves slaves to the power and glory of Rome, and forced to pay tribute to an alien ruler. Known fighter of abuses: socialist-democrat of the first water, it may well have been expected, pointed out the preacher, that the young Prophet and Teacher would rate the Jews for their indolence and servility; and that He would denounce in no measured terms the arrogance, and question the authority, of Caesar's pro-consul. But with that sound inspiration which governed all the utterances of the Son of Man, He drew himself out of the excitement of the day; turned confusion on His enemies and preached what He was to send thundering down the ages; and rendered service unto God—the thing that was God's. Harold then dwelt at some length on the political aspect of the people of Trinidad, and how freely they " rendered unto Caesar the things that were Caesar's." How loyal were the people and how pure their judiciary! Justice was meted out to the humblest litigant, if not always as perhaps it might be expected, certainly at least as the Judges conscientiously saw; which was a vastly different thing to the same pronouncement at the instance of outside interference, or venal suggestion. Thus did the judges render unto the people that which was the people's. He, Harold, however, was afraid that they were all sadly lacking in rendering the greater tribute of the things which were God's. " How many of you," he thundered, " could hold up your heads as you swagger down Marine Square if God were to look you in the face and demand if you had rendered unto Him the things that were His. " Yes," he cried, " you come to Mass regularly, you perhaps go to confession, and are righteous for five seconds as you kneel at the rail of communion and join in the great mystery of the Church; but, I ask, how many of you really render unto God the things which are God's. The things which are God's, are an upright life, and a due performance of your secret obligations to your fellow man. Your public and chartered obligations, the law of the land takes care that you discharge. But what about those obligations of which God alone is the witness? You are afraid, as a rule, to cheat, and ashamed to steal: but, when you neglect those obligations you cheat God of his fee as a witness, and you rob the High Altar of the costs of the cause. You doubtless," he continued, " give some alms, which scarcely touch your incomes; but you leave unpaid the costs and charges accumulating on your conscience. Look," he cried again, " at the published tables of the birth rate. Look with horror at the startling percentage of illegitimates. And there are greater things than disclosed in those tables. No count is taken of the mothers broken and deserted. No record is kept of the result of children denied a father's love and care: neglected and abandoned on the sea of life, to become flotsam and jetsam: wastrels in Society, and a rebuke to their fathers Those are the things that are God's; those are the things that are neglected. And I charge you men here present to see to it that in future you render unto God the things that are God's. And you women," he whispered, as he faced another side of the congregation, " Have you renderd unto God the things that are God's? As you kneel here this evening, shining in your graces, and clothed in the radiance of the earth, does any whisper reach you that you have not rendered unto God the things which are God's? Have your lives been pure, and your consciences clean? Those be the things that are God's."

Handling this subject with a delicacy and a touch of sympathy, which was marvellous in one so young, Harold passed to his hearers obligations to the Church.

" And my children," he said, " what do you render unto the Church? This is the great Mother of Churches and to her belongs your allegiance. Do you speak no slander, think no evil of her? Do you, by precept and example show that with a Catholic there dwells the spirit of the Lord? Those things belong by right of primogeniture—if by no other right—to the Church. What though she has been maligned and libelled: what though she has been ill served, and even betrayed, by some of her high officers as the years have gone by. She has stood the test of centuries. What though some accusations have been proved true: I say of those things, that the priests and prelates responsible did not render unto the Church, nor unto God, the things which were theirs. But your duties are not affected thereby."

So spell bound had the congregation been held that few realized that Harold had come to the end of his great exhortation until they saw him descending from the pulpit. That sermon made his name in Trinidad, and the legend of his ancestry helped not a little in the doing.

That night as an old Bonapartist, well known in island circles, left the church he muttered to himself but loud enough for his companion.

"Napoleon! Napoleon! Vive L'Empereur."

At the which his companion as much out of mischief as anything else replied:

"Gravelotte, Sedan; Strassburg, Metz!"

"Bah!" cried the old man, "Napoleon III. was only imitation Bonaparte, or may be ze first Consul not Bonaparte: Mother Letitia may be had une petite officer of ze Garrison Francaise in Corsica. Or, maybe, Louis Napoleon was a de Morny, or ze son of some Dutch garcon. Hortense Beauharnais been veerai careless with her amusements. Bah! there been no Napoleon, again! Perhaps this boy: Perhaps!" and then again he muttered

"Napoleon! Napoleon! Vive L'Empereur" and passed into the night.

"Father Dominic" became a name to conjure with, and his congregations continued to grow. Then came the great shock to the people of Port-of-Spain, for it became known that Harold had been ordered to assume charge of the mission in Tobago. Loud were the protests in the press, and much was the influence brought to hear on the Presbytery. But none may measure the policy of the Church, nor outside influence dictate her changes. So Harold, at last, as he looked from the prow of the steamer which bore him to his new charge, saw his island mission, and erstwhile home, rise on the mists of the morning, full in front of him.

As the steamer drew near, the points of familiar interest gradually discovered themselves to him. There was the old fort, with its bristling and empty walls and silent guns. There was St. Seriols nestling snugly at the foot of the hill; there was the little white landing Jetty in the offing. Everything exactly as he had left it, and all spelling 'home' to him, for he scarcely had known Demerara. As the steamer swung to her anchorage he looked for his little church and Presbytery. There were they in their little compound close by the sea; and as he looked, he dreamt many dreams of the days to come, and his plans for the good of the people.

Mrs. Walton anxious to meet her son, whom she now shared with the Church, rose early, and unable to constrain herself, decided to travel straight down to the Jetty to meet him. Marjorie more self contained, and perhaps a little conscious of her dawning womanhood, decided to wait him at the Presbytery.

As the boat, which bore Harold to the shore reached the landing stage, he sprang lightly to the stairway and ran to the top: as he stood there he glanced uneasily around as though looking for faces that were not. For a moment a wave of disappointment swept over his features; in a moment it was gone, and a harbour official came up to him. They had known each other well in the old days and they shook hands warmly. Harold looked very picturesque as he stood at the head of those stairs. The boisterous sea breeze swept the lappets of his gown in fluttering folds about his feet, the black overcoat tossing riotously in the elements. The wide brimmed black sealskin hat completed a graceful picture of a tall and well built man clothed apart from his fellow men.

Greetings exchanged, the official led the way to his nearby office where stood Mrs. Walton anxiously awaiting the coming of her son. When Harold reached his mother's presence she folded him to her bosom, and he kissed her on her brow and on both of her cheeks: loosening himself from her tender clasp he looked around for the playfellow of his childhood, but saw her not: neither did any word of enquiry escape him. After some commonplace exchanges about the trip, and his successes in Trinidad, they took their seats in the small waggon which one of the wealthier of the faithful had sent to convey him up to the Presbytery, though the distance was little enough indeed.

What little distance there was, was speedily negotiated and Harold found himself assisting his mother to alight at the Presbytery gates. Then he saw Marjorie, in the portico of the Presbytery, awaiting their coming. But oh! what, a Marjorie!

Harold had not been unaccustomed to the meeting of grace and loveliness in women. In Budapest, in Brussels, in Paris and in London, as lad and priest, Harold had seen women of ravishing loveliness. In Trinidad, that Paris of the West Indies, where Spanish and French blood mix to produce some of the fairest women on earth, many had stormed him in the confessional and left him unmoved; but there was a charm and grace in Marjorie that eclipsed them all. The subtlety of right, and the joy of morning seemed blended in the easy looseness of her limbs, as she advanced to greet them. Priest and celibate that he was, he, at it were, turned aside from the radiant loveliness of his cousin, as his Master of old may have turned from the glittering minarets of the cities of the world, when the Prince of Darkness spread the mighty panorama before him and promised dominion over them.

Marjorie advanced with hands outstretched and a cheerful, " Well! Harold!"

" Harold " as she called him smiled, and thought that it would be some time before he could wean his wayward old playmate from that " Harold," and teach her that he was now " Father Dominic " with charge over her spiritual welfare. He was glad indeed of their meeting in the open, where he might well be excused the affectionate greeting that he had given his mother. For a moment they both stood irresolute: then he took both her hands in his own, called her " Marjorie," and spoke with evident affection of his long delayed home coming.

Immediately the priest asserted itself, and they moved to Mass in the neighbouring edifice, which, perhaps, may be more accurately described as Chapel rather than Church. A small congregation of the faithful waited the Father, at the entrance of the sacred edifice; and, as he approached, knelt dutifully in turn, kissed the scapula of his gown and received his blessing.

From the time when Harold descended from the little waggon, Marjorie's eyes had followed him step by step. His easy grace and open countenance marked him as one by gods beloved. When he entered the Chapel she followed with the little crowd and took her seat with the meagre congregation. As Harold proceeded on his way to the sacristy the aureole formed by the tonsure of his crown showed up the graceful proportions of his head to perfection. As he genuflected, on reaching the altar, and passed into the sacristy, which stood at the rear of the altar, with that grace and litheness of limb which belong to youth, Marjorie again thought that Harold was good to look upon.

Through the solemn and picturesque phases of the Mass Marjorie's senses battled with her instinct of propriety, and the fitness of things. Harold was good: Harold was devoted to the Church. A little bit of a pity—but really what difference did it make to her. In a little while she would give herself to some Lord and Master, and Harold would himself perform the marriage rites with as much punctiliousness as he now said the Confiteor or pronounced the Oremus. She had heard that Gaston de Garcia had been appointed Doctor of the Windward District, and had indeed arrived on the Island, but she had neither been introduced to him nor had she even seen him. Now that Harold had come he would introduce them; and she smiled as she thought of the possibilities: if he were not still inclined to " put even money on two horses and a ' kicker ' on the " outsider." " How," thought she, " they both would laugh at Harold, and lead him a dance in between times."

Marjorie's thoughts were as far from the solemnities of the ritual being enacted before her eyes as if they never held claim to her devotion. She pictured her young kinsman, who pulled so lightly at her heart strings, in all manner of positions, with herself and Gaston de Garcia as the leaders of every *outre* act: until his heart should beat and throb like her own. " Gaston de Garcia!" she liked the music of the name; and he would be the companion of her rides and excursions, and at each they would wave a tantalising farewell to Harold.

As Harold gracefully kissed the spotless linen of the altar in allegory of the kiss which betrayed his Master, Marjorie started guiltily and her heart leapt within her bosom. Should she permit a stranger to kiss her; would Gaston de Garcia be content with less, or would he rush the battlement of her defences by assault, and abandon all policy of division of risk. Her face gradually flushed crimson and she concluded with a " why not, if he loves me." Harold had greeted her with coldness: and she smiled— evidently more interested in kissing the spotless linen of the altar than the spotless radiance of her own face. But, suppose the partner-to-be of all these musings saw her with a cold and indifferent stare: at this her face blanched. Suppose he were married. Suppose he loved another. **Suppose,**

IN BONDAGE.   129

worse of all, he sought her kisses to betray her, as illustrated by the imagery of the ritual before her? A catching at her throat caused her to gasp as for air, and at that same moment the little altar bell rang to call the faithful to their knees for the most solemn part of the service—the consecration of the Host. Marjorie eagerly seized the opportunity and, kneeling, buried her face in her handkerchief.

As Marjorie knelt, her pent up feelings melted into silent tears; and when she rose from her knees her eyes were soft and humid with newly shed tears. When, shortly after, Harold turned to the congregation with the whispered " Oremus " their eyes met, in the narrow compass of the little Church, and the soft appealing gaze caught his heart as in a vise. Could the solemnity of the consecration have melted the heart of his young kinswoman? Or had she shed tears over something else;—maybe—the gulf which now separated them? For half a second Church and Cloister were forgotten, but in another instant he had driven from him every mundane thought which sought to invade the sanctity of the solemn hour, and, bending to the task at hand, soon completed the service and descended the altar steps, without giving one more thought to his fair young cousin.

At the completion of their devotions the family party once again adjourned to the presbytery; where Harold—or to give him from henceforth his new designation, Father Dominic—insisted on his mother and Marjorie remaining for the day with him.

In the course of the day, while Mrs. Walton had retired for her noonday rest in the room specially prepared by the old housekeeper, Marjorie and the young priest were left alone for some while.

" You know," she said, " I really do feel queer having to call you ' Father Dominic ' like the others. It sounds so far and distant; and every now and again I find the "Harold" jumping out."

"Never mind," answered the young Father, "you will soon get accustomed to it. Anyway you won't get imprisoned if the 'Harold' does 'jump out' occasionally, as you put it. But tell me," he added, "what all has happened since last I was here."

"Oh, one thing at least that I was bursting to tell you. Poor old Cudjoe, who took us to the cave died, the other day."

"Poor fellow!" ejaculated Father Dominic, "What went wrong?"

"I don't exactly know," answered Marjorie, "but I have heard that if Medical skill had been available his life might have been saved. But the delay in filling old Doctor Wessell's place left that side of the island without a doctor."

"So Garcia did not get there in time?" asked Harold

"No," answered Marjorie. "Then, you know," she enquired, "that 'Garcia,' as you call him, has been appointed to the island?"

"Oh! yes," laughed Father Dominic. "He looked me up in Port-of-Spain. He was present at my first sermon in the Cathedral; and when I was appointed to this mission he forthwith sent me a 'wireless' full of welcome and noisesomeness. Have you not yet met him?"

"No," answered Marjorie, "few people come our way, as you know, and he is stationed quite the other side of the Island. I should like to know what he telegraphed you," she added laughingly.

"Oh, some nonsense about welcome to the rock; and intimation that his side was wholly heathen, and his house open for Missionary work, and the like."

"But that was very good," urged Marjorie.

"Yes, if you did not know the sender," replied the young Missionary. "If there are heathen in that district you will find Gaston the most pronounced; and his offer of his house mere gallery work: but I shall certainly avail myself of it."

"I should like to meet him," naively urged Marjorie.

"I hope not because of his heathenish tendencies," laughed her companion. "I have no doubt however that he will find himself down here some Saturday afternoon with the pious intention, as far as excuse is wanted, of hearing Mass next morning. You shall then have plenty of opportunity of meeting him."

With such small talk the day flew and Marjorie completely forgot the momentary bitterness of the morning.

CHAPTER THIRTEENTH.

With the cool of the afternoon Father Dominic set out with his mother and Marjorie to do the walk from the Presbytery to St. Seriols. The road along which they travelled was the same as Harold and Marjorie had taken on some of those riding excursions herein before referred to. A level stretch skirting the foot of the hill on which stood old Fort St. George, for a pleasant walk, it has few equals: fanned by the salt sea air and with the sea constantly in view it might almost be called a Marine road, though some couple of hundred feet above the level of the sea; and in some instances, some hundreds of yards away from it.

The conversational current in the course of this walk was bright and witty. Many were the subjects discussed; they flitted from Mission work to the Island steamer service; from the Road Commissioners to the state of the peasantry; and from the price of Cocoa to the demand for Cattle in Port-of-Spain. Marjorie denounced the paucity of young men and the shallowness of the girls, and declared her own intention some day to fly from it all.

"I don't know," she petulantly exclaimed, "why Auntie would never return to Demerara. I am sure that things are better over there."

Mrs. Walton sighed. "My child," she said, "happiness is in every place; and so is misery. If we have less excitement here, we also are less open to sorrows. You are young; be not impatient. The pleasures of life will come to you."

And the rebellious young heart flew unbidden to Gaston de Garcia; and raced back to the stalwart young kinsman beside her.

At a bend in the road the strollers came into full view of the little bay of St. Seriols where Father Dominic well remembered to have spent many a happy hour with Marjorie. Turning to her he said:

"I hope you have outgrown those days down there," and pointed to the masses of stone, honeycombed by centuries of time.

"I don't know if I have;" she replied, "but your dignity and soutane will certainly be beyond it.' And she remembered with laughter the sometimes sudden swoop of the incoming waves which had drenched her companion to the skin. "Perhaps, however, I may induce your friend to try his luck one of these days." Then she wondered what sort of remark the elusive Gaston de Garcia would make on emerging from the sudden embrace of some riotous and impatient wave.

Father Dominic laughed, and replied that he had no doubt Gaston would be ready most any time he could get away from his heathen.

After a few more yards of walk they were at St. Seriols and in the presence of Mrs. Keith; that good lady was overjoyed at the home-coming of the stranger. She however could not restrain her amusement at the metamorphosis of the "Harold" she was accustomed to.

"Although, I suppose," she added, "I must say 'Father Dominic' now. Well, I never!" she exclaimed, as she looked him from head to heel, "you look like one of the pictures given away at the Presbytery."

The old lady was not without a sense of humour, and her comments were keenly enjoyed by all. Meantime tea was brought in and Mrs. Walton dispensed it; and, eventually induced the young cleric to remain for dinner.

As the shadows of evening approached the charm of his cousin stole upon Father Dominic like the effects of strong wine. If she looked radiant in the morning, in the stillness of the evening she seemed clothed with a mysterious softness and langour. When she made her appearance dressed for dinner he thought of some of the women he had seen in Buda-Pesth, and of another he had seen at the Madelaine in Paris. Dinner over, Mrs. Walton withdrew early and left her son with Mrs. Keith and Marjorie. Eventually the former also retired and Father Dominic, left alone with his cousin, decided to take his departure. Immediately as he rose to go Marjorie passed swiftly to the piano and called out:

"What! going already! and you have not even asked me to sing to you."

"I did not know you would care to," answered her companion simply, "but if you will sing, I shall be glad to remain and listen to you."

Not a touch of flattery did he offer: not a sign as to whether he would listen with pleasure or otherwise. And Marjorie felt the sting of his coldness.

Lightly picking out some notes on the piano, it was easy to see that Marjorie had largely been self taught. No professional pedantry marked her notes: no 'book work' did she give. Straight from the cords of her heart touched she the ivory, and in another moment she melted into the sweet swinging notes of the beautiful ballad, "Down the Vale." Whether Marjorie was idealising Gaston de Garcia, or singing to the young priest in the room, she never stopped to consider. Gently, passionately, she warbled through the first verse:

*" When you come down the vale, lad, there's singing
   in the trees,
There's music in the gale, lad, and music in the breeze;
There's welcome and there's rapture, o'er moorland and
   o'er dale,
But none so glad as I am, lad, when you come down
   the vale."

Pausing for a moment longer than usual Marjorie expressed some further notes and then bursting into a louder key she sang on:

" Stars up above, find ye my love,
   Tell him the night is fair;
Peep from the skies into his eyes,
   Leaving my image there."

With scarcely a perceptible pause Marjorie stilled the vibrating notes and passed gently into the next verse:

" Where vale and coppice meet, lad, my tryst for thee
   I keep,
The harebells at my feet, lad, are smiling in their sleep;
And every bonny bird, lad, wings home his mate to
   greet,
And croons to me of love and thee, where vale and
   coppice meet."

Again she keyed her notes up higher and burst to the full timbre of her splendid native voice. Calling out her heart to the wilderness, as plain as though she sang from a desolate ship, she sang on

" Stars up above, find ye my love,
   Tell him the night is fair;
Peep from the skies into his eyes,
   Leaving my image there."

* Copyright by Boosey & Co.

Then, as though exhausted by the effort, she hushed the notes of the instrument almost into silence, and her voice sank to the tenderness of a caress:

When we go down the Vale, lad, the last long Vale of Tears,
No terror shall prevail, lad, and there shall be no fears;
For though the shadows darken, and every star be pale,
I shall not fear, if you are near, when we go down the Vale."

Raising her voice slightly she sang the concluding words:

Angels above shall sing our love
In a divine refrain;
Where Love alone homage doth own,
Where Love alone doth reign.

Without lifting her fingers from the keys Marjorie fingered out, with truly artistic sense, the music of the last verse and its refrain, in slower time than she had sung, and melting the final notes into silence she turned and faced Father Dominic.

"I did not know you sang so well," he said.

"Auntie says I do not always sing well."

"Perhaps it is her fancy," he ventured.

"No. I think I only sing well when I attune my song to my fancy," she replied.

"Well good-night," he said abruptly, "I must be gone;" and taking her firm fair hand in his he pressed it gently and passed into the night.

The lonely walk back to the Presbytery that night, with the refrain of Marjorie's song in his ear, and the " stars up above," would have moved to idealism a far less impressionable man than Father Dominic. As the waves of the sea beat their refrain on the rocks and cliffs below him, in the stillness of the evening, so did the words of Marjorie's song beat their refrain on the ear of the young priest. It was not alone the words of the song, perhaps, so much as the whole setting: the silent room, the passionate tone of Marjorie's voice; her grace and loveliness, all bleared his vision, and for the moment he wondered again whether he had been all wise in choosing the way of the Church, and forever denying himself the possibilities of a love like hers. Like treason, or hot coals, he thrust the thought from him with repugnance, and tried to busy himself with the "heads" of his sermon for the coming Sunday's High Mass. He had selected the great theme of Christ weeping over Jerusalem, for his maiden effort: but to-night his mind was chaos. Perhaps only a futurist drawing of conflicting emotions could really depict what his mind was like. In the midst of some flowing period of his sermon would obtrude the lines.

 And every bonny bird, lad, wings home his mate to greet.
 And croons to me of love and thee, where vale and coppice meet.

He alone of them all, he thought, "winged" not home his mate to greet: and, worse, had taken solemn vows to remain forever celibate. Again he would chase the demon from him and turn to the sermon by which he hoped to bring some souls into the holy fold of the Church; but 'the stars up above' would tell him the night was fair, and that "she" was near; and again he would seek refuge in the solaces offered by the Church to a stricken heart. At length he reached the gates of the Presbytery, and, once safe within its walls, shook all the dust of doubtings from his mind, as he shook the dust from his garments, and knelt at his breviary to complete the sacred offices of the day.

 * * * * * *

The waning of the week proved Father Dominic a good judge of character, for Gaston de Garcia, lusting up at his hill station for familiar companionship, had no sooner learnt of the arrival of the new comer than he notified him that on Saturday he would arrive for " bed, board and lodging " and would stay " until Monday, D. V. (and Father Dominic) if no more mundane call summoned him away before."

When Marjorie heard of this she was on the tip-toe of excitement; and it was soon arranged that Father Dominic would bring his friend to St. Seriols as soon as he arrived, and that they would both dine there and then return to the Presbytery.

It had been a busy week with the young Father and he hardly realised it was Saturday until somewhere about 3 p.m. when he heard the even foot fall of a horse's hoofs on the gravel walk leading to the dismounting block. Looking out of a bay window, he was greeted by the half quizzical half cheerful:

" Hallo, Father, is that you in the flesh?" of Gaston de Garcia.

" In the flesh, but not all flesh," answered Father Dominic, with a brave attempt at raillery. " So it is evident the heathen at Windward have not eaten their doctor."

" Me! oh fear not: I keep them at bay with castor oil and boat hooks," replied Gaston.

Thereafter Gaston was soon well established in the most comfortable chair the Presbytery could offer and bounding along in his racy comments on every thing in general and nothing in particular, at a rate that old Rapfuller, of blessed memory, would have described as being " ten hogshead to the acre, and yellows at that."

It was not long, either, before he had enquired in very good grace for the Father's kinsfolk at St. Seriols.

" You know, Father," he added, " at college I had always hoped that some holiday you would have asked me up to Tobago,"

IN BONDAGE.

"Indeed, then why did you not hint at it," answered Father Dominic, "you are not over bashful."

"Me! well, you are a tickler," jerked out Gaston, "why, man alive, you never once led in the suit, so how could I take you up?"

"Anyway, everything in the fulness of time," replied the young cleric. "This afternoon I shall take you thither: you shall have tea, and stay to dinner."

Indeed! indeed!" cried Gaston, "just see me balancing refined dough on your mother's best china. I will go upstairs and scrape the old chin right away."

"What, going to shave again?" chevied Father Dominic. "But I suppose if you must, then you just have to. I shall however take care to tell Miss Hamilton of the high honour done them."

"No nonsense, Father, no nonsense. Give me a fair chance to lead up. Don't spoil the game so early." Saying which Gaston bounded up the bedroom stairs three at a time.

By 5 o'clock Father Dominic and Gaston were well on their way to St. Seriols, and in less than no time were within its charming portals.

Gaston, presented to Mrs. Walton, bent low over her hand and murmured of his pleasure in the opportunity to do homage to the mother of his friend and a distinguished member of a great order.

To Marjorie he was utterly silent. Her radiance had struck him speechless. Even when she expressed their pleasure at his having come along after such a long ride, he barely smiled feebly; bowed, and sat down with a numbled "thank you."

Father Dominic watched his friend and was gently puzzled. Could this be the voluble and witty Gaston de Garcia bending over the hand of a woman in silence?

With all the vivre of her youth Marjorie sent the ball of conversation whizzing to each in turn. Boldly advancing on Gaston she required to know of his station and the state of the roads. Gaston ventured a weak reply and then drew in Father Dominic. Mrs. Walton calling back the faculty of the time when she was a brilliant ornament of society also joined in, and soon had the conversation running in easy channels.

It did not take a man of Gaston's temperament long to recover his self possession and soon " Richard was himself again."

Marjorie took opportunity to furtively study the new comer from tip to toe: and he was not an uncomely subject to study. Built, as he would himself have put it, in a lighter vein than Father Dominic, he was yet well knit and of a pleasing presence; standing some five feet ten inches in his socks. His features were soft tinted as may be so frequently met with in those creoles of Trinidad who can trace their ancestry back to the Spanish occupation. His hair was jet black, and he wore a moustache trained with punctiliousness to take a graceful, but not ferocious, upward curve. As he sat there between the soft shadows of oil lamps—the fierce glare of electric carbons not having yet forced its way to Tobago—Gaston de Garcia made a picture that would have fascinated the heart of any woman.

Marjorie noted him with approval, and then " pointed him off " with her cousin. There was a certain witchery in the atmosphere of Gaston which was sadly lacking in Father Dominic. Yet what the latter lacked in that respect he made up for in others. His clean shaven features were bolder, and, perhaps, handsomer: his soft winsome eyes gave a wistfulness to his features which brought him level with Gaston's more Cavalier look. And in the end Marjorie summed up Gaston's total points with a " check number " of disappointment.

It is not to be supposed that Marjorie did all the " pointing off." Gaston, when once he had got into his stride, studied the charming Marjorie completely and with the knowledge of the born appraiser. To Gaston a covert glance, and an airy stare, occasionally, sufficed him: yet he appraised her with completeness and judgment.

The langour of her eyes, her sweeping lashes, the delicate pencilling of her brows and the crowning glory of her raven tresses. all marked her to Gaston as a thing of beauty and a joy forever. Had she lived in Demerara there would have been many to declare that she had inherited many of the most salient points of her aunt's prepossessing appearance as a young matron.

Although a maid, and barely on the threshold of her twentieth year Marjorie yet showed all the graceful development of young English matronhood. Her limbs moved easily and with the grace of supreme self possession; they seemed to take joy from her royal beauty, and to move with the whole music of her being.

After a while Marjorie herself brought in a dainty waiter set with everything for the dispensing of the useful cup of tea. What was left of restraint, in the for once shy Gaston, vanished under that cheerful familiarity which seems to be generated within the radius of the tea table; and by the time the soft sea-side afternoon had melted into the warm tropical night—for there is no twilight in the tropics —every one was as familiar as an old family gathering. As Mrs. Walton and Marjorie withdrew to dress for dinner they bade Father Dominic take Gaston to the old bedroom which was still kept for service of the young cleric, what time it should be necessary.

When the little party again foregathered for their march to the dinner table it was as the reunion of old friends. If Gaston was weak at the first meeting he by now had found his strength, and caught up to Marjorie as gay as any old Cavalier of the 17th century. At dinner the conversation sparkled with wit and Gaston kept Marjorie in ecstacies of delight with his pretty witticisms and charming compliments.

After dinner was a more extended operation; and Gaston soon felt himself losing all control to his charming young companion; when, during the evening, she asked him if he danced or liked dancing, he felt himself murmuring that while he liked dancing he would infinitely prefer to keep step with the music of her life. Marjorie laughed. Her life had been so free from the homage and flattery of men that the delicate homage of this man was now like strong wine to her veins.

"Music of my life!" she echoed, "How do you know there will be music to my life?"

"Believe me, Miss Hamilton," Gaston replied "there will and must be music to your life. It may be *a Te Deum*, or a *de Profundis* but it will be music in crescendo—with all the stops out," he added with an attempt to return to his lighter vein.

Father Dominic watched the approaching tendresse, in Gaston's manner, with a peculiar sensation that was foreign to him. Why this catching at his throat? Why the stifling atmosphere of the room? Excusing himself for a moment he stepped out on the verandah and then crossed the yard to the residence of Mrs. Keith. There he could scarcely contain himself, and, barely exchanging greetings with that good lady, retraced his footsteps. All at once he felt the burning desire to hear Marjorie sing again the ballad, 'Down the Vale,' as she had sung it the evening of his home-coming.

Entering the room he quickly suggested that Marjorie should sing something; but that lady was in no singing mood, for she had enough music and rapture without. When her young kinsman suggested that she should sing 'Down the Vale,' she declined, with a laugh, and pleaded that she was "not in the mood for that song to-night." Eventually Mrs. Walton joined her solicitations to those of her son; for she could not bear to see him denied anything, and Marjorie, out of mere gladness of heart, moved to the piano.

After idly fingering the keys for some moments she at last broke into the old hymn 'Rocked in the cradle of the Deep,' and never had either men heard it so sung before.

Gaston listened enraptured, but it made no ease to Father Dominic; and, shortly after, the visitors took their departure

The walk home in the soft night was one long penance to Father Dominic. He had to listen to the enraptured praises of Gaston; reply with easy good breeding, and vainly try to bring his own heart to reason. She was his playmate and cousin. He was a priest of the Church, and vowed to eternal renunciation.

That night, long after Gaston was wrapped in the arms of Morpheus, and probably dreaming of the rare beauty of his new acquaintance, Father Dominic wrestled on his knees with his yearning after the charms of the material. The next day would be Sunday and his sermon had to be finally polished and brought to that pitch of perfection for which he was justly noted. He brought out his notes, read and re-read them, spoke some parts: but, good God, what was this agony? When he spread out Jerusalem before his congregation, stretched his arms out to it, and would gather it as a hen gathereth her chickens; it was Marjorie who came to his arms, while Jerusalem " would not." Down on his knees again he went, and, like in the greater agony of Gethsemane, pleaded that the cup might be passed from him. Eventually, it was well on to 3 o'clock in the morning before the harassed priest threw himself into bed, to snatch a few hours hasty sleep before the day came.

CHAPTER FOURTEENTH.

True to all the portents of the preceding week Father Dominic's first Sunday in Tobago brought such a congregation to the little parish Church as it had never seen before. Nor had the agony of the night before stilled the eloquence of the young preacher. Possibly, like steel from the flame he had emerged of more highly tempered metal. Preaching from the text:

" Oh! Jerusalem, Jerusalem, ... how often would I have gathered thy children together, even as a hen gathereth her chickens, under her wings, and ye would not."

The young missionary electrified his audience. Dealing in easy stages with the state of morals in Jerusalem Father Dominic led up to the coming of the Divine Reformer with all His poigant sense of love and pity. First, pointed out the young preacher, was Divine enthusiasm for His great work, and then fearful disappointment, as He realized how uphill was His task and how deaf the Jews had grown. Then, with telling effectiveness, he pictured the young Prophet on the Mount overlooking Jerusalem, as He saw with His Divine vision the ruin and desolation that was to overwhelm the fair city: and, as He reflected how He had laboured, and prayed, and was to suffer, and that the desolation was yet to descend, He wept those tears of love.

" How many hearts to-day," cried the preacher, " within the walls of this little church, represent in the arc of their own circumference the situation of Jerusalem as Christ saw it eighteen hundred years ago? With how many had He struggled and prayed and suffered. Over how many is He now weeping the tears of sorrow, as He foresees the desolation to come."

Search your hearts," he cried again, " Cast out the tempter. Lay hold of the Rock of Salvation."

If Father Dominic preached to the congregation he no less preached to himself: and what preacher can be so eloquent as when, under such circumstances, he lays on the scourge to his own conscience.

Possessing in a rare degree the gift of persuasive eloquence the young preacher rose to the full measure of the pathos of his subject; and many a man and woman resolved on better things for the future: that some failed to carry resolution to fruition is to be regretted; but, who knows not, that even the sincere registration of a vow is something gained in the life of a soul.

When the congregation filed out of church that morning loud were the praises heard on every side. Never had such a sermon been heard in Tobago: never such a preacher: so young, so manifestly earnest. So pure of heart, so pure of speech.

The next month saw Gaston de Garcia constant in his visits to Scarborough, and in his attentions at St. Seriols. And, best of all, when the Government Medical Officer stationed in Scarborough had to be invalided home, and Gaston was ordered to act in his place, his visits at the chief point of attraction, became one daily pilgrimage. He rode, danced and sang with Marjorie, and therefore it surprised no one when the betrothal of the young medico and Mrs. Walton's ward was announced.

Father Dominic meanwhile threw himself into his labours with increasing vigour. Trained by the Church as an Architect-Priest he was forever busy in embellishing and decorating. Out stations had to be visited and Masses said in all manner of conceivable places. A secondary school had to be established and the whole fighting efficiency of his mission placed on a sound basis. His sermons rose in eloquence and his church was filled to over flowing. Even dear Mrs. Warrington journeyed into the town to hear the " poor boy." Strong Non-conformist though she was, she freely expressed to Mrs. Walton that she had almost been persuaded to embrace the great Mother of Churches. Oh, Agrippa! how many like your illustrious self stand halting at the parting of the ways! And poor dear Mrs. Warrington, you stand not alone in sudden inclination to change the form of your faith on the popularity or the reverse of some exponent of a particular creed.

Moved by the growing reputation and popularity of the young missionary, and possibly by some occasional hints of heterodoxy, for already he had been referred to as " another Dominion Savonarola;" the Trinidad Presbytery sent word that Father Dominic was to hold himself in readiness for " Lenten duty " at the Port-of-Spain Cathedral, and that relief would be sent him accordingly.

About this time Father Dominic had temporary quarter at St. Seriols; for his Presbytery, long in need of repairs, had been handed over to workmen at the earnest request of Mrs. Walton, who herself undertook to disburse all the costs and charges.

It must not be thought that the young cleric consented to live at St. Seriols without a struggle. First his enthusiasm as an architect urged him to live among the scaffolding and workmen's turmoil at the Presbytery: again he thought it best to keep away from Marjorie as far as possible. Then, seizing his courage in both hands, he finally concluded that the best plan was to meet her daily; see her in the full possession of another; and, grappling with the sinister temptation, tear it out branch and root once and forever.

The more the face of Marjorie had haunted him the more of an ascetic had the once cheerful Father grown. Nor was Marjorie unmindful of the change in her kinsman. She constantly studied him under her lashes, and the more he drew into himself, the more her heart yearned in sorrow for the playmate of her childhood. Thinking herself supremely happy in Gaston's unceasing attentions, she yet felt wounded and guilty that "Harold," as she still thought of him, should be unhappy and not sharing in her joys.

Thus was the state of affairs when the night came on which the young priest was to take his departure for Trinidad. The little coastal steamer which keeps the island in touch with the outside world was due on its return from around the island that night, and would leave for Port-of-Spain in the early hours of the morning; and, it was arranged, that Father Dominic would board her at 4.30 the next morning; Marjorie, as usual, the stay and support of every executive action at St. Seriols, undertaking to see that he woke early enough to get away in time to be on board as appointed; for a priest may not trifle with his orders. The Church is set over him like the famous Centurion who saith unto one man "go," and he goeth; and unto another, "come," and he cometh.

That night Marjorie, pained with the idea of parting, and morose at the "drift" that had set in between herself and her cousin, was long in hushing herself to sleep; long after the whole household had been wrapt in slumber Marjorie tossed on her pillows. She could not have been asleep for more than two hours when she awoke with a start and a stinging sense of betrayed trust: looking out into the starlit morning it seemed to her that she had slept for hours and hours, and that it was now well past four in the morning. Without a moment's further pause she rushed to Father Dominic's bedroom, and, turning the handle of the door, passed right in.

To Marjorie " Father Dominic " had ceased to be: it was
" Harold," and a broken obligation, and she stood not upon
the order of her action. As she stood within the room,
however, her ear detected the tick, tick, of the little time-
piece which the young cleric always wore, but now
on the dressing table; taking it at once to the
window she made out by the feeble light of the waning moon that it was then just past 2 o'clock. Smiling to
herself she turned to leave the room, when the sleeping priest,
possibly disturbed by the movement in the room, sighed
heavily and turned on his pillow. The sigh went to Marjorie's heart, and turning to the bedside she lifted the curtain
and looked down upon the sleeper. The pensive sweetness
of his face in the soft morning light went to her bosom, and
the tonsure around his head seemed, for the first time, to
add something to be sorry for. Like on that morning some
years before, when she woke him for another journey, the
maternal instinct of pity swelled strong in her, and she stoop-
ed and kissed the silent priest.

Marjorie, in that instant wafted back to the morning
when no vows stood between them, spread her arms caress-
ingly around the head of the sleeper and kissed him again.
Turning restlessly he murmured " Mother?"

"Harold, it is I," answered Marjorie, in the exact
sentence she had used those years before.

Whether "Harold" also stood back in the years, it
would be difficult to say: as though to gather consciousness,
he was silent for a moment. In another instant his arm had
stolen around her supple waist, innocent of all garment save
her simple night dress, and his hand tasted of the fulness of
every line and contour of her form.

"Marjorie, why have you come?" he asked.
Then the priestly office forgot, drawing her to him
he kissed her on the brow, and, by a sudden impulse, on both her eyes and cheeks, and, last of all,
their lips met in one lingering caress: long as eternity, sweet
as death. In a flash of time the divine right of mother-

hood flew to Marjorie's breast, and a woman was born: subtle, strong, weak, imperious in her will, as the stern and clamant instinct of budding maternity seized her in its relentless grip. Forgetting all that bound them each, Marjorie whispered:

" Oh, Harold! you do not love me."

The soft whisper, the witching tropical night, the daze of half dream-land, all stood upon Harold, as we shall now once again call him, and before the warm lust of her blood, and the charms of her ample bosom, the priest in him went down, battered and beaten, and was not.

   *   *   *   *   *   *

The great white crested waves of the Sandy bay curved and curled and lashed themselves to foam on the white stretch of beach, right beneath the bedroom windows at St. Seriols, throwing high on the foreshore such things as the sea gives up. The casual promenader, or visitor with some time to spare, will find much to interest and more to wonder at in the flotsam and jetsam that may be picked up on a topical sea shore. Here is a gnarled stump, which shows signs of the struggle through which it has been, yet exhibiting all the native strength of its once vigorous life. Here are lovely sea shells; some burnished and wistful in their beauty, some shattered and broken. Here again in large numbers are the knotty looking " Sea gru-grus," each a poem unto itself: some are disgusting looking, rough and unclean; some show the polish of the sea, fresh as from the cabinet-makers, softly shaded in slate and mahogany, smooth as a billiard ball, and nearly as true. Here are " Portuguese Men-of-War," filmy and irridescent in the sunlight, beautiful as a dream, yet stinging like an adder if handled carelessly. Let those who have studied life on a tropical sea shore bear out the claim that there is nothing so beautiful or more interesting than such a study.

Even as the waves of the sea seem to exert contrary influences on each little thing which they send rolling to the shore, so does it seem that the waves of life's great ocean deal with us all. To one is given purification and ennoblement: to another despair and despondency, and to another the colourless drab of just flotsam and jetsam.

Before the priest under orders had time to dress at the appointed hour, messengers arrived at St. Seriols bearing the news that the little coastal steamer had been delayed by an accident to her machinery; and that she would not call at Scarborough for passengers until well into the day, and there was much rejoicing accordingly, except by the person principally concerned.

Broken and dejected, Harold moved as though under sentence of death. Marjorie, radiant and joyful in her new found love, was blithe and gay; and her heart beat tune to the music of her thoughts. In her happiness she neither thought of Gaston, nor noticed the misery of her kinsman; indeed, had she noticed it she could not have understood misery under such circumstances: did not life spread out at their feet its prismatic hues of gladness, and of rapture? Did not it give promise of as great a fulness as there had been emptiness before. Harold, on the other hand, saw his career blighted at the outset, and himself standing on the threshold of a desolate waste.

Marjorie, pulsating with joy, soon felt the house too small to contain her, and she called to Harold to go with her to the sea-side. Harold begged to be excused, in an uneasy manner; but Marjorie was insistent, and Mrs. Walton, joining them at the same moment, urged him to go down and let the fresh air straighten out some of the furrows on his brow: "which seemed to have grown there since last night."

" I suppose your heart is sad to leave," she added.

Making the half sad rejoinder that " Each heart knoweth its own bitterness," Harold rose, as much to follow Marjorie as to escape his mother's further comments.

As soon as they had gone beyond earshot Harold turned to Marjorie and said:

"I am very sorry."

"Sorry for what?" asked she blithely.

"You see," he started tentatively, "My vows are such that I may not marry."

At that word, and the memory which it brought of Gaston, the blood flew from Marjorie's cheeks and she felt a choking sensation at her throat, for she was fond of Gaston, and, indeed, loved him in a measure.

She had not seen him for some days, because a new man had been sent to act in Scarborough, and Gaston had returned to his district to find many cases of pressing importance, and, in consequence, he had to discontinue his visits to St. Seriols for some time.

"Who asked you anything about marriage, anyway?" Marjorie replied, seeking time to recover, under the influence of one of their old time squabbles.

"I did not say you asked anything, Marjorie," replied Harold, "I merely remarked on the great sorrow and cross of my life."

"Oh, Harold," she cried impatiently, "don't be stupid; nobody ever said anything about marriage; but if it did come to anything like that and your precious vows——."

"I know what you would say," answered Harold, scarcely remarking that Marjorie no longer addressed him as, "Father." "You would say that my 'precious vows' are broken already." And gazing full upon her beauty as though to steel himself for the thrust he added, "But falling in the dust and lying there are two greatly different things. I must fight you out of my life and forget you in penance and repentance."

"Do what you like," she replied airily, but nevertheless the thought came to her that no more could she take joy in Gaston's presence; and, flitting with that thought came the idea to retire into a convent at once and forever. Her warm heart.

however, and the handsome presence of the man beside her, drove the last thought wildly away, and, turning impatiently to Harold, she said:

"Do, go and leave me."

By this time they had reached the foot of the little path leading to the shore and Harold bowed his head and went to the West. Marjorie stood for the moment irresolute.

The old target range at St. Seriols bay stood on a promontory of stone jutting far out into the deep of the sea, and thither Marjorie now wended her way. The soldiers of the old garrison had concreted the path leading to the point on which was embedded the upright irons of the old target; reaching that point, Marjorie sat and looked in the deep sea at her feet. And such a sea it was: one moment green, another blue, and yet another grey. Looking down she could see clear to the bottom with its stones, and its sand, and its seaweed. Ever and again she could see fishes, in the joy of the clear sunlight, swimming in and out of the little ponds made by the stones and the sea plants; and she wondered if God had not made all his creatures to be as blithe and as happy as they. She revelled in the memory of the cup from which she had taken her first draught, and grew bitter as she thought how soon fate threatened to dash it from her lips. Then came the temptation that life was not worth living. "The sea is blue," said the voice of the tempter, "and will take you in its loving arms and hush you to sleep forever."

Glancing round at the distance to the shore, Marjorie smiled: "why,—" she thought, "I could swim the distance with ease." Then came the suggestion: "suppose an outward tide!" and she saw herself swept out to sea and back on the sea shore, dead;—perhaps, washed far down to some bay among unknown people, who would gaze at the cold stiff corpse with unfeeling eyes; much as she herself had gazed on the trunks of trees she had so often seen washed to the shore. Perhaps ravenous fishes would lacerate the warm flesh of her arms, and she shrank from the very contemplation of the subject. No, certainly not: she would live it out. She would leave Tobago as soon as she could, and, assuredly, life would bring her some man whom she could love better than Gaston, and as much as Harold.

CHAPTER FIFTEENTH.

The trip from Tobago to Trinidad in broad daylight is one of never ending beauty. As the steamer takes its diagonal line from out the Scarborough harbour the towering hills of Tobago loom largely in the background: hill and valley show up in beautiful relief in the sunshine; and the deepening blue of the sea lends enchantment to the colouring. In front, the irridiscent sea spreads in every direction while the easy motion of the comparatively short compass of water set tavellers at ease, and all may be at peace with themselves, and in pleasure with the world.

Harold, however saw little of the beauty of the crossing. Wrapped in the remorse of his scourging conscience he avoided his fellow passengers, and enveloped himself in the sacred offices of the day. Ay, one time as he leant over the rail looking into the deep waters of the sunlit Caribbean he heard those same siren voices, that had called to Marjorie earlier in the morning, calling to him and promising rest and oblivion. But his warm young flesh quivered in protest: silvery voices reminded him of the raptures of the Golden Chalice so recently held to his lips by the most ravishing High Priestess he had ever seen; and stern voiced came the teaching of his faith. " Thou shalt not!" But, again returned insistent the voice of the tempter: " Cleanse thy sin in the one bold sacrifice." Distracted Harold rushed to his cabin, and there, upon his knees, wrestled with the spiritual powers as he knew them. Confessing to utter unworthiness to approach the Great White

Throne he invoked the aid of the Saints, but blushed to approach the Virgin Mother. For some two hours Harold scourged himself and tossed his spirit with remorse and self condemnation. When he rose from his knees the sweat stood upon his brow, but his course was set.

Arriving back upon the upper deck Harold saw that they were within a Homeric stone's throw of the bold North cliffs of the coast of Trinidad. He watched the narrowing distance with mixed feelings. On the one hand was he leaving the temptation which tugged at the very roots of his soul. On the other, the steamer, with every revolution of her screw bore him nearer and nearer to the sacred offices—within the very sanctuary itself—which he dreaded with all the power of his sensitive conscience—and then, and then. On drew the steamer past the frowning Bocas, up the Gulf of Paria, through the lovely fairy islands, all studded with little summer houses and bathing pavilions; there in front lay Port-of-Spain. Port-of Spain, nestling at the foot of the Laventille hills, close to the water's edge; the Port-of-Spain which had surrendered itself to all the excesses of Carnival for the last two days, and now to-day, Ash Wednesday, stood ready to commence the long forty days and forty nights of Lenten penance.

As the little steamer drew alongside the quay Harold espied two of the Cathedral Clergy evidently awaiting his coming. The work of disembarkation took but a few moments and then Harold learnt how the delay in his coming had thrown the Presbytery into consternation; for it had been arranged and announced that he would preach the sermon for that evening. So persistent had the demand for seating grown that it had been found advisable to issue tickets to control the crowd. When Harold heard that he had been assigned the sermon of the evening, his face lit up with a strange smile. He however, confessed that he had no sermon prepared; at the which Father Hyacinth, for he it was, who, still proud of his one time pupil had volunteered to immediately prepare him for his duty, patted him on the shoulder and said that the young Savonarola had no need to prepare his sermons, they all seemed so ready and well." Then he added.

"But Father, have a care you do not follow too closely in the wake of Savonarola."

Harold again smiled whimsically and thanked the good old man for his compliments, barely adding:

"Poor Savonarola!"

They all then set out on the short walk to the Presbytery.

The evening did not belie the promise of the morning: the spacious Cathedral was filled to overflowing; the steps, the church yard, all were filled to their uttermost. Inside, could be heard the murmur of incessant conversation: yet none could have dreamt what was in store for them.

When Harold mounted the pulpit a gentle hush descended upon the vast concourse of people. With deliberation he read out the text of his sermon: chosen from one of the lessons of the day: Joel II, 17-19.

"Be converted to me with all your heart in fasting and weeping and in mourning . . . . Rend your hearts and not your garments, and turn to the Lord your God."

"You good folk of Port-of-Spain," he began, "have been spending the last two days in almost pagan excesses, to counter-balance the commencement of Lenten denials to-day; and to-night you are foregathered in this temple of God to make show of your piety and religion: but I would charge you all in the words of the prophet, and ask how many of you are come with all your heart. Fasting no doubt many of you have been; but have your hearts been in your fasting: or have you taken up your fasting as you would take up a garment for the sake of appearance; and would now render unto God your garments like your fasting, without your heart in either?"

Burning to his subject the young preacher lashed out at the sins of the day, that stalk unashamed in the midst of the multitude.

"Not many months ago," he continued, "I preached my first sermon in the West Indies in this Cathedral, and I then hoped for some reform; the Church has furnished you with good men devoted to your welfare, labouring unceasingly at the Vineyard of your hearts, but how have you repaid it? Was the Carnival just ended one whit more chaste than those that have gone before; or did not each of you strive with the other to make terms with the devil? And now you come ready to render your garments."

Much in this strain, towards purity of heart, did Harold continue: with his whole frame knit with the intensity of his feelings, and his eyes blazing at the congregation, he continued to thunder forth on the subject of his text. Never had Harold been heard to such advantage. He seemed etherealized with the keenness of his battle for purity; until drawing to the close of his great exhortation he leant low over the pulpit rails and made the dramatic announcement to which he had bent his will.

"And now my brethren," he said, "I come to the announcement with which I purpose to close this sermon to-night. An announcement of which I have not advised my Superior, nor any one else, because, making it here, I intend that it shall be irrevocable. I have ministered to my flock for some short months, but in that time I have felt how futile has been my labour: and how unworthy a labourer am I. There are many good men and true who feel that they can serve the Church and people from the inner pale of the Church: I feel like a man on the bank of a dangerous stream shouting directions to some unfortunates in a frail craft. The call comes to me to breast it out into the danger and lend a helping hand, even though I go down in the effort. The hour has come when I can no longer stand in the pulpit and shout directions to the people."

At this stage the congregation moved uneasily and priests were to be seen hurrying in and out of the sacristy: Harold continued, " I feel," he said, " that I must come out into the market place, and share the temptations of the people. I must fight their battles with them, raise the fallen and salve the wounded," then he continued rapidly. " From the pulpit I cannot see enough. From to-morrow I lay aside my robes and gown, and become one of you—sharing your trials, and helping to bear your burdens. No more shall I render my garments: thus I hope to render my life with all my heart: thus I hope to help some of you through to God: thus I hope to help you all in rendering your hearts and not your garments, to turn to the Lord your God."

By the time Harold had uttered the last words and turned to descend, without so much as blessing the congregation, the threatening trepidation had turned to a panic. Here a woman fainted, there another was taken in hysteria. Hundreds inside the vast edifice surging to go out: hundreds outside pressing to go in, to witness, if possible, the closing scenes of the great drama. For a moment the situation looked ugly; then the venerable Pere Hyacinth, sizing up the essential dangers of the situation, rushed into the pulpit and summoning up all the past vigour of his youth called aloud to the congregation:

" My children, be still. I beseech you to bend your knees, for five minutes, in silent prayer for the overwrought and saintly young Father."

The electric command, the appeal to the sense of pity caught the congregation, and in a moment all were kneeling, and no sound broke on the air, save an occasional sob from some emotional woman. At the expiration of the awarded five minutes the voice of the aged priest was heard again:

" My children," he said, " His Lordship the Bishop will pronounce the Apostolic benediction, and, at the close of the service, I would ask the congregation to leave quietly:

always remembering in your prayers a petition for the recovery to health and grace of the good and youthful Father Dominic." Saying which, he descended; the consequences of a panic were averted, and the ritual of the service proceeded in its even way.

Readers will wonder what had meanwhile become of Harold. Met, as he descended the pulpit and made his way into the Sacristy, by several priests with every degree of exclamation, he had swept them all aside and proceeded to disrobe. On being approached by the Bishop's chaplain with a request to attend on his Lordship, and on the Superior of his order, he begged to be excused to both; and, rushing out of the Cathedral, made his escape by one of the side gates and hurried down a cross street. Persons meeting the hurrying, or rather flying, priest, blessed themselves and wondered what soul *in extremis* had called for his ministration.

Rushing he knew not whither Harold soon cleared the vicinity of the Cathedral, and, boarding a passing street car, was soon whirled to the far end of the town at which stood the great open Savannah known as the Queen's Park. Beseating himself on one of the rustic benches, placed there for weary pedestrians, Harold for the first time commenced to take stock of what he should, and should not do, after the great renunciation of his life. High principles were one thing, but he knew that in this mundane world a man must work, receive alms, or starve. He did not intend to starve; true his mother was well off, but not even from her would he receive alms, nor know money from her by any other name. He indeed had his profession as an architect, but how much could he earn in a little place like Port-of-Spain? He thought of the place of his birth—British Guiana,—and wondered what were the chances. He thought of Europe, but felt too diffident of his unknown capacity to risk the venture, if even he had the money for the expensive journey. At length he thought of his immediate wants and wondered where he could turn to lay his head for the night. The only person he could think of at the moment was Gaston's mother, whom he had often visited; but he felt that recent events prevented him from seeking the hospitality of that lady. At last he bethought him of the genial captain of the coastal steamer who had so frequently accepted the hopsitality of the Presbytery, and also that of St. Seriols: Harold thereupon decided to risk a call upon him.

Fortune stood in favour of Harold, for, as he rounded the corner of the street leading to the captain's house, he came across that good man just " making port anchorage " as he called it.

" Hallo! Father," he cried, " through your sermon already and on service bent."

" Yes," Harold answered simply, " through with my last sermon, but not on service bent. I am in search of lodgings, for I am no longer ' Father ' but merely Harold Walton again. I, to-night, left the priestly service of the Church."

Captain Markham wondered whether he heard aright, or if the young man's high strung metal had affected his brains, and then cried aloud:

" You have done WHAT ? "

" From henceforth, my good friend," answered Harold, " I will be no longer ' Father Dominic.' I made the announcement from the pulpit to-night."

" But is that not rather a serious step?" queried the captain.

" Oh yes, serious indeed," half laughed Harold, " and that is just what brings me to you. For I know not where to lay my head to-night."

" Oh, you don't mean it," replied the genial hearted captain, as they reached the gates of his bungalow, " just walk right in here, and be as happy as you like for as long as you like."

Harold thanked him profusely and explained that while he had not been turned out of the Presbytery he did not feel justified in accepting its hospitality any longer; and he would therefore avail himself of his host's genial offer for a few days, at least until he had time to turn around.

" Quite right, too, Father, 1 mean Mr. Walton—though that sounds funny! Meanwhile, my purse also is at your service, for you priests are never burdened with much cash, if you will excuse my saying so."

" Thanks, a thousand times," fervently answered Harold, " maybe I shall have to avail myself of your kindness, for I must change my habit with my occupation."

Before retiring that night Capt. Markham told Harold that next morning at daybreak he would sail round the island of Trinidad; picking cargo at different points, and if he, Harold, desired to be out of the way for some few days, he could do no better than do the round trip in the little steamer as the captain's guest. " Some diversion will do you good, otherwise," he added, " you might be a little lonely and too retrospective in the house all by yourself."

Harold, overwhelmed by so much kindness was anxious to decline; but, remembering that it would take some days of growth to obliterate the tonsure of his crown, and, that it was best to be away while the hubbub was at its height, gratefully accepted the offer.

That night, before retiring to the spare room which Capt. Markham's bachelor establishment boasted, Harold sat and wrote two letters: one to his mother, the other to Marjorie. To his mother he briefly explained that he found it impossible to remain in the service of the Church, and while he hoped that his vows would remain upon him to the end of his days, he yet found it necessary to mix with the people and understand their temptations. He begged that she would think of it in the best light possible and bear to him the same loving regard that she had always shown. With respect to money he begged that she would offer him none as he proposed to earn his own living by the sweat of his brow.

To Marjorie he wrote a passionate outburst. He upbraided her for nothing and took all the blame upon himself; but he confessed that it was impossible for him to remain in the service of the Church or perform her sacred offices with the stain of his broken vows upon his soul. While he was leaving the Church he trusted to be able to devote the remainder of his broken life to the uplifting of his fellows in the warfare against temptation. For herself he dared not offer any advice. He, who had made such a hash of his own, would be a poor mentor to one whose happiness he had so sorely jeopardised. If it were any satisfaction to her he would add that she would remain the one consuming passion of his life; and but for the burden of his vows, which remained vows still, he would have asked her to share the remainder of his life with him. This admission he made so that she might realize how complete was his renunciation of her, and he asked that she forget him forever.

Next day the local newspapers were full of the dramatic withdrawal from the priesthood of ' Trinidad's most eloquent preacher ": " the Dominican's second Savonarola," etc., and those which referred to the strain in his pedigree asked, in headlines, whether it was " Elba or St. Helena."

The emissaries of the Presbytery were sent to search high and low for " the wilful brother "; but he had vanished as completely as though the earth had swallowed him. Meanwhile, Harold sat on the deck of the little steamer and watched her plow her way on the " southern journey," through the gulf of Paria to the rolling waters of the Atlantic: and thence, eventually, back to the Caribbean and the Gulf of Paria by another entrance. For the next few days, Harold was of the world, yet out of it: he drank in the lovely scenery of the southern coast of Trinidad and followed the life of the people he was thrown among with zest. No one in these bays and landing places had yet heard of his abandonment of the Church, for he yet wore

IN BONDAGE.

his flannels to keep tune with his tonsure. The continuous life and movement from bay to bay, the varying types of humanity: the constant warfare between shippers and ships' men, all helped to keep Harold from too much introspection, and helped to fill in the awful chasm he had made:

Stretched at full length in a deck chair Harold saw himself slowly steaming past what the people call the mud volcano; probably one of the most unique geological features in the world. As a matter of fact it is not one volcano at all, but a series of small vents in the earth, each spurting out its mud and pebbles, and then closing up exhausted, to burst out afresh in some new place on the hill side. The hill side looked bare and desolate: no trees, nor sign of animation; just these mud geysers old as well as new. Inhabitants say that occasionally one of these geysers gets " wicked " and throw up mud and stones to a great height, and that even flame may be seen. But, Josephus like, it must be said: let every man believe as it pleaseth him. Certainly it has been recorded on no less an authority than Chas. Kingsley that they throw up quartzose and jasper, all bearing evidence of having been long rolled on a sea beach. Geologists have also recorded pyrites and gypsum; all of which must have been carried up from a considerable depth by the force of the same gases which make the miniature volcanoes. Steaming on, Harold found himself brought to the mighty bay of Mayaro. And what a " sandy bay " that was! In Tobago the " sandy bay " was not more than a few hundred yards in span. Here was a " sandy bay " indeed, with one mighty sweep of miles and miles of open beach, breasting the sweep of the wide Atlantic. Communication between ship and shore becomes one of difficulty: heavy surf boats have to be used and these not infrequently get swamped by the mighty rollers which sweep in on the beach. Harold was informed that two trips before, a most promising young officer had met his death in the journey to the shore: his boat was caught and overturned in the surf and two seamen and himself were drowned: two others escaped. "Poor fellow!" sighed Harold, "may he rest in peace."

Eventually the North coast was reached, and the little steamer commenced to take cargo for Port-of-Spain. Toco was the commencement. Then Harold saw life in all its phases, and saw humanity dressed and undressed. Here was a buxom woman, spluttering French patois, and broken English by turns, dragging a weary looking child with her. There was a boatman, jawing the life out of one of the seamen over two pigs which did not seem to enjoy embarkation; and to which, the seamen aforesaid insisted that something or the other should be done. At which, eventually, the boatman declared.

"De man gie dem so; and 'e tell me to lef' (leave) dem so; and I leffing dem so," saying which he pushed off and left the seaman to make shift as best he could.

Eventually with exhausted patience the chief officer dejectedly announced to Harold that he scarce knew what to do with these Tobago people. Harold, always loyal to Tobago, ventured that he thought the ship was yet in Trinidad waters.

"Yes," answered the chief, "But don't you see Tobago off there?" Jerking his thumb North. "Well, this is the back door to Trinidad for them: they swarm over, and they think themselves God's people. Look here: see that woman coming; I bet you she is one. She is done with the mate, and is now looking for me. Why, if I gave them half a chance they would have their pigs in the berth, their cocoa on the dining table, and their poultry God only knows where.

Ere he was through his caustic comments the woman aforesaid was hailing him.

"Mister," she said, in a sultry aggressive tone, "Is you de cap'n?"

"No, I aint de cap'n," replied the chief in faithful imitation of her tone: then straightening himself he resumed his own voice, and, almost sternly, said with rising inflection:

"But I am his Prophet."

"I aint know if yo' is a prophet," calmly replied his interrogator, "but if yo' is, yo' better come and 'prophesy' to dis nigger man," (she was a full blooded negro herself), "wha' will happen, ef he don't put me fowls whe' I kin feed dem," and marched majestically back from whence she came.

The prophet laughed and hastened in her wake to "prophesy" unto the aforesaid "nigger" man.

On his return Harold enquired as to his annexing the high office of prophet.

"Well, it's this way," answered the chief, whose name by the way was Ferguson, "There is 'no other God but Allah and Mohammed is his Prophet.' Do you tumble? I am the captain's "prophet"; saying which is interpreted that I am everything: Cook's boy, Carpenter's boy; Ship's boy; Mate's boy; Engineer's boy and great Jehosaphat's boy."

Harold laughed heartily, for diversion indeed he was getting; and then witnessed another call upon the "prophet" by a boisterous Barbadian (for all islands are represented in these nooks and crannies) who wanted, according to the aforementioned "prophet," "one and sevenpence value for his shilling."

Amid scenes such as these Harold lived his hours until Port-of-Spain was again reached and he had to take up life in earnest.

CHAPTER SIXTEENTH.

The news that reached Mrs. Walton seemed to her to be the complete overfilling of her cup of sorrows. She discussed it with no one, and declined to allow it to be discussed in her presence. She simply sank into herself; and those who watched her knew that it boded no good. Marjorie took it inwardly like a sport; and concluded that "if he felt that way, it was the best way, that's all." Outwardly she counterfeited the sorrow of her Aunt, and seized the occasion to give Gaston his liberty. He pleaded and argued but in vain: Marjorie was obdurate. She claimed that she could not think of marriage with that great shadow overhanging their household; and she could think less of keeping one whom she so sincerely appreciated—she did not say loved—tied to her apron strings. Gaston was hard hit, but a temperament like his carries its sorrows lightly, and he was not likely to die a bachelor. When some of his boon Trinidad companions wrote, chaffing him, to those to whom he did reply, he was spirited and witty; he claimed that even if he had lost it was something to have ridden in a great race, if even he was classed among the " also ran."

In Trinidad, Harold quietly remained in seclusion awaiting the full growth of his crown. Like most things, his sensational withdrawal from the Church was passing away, so far as the people were concerned, like the proverbial nine days' wonder. Good Captain Markham begged Harold to make his home at the bungalow and help to make company; and meanwhile gave him *carte blanche* at his tailor's. Reluctant though Harold was there was nothing left to do but avail himself of the offer, and meantime his hair grew. his clothes were in the making.

After some while an announcement appeared in the local press signed "Harold Walton'" offering continuation and preparatory classes to young men, together with lessons in drawing and architecture. The advertiser also offered his services as an architect to prospective builders. This advertisement brought in some few pupils and Harold stood to earn a paltry $25 per month. Soon, however, some mysterious power seemed set against him and his pupils began to leave his classes. Of course he suspected early that the influence of the Presbytery was at work; and indeed he was not far wrong, for the Presbytery had taken double umbrage, as Harold had resolutely declined to obey the summons of his superiors. Port-of-Spain is an almost entirely Catholic city, and it did not take the Presbytery long to bring pressure to bear on parents and even young men, and to secure attention for the view that it was highly improper to have dealings with an infidel and a disobedient son of the Church. Taking that lead, some unscrupulous zealots even freely ascribed an immoral life to the struggling young teacher.

Now in the City there lived a very wealthy Portuguese Colonist whose name was Espindula—Justino Espindula. His wealth was estimated to be close on one million dollars, and in a small colony that is a colossal fortune; and he was a character unto himself. Son of the Church though he was, yet he carried all the traits of a self made man, and was as little likely to allow the Church to dictate to him, as to allow one of his employees. On occasion he did not hesitate to say that " the Church was the Church, but business was business."

Early one morning the post brought Harold a characteristic letter from this man asking him to submit plans and specifications for a new Hotel which he proposed to erect on a central site in the city, which he had recently acquired. The note, even the caligraphy, was typical of the man.

It was short, curt and jerky—almost rude in its brevity. His writing was characterized by broad slanting letters: the tails of his "ys" and "gs" swept the line underneath, and he signed his name in full "Justino Espindula" in a plain, bold hand, without flourish or addition.

Harold hesitated. In the first place how could he "submit plans and specifications" without instructions: then, plans and specifications could not grow in a night. There were lots of things to be decided, even the—to him—least of all, the question of remuneration. Then, Harold again considered: Hotels were hardly erected to the glory of God, and he questioned the propriety of aiding in the erection of one. Healthier views however prevailed over these last objections: Hotels were after all for the rest and comfort of strangers, and for the abode of the homeless; and even a church could become the vehicle of vice. At length he decided to wait on the great man; for his wealth made him great in the eyes of the people.

Harold acted immediately his mind was made up, and on reaching Espindula's place of business asked one of the clerks to enquire if he could see him, as he had called in connection with a letter received that morning.

The clerk for reply informed Harold that he was just to go and "knock at that door. If he wants to see you he will say 'come in'; if not, he will say 'go away,' and it does not matter whether he sent for you or not you will have to go away."

Harold felt a little nervous at the possibilities, but did as he was bid and heard a deep, though not unkindly, "Come in."

He no sooner entered the room than the great man greeted him with:

• "Well, what is it: money or work?"

"Neither or both," answered Harold, "I am Walton and come in connection with your note."

"Oh, Walton, yes: sit down. Have you brought any plans?"

IN BONDAGE.

Harold suppressed a smile.

"No," he replied, "I have not brought any plans. I called to get details and directions as to what you want and how you want it."

"My good man," almost sourly jerked out Espindula, "I am no architect. You are the architect; or supposed to be. I want a Hotel: a great big one. The best that money can buy—that is, in keeping with the business of the place. Its no good building a Waldorf Astoria at the North Pole. You figure it out; tell me your fee: hand over the work."

Harold was at a loss how to reply. He had never been in a Hotel in his life.

Seeing the hesitation Espindula added:

"Well, if you don't feel like making plans for a place of that sort: cut it out: If you do, and want to look over the idea, meet me here at 4 o'clock, and I will take you over to the General Picton and you can gather up—Good morning." Saying which the "great man" turned to the papers at his desk.

Harold with a "Very well, Sir" bowed himself out and homewards. Assuredly, he thought, Hotels were no strong point of his. Were it a store, or a Church, alright. But now he would have to pick up what he could.

At 3.55 Harold was in attendance at Espindula's, and promptly at the stroke of 4 that goodly man emerged from his inner office, and on catching sight of Harold, gave a grunt of satisfaction.

"Oh, you here eh? Good. Come along."

Entering the roomy Victoria which awaited them at the entrance they were quickly driven to the General Picton Hotel. There Espindula thawed somewhat, after ordering two whiskies and sodas and duly disposing of them. Harold lending a dutiful hand, thereafter suggested that they should walk around: and so they did. As they moved aound, Espindula pointed to a feature here and indicated an error there: eventually he grew quite communicative and at last enquired:

"And how are your classes?"

"Not flourishing," answered Harold.

"Pupils leaving, eh?"

"Yes. The old influence is against me."

"Thought so," said Espindula, "The Church is alright, but some of her men are very narrow-minded."

Soon after, Espindula indicated that it was about time to leave. On the drive to Harold's quarters Espindula handed him an envelope, saying that it contained something "on account," as "while the grass was growing the horse might be starving!" Harold thanked him cordially and pocketed the missive. When in the privacy of his own room he did examine the contents he found two cheques of $250 each. His first impulse was to return at least one of the cheques, but neither Capt. Markham nor the "Prophet," who was now a frequent visitor at the bungalow, would hear of it, and, added the "Prophet":

"I know Espindula so well that I am at liberty to say he would go fairly crazy at the suggestion that he did not know his own business best. You bet he had some notion in coughing it up."

Of course Harold was badly in need of funds and deeply indebted to his host, so the handsome payment was just in time to put him "high and dry," as the "Prophet" said.

Some two weeks later Harold seriously confronted his host.

"You, know," he said, "I can't do Espindula's work: and I have spent a good deal of his money."

"Well I am blowed," was the captain's eloquent reply.

"Fact, though. I have already destroyed two sets of plans; for as they commence to take shape they seem to exude the very atmosphere of the Church and the cloister. My very will seems dominated by those influences."

"Serious case," answered Captain Markham, "You had better read up your architecture."

"Reading is no use. I have spent days and days in reading. It is the spirit of the place I can't catch."

"Spirit! Look here, sonny, you had better take another trip around the island wth me. Your nerves are going "creketty."

"No, thank you," replied Harold, "I don't want any trip. What I want is to catch the Hotel spirit. But I don't want to go and live in one. My plan is that you and the 'Prophet' should come along with me some evening, to some place or the other, and let me get my bearings."

"Right ho," answered his host. "What say; tonight?"

"This afternoon, and to-night," suggested Harold.

"Very well. I will connect up with Ferguson; for, I am sure, I don't know where you get that outlandish title for him from."

Harold laughed.

"That's one of my fancies," he said.

That afternoon the trio "did" one place; but the results seemed poor, to Harold, and he suggested that they should dine at another; to that plan they all agreed, with stipulation for early assembly, all to be dressed for any event.

At the appointed hour the friends were again together at the General Picton. The first thing that Harold did was to order swizzles; then they walked around and smoked; establishing themselves in the lounge for a little while, they followed the example of the crowd and ordered more swizzles.

By the time they got to the table which had been duly bespoke and planned for by the "Prophet," Harold's face bore a hectic flush, and his eyes shone brilliantly. Wine was ordered and Harold seemed to take a delight in plying his guests—for he insisted that for the night he was host —and he did not hesitate in setting a fairly fast example,

When dinner was through Harold was a changed man. The wine, the lights, the crowd, all seemed to leave their impress on him; and he brought a laughing comment to the lips of the " Prophet " by suggesting that they should adjourn to the Theatre and then flit to the " Carlsbad " for supper.

" Well, sonny," added Markham, " that does seem a Lit ' of a cotter's Saturday night ' but since I am in, I will stay in: that's all there is to be said."

They were late for the theatre; but that made little difference to the trio, and when the " Prophet " suggested that they should invite a couple of ladies back to supper with them Harold eagerly assented; but asked whom could they pick up in that casual sort of way. The " Prophet " confessed that he had no one in view but he would " spy out the land."

Sauntering round to the side of the building Ferguson shortly after returned with the report that the gay and festive widow du Saumaris was present with her niece and " that young ass, Smith." Hurriedly holding a council of war it was decided that they should join the ladies in the vestibule when they were leaving and trust to luck.

Thanks to the clever manoeuvring of the " Prophet " all fell out to their desires, and they were all soon established at a supper table at the Carlsbad.

The supper was but an extended edition of the dinner, save that there was more wine and less to eat. The crowd was bigger and more brilliant than at the ' Picton.' There was a constant stream of fair women and immaculately dressed men; and through it all Harold acted as to the manner born: full charged with wine, he felt that he was living his part to perfection. At last the ladies announced that the time to leave had come, and soon they were bowed to their carriages; but not until the elder lady had pressed a cordial invitaton on Harold to join a party of excursionists to one of the islands in the gulf " when all would be gay, and every man gallant." With the withdrawal of the ladies. Captain Markham suggested that a cab should be called and the charming example followed, for he was feeling fairly full.

"Oh no," cried Harold, "It's a night, and a night it must be"; and with that he headed straight back to the staircase.

On reaching the verandah, and being joined by his companions, he rang and ordered more wine, as cool as any old offender. The "Prophet" was a 'toper' from away back, and the captain could hold his own in any meleê, as he put it. Shortly after an adjournment was made to the billiard room. Here the crowd was at its best. The musical click, click of the ivory balls, the skill required and the noiseless moving to and fro of white coated waiters, with trays of sparkling refreshment, all helped to a scene of pleasant good humour.

Harold however did not fail to notice a visitor occasionally flit into an adjoining room, and again some other emerging from the same place: by duly "pumping" the "Prophet" he discovered that within that room were the green tables of chance. Harold insisted that all things must be uncovered, and accordingly the entree was obtained, and the companions were soon within the presence of the blind goddess.

Many games were in progress and as many types of humanity represented: and there is no place that humanity can be seen with its clothes off like unto a gambling table. Bent on participating, Harold soon found himself at a table, round which was gathered a motley crowd with dice and cup. No skill was required; none was asked. You shook the cup, emptied it, and took your chance under certain well defined rules. Harold, like all beginners stood well in, and was winning handsomely; but he grew tired of the sameness of effort and, after ordering more wine, suggested to the "Prophet" that a game of cards would be more interesting.

"Cards! boy," answered Ferguson, "why, you would be skinned alive in a minute, for the only card game you could look in at would be poker."

"Oh, poker," airily answered Harold, "I have heard a little about. Gaston de Garcia initiated me in college days; though I can't say I remember much. Two or three lessons however will set me right."

Calling for cards the three companions sat at a vacant table, the Prophet dealt a few hands, and they played for nominal stakes; in a very little while Harold had the hang of the game.

Some nearby players, seeing a greenhorn being initiated, drew near, and, scenting easy game, asked permission to join the table if play was meant in earnest. Harold promptly agreed, and on Captain Markham withdrawing, three new comers joined the two remaining players.

For the first few hands Harold lost with judgment, the "Prophet" won a hand or two, but, on the whole, fortune favoured the strangers. Ordering more wine Harold commenced to play with a good deal of recklessness, and fortune ever favouring the brave, seemed to set his way: but the play was small and money changing hands slowly, until one of the strangers suggested a doubling up of the limits. To this, Harold agreed, though the "Prophet" demurred. The latter, though forced to follow, took no chances and played with extreme caution. Thus the game was practically left between Harold and the strangers. What Harold lacked in skill he made up in luck, and the game stood fairly even when Harold suddenly remembered Gaston and the holding up of a "kicker." Immediately the cards were dealt he discarded four and held one for the new deal. After the second deal every one seemed pretty well satisfied with himself, for the betting at once commenced with strength. Never leading, Harold yet followed every " rise " with perseverance. When things got warm the "Prophet" declaring the position " no place for a parson's son," threw down his hand: though he declared it a "full house." Harold laughed boisterously: but his laugh was an enigma. Whether he laughed at the "Prophet's" folly, or wisdom, none could say. He ordered more wine, and the pool rose steadily to about $450, then it came to a standstill, and the first in hand declared in a small piping voice that he held "a straight." "Nothing doing," cried a boisterous fellow "I stand on a flush in hearts." "Shut up," gruffly called the third "I walk through you all with four Kings," and suiting his action to his words, he made one full sweep at the piled money on the table. "No, you don't," solemnly announced Harold, and imitating to perfection the small piping voice of the first speaker he cried, "I hev' five little wan spot cards," and, with that, he disclosed the "kicker" ace that he had held up, together with three others, and the "joker" that had been dealt him.

The last speaker blanched: it meant "broke" to him, and suddenly remembering how he had regarded Harold as easy game he lost all self control and continuing the mimicking of manner cried sarcastically:

"You hev', hev' you: you preaching son of a"——.

Before he could complete his sentence Harold's right arm had shot out straight from the shoulder, and his fist, catching the speaker fair in the mouth, sent him reeling from his chair. In an instant all was confusion. The "Prophet," trained to act in emergencies, swept the table, and then sprang into the crowd of struggling men. Harold was bitter and excited: it was the first time any one had referred in such terms to his previous life, and he was prepared to fight the whole assembly. Men gripped their hip pockets ominously and waiters sprang from everywhere. Captain Markham elbowed his way in, and catching Harold by the arm hurried him out of the room. Meanwhile others soundly rated the offender against good manners. Soon after, the Prophet joined Harold and the Captain, and together they all made their way home.

Next morning Harold woke with a "head as big as a house," and the Prophet was in early attendance, ministering to his wants and salving his wounds with his winnings. Of course his prime prescription was the "hair of the dog that bit him." But Harold would have none of it. His lesson was through, and now his work was before him.

Once begun, that work was done mighty fast. He had caught the spirit of the place by drinking deep down to the dregs of the cup which he had held to his lips. The lines and columns of a Hotel rose in his imagination, with startling rapidity, and, as quickly, he had sketched out such a place as he felt sure would mark a period in West Indian Hotel architecture. He then set to work on interior plans of saloons and staircases; of boudoirs and bed chambers. Harold worked with feverish anxiety. Day and night he worked without ceasing; lest he lost the spirit, he said; and in three weeks after his famous night out he was ready to wait on Espindula.

Arriving at the office he hazarded the knock and heard the welcome "Come in." Harold experienced his first pang of disappointment when Espindula barely glanced at his plans and threw them aside. Then, turning to a drawer, he drew out his cheque book and curtly enquired:

"What is your fee?"

Harold was so disgusted at the treatment that he almost savagely replied.

"Two hundred pounds: and you have been good enough to let me have one hundred already."

Espindula took up his pen and wrote, deliberately as usual. Blotting with care he handed Harold a cheque for two hundred and fifty pounds saying.

"Two hundred pounds, your fee. Fifty pounds a personal gratuity from me. And the first hundred you may regard as consideration for that wasted month, and part payment for the blow struck that night. You were damn right. Good morning." Saying which he turned to other business in hand.

Harold could just thank his patron, outside the building, he ejaculated. "Well, I never!"

CHAPTER SEVENTEENTH.

The six months that elapsed between the handing in of Harold's plans and the completion of the Mount Athos Hostelry seemed to have slipped away like a midsummer's night dream. It is true that Harold had his sorrows, and felt to the full the freezing effect of the ban of the Church. His classes had dwindled to zero, yet was he happy. His living expenses were small, and Espindula's fee lay still fat at Harold's bankers. True, also, that the letters from Tobago were far from being reassuring. His mother scarcely allowed his name to be mentioned in her presence, and she continued to suffer visibly. She would sit for hours looking across the fair blue waters of the Caribbean without exchanging words with one mortal. Such was the relic of the once brilliant Marion: fair chatelaine of the house of Walton. Marjorie had written, frequently urging Harold to come home; but he dreaded the sweet sad eyes of his mother: and he dreaded other things more. Through all these sorrows and anxieties his spirit rose jubilant, for his never ending joy was to watch the rise of the scantlings and columns, the high peaked towers, and nestling minarets which gave life to the child of his imagination, and being to the Mount Athos Hostelry.

Many a day, as the building took form, the effect of the whole startled him. As he gazed on the nearly completed building he could see reflected as in a mirror the features of that ghastly night in which he captured the Hotel spirit, and saw scarlet. There was no mistaking in the voluptuous sweep of the low treaded staircase, and its crystal banisters, the bold curves of Mrs. du Saumaris' ivory bosom which had sent his blood, full charged with wine, tingling to his ears: nor was there any misconceiving in the low cast of four little minarets and one spire, when the sun would shade them in its long western gleams, that card squabble when his own right arm had shot home like a bolt.

On the completion of the building, controversy raged wild around the "Mount Athos Architecture." One school described it as a poem in stone; while another referred to it as the most ghastly and immoral looking place it was possible to find. Through it all, Espindula, under his grum exterior, rejoiced to his heart's content. Always he took a delight in giving a black eye to convention; but now he had landed one fair and square in its solar plexus.

At the height of this controversy Harold decided that he would flee the country: his bank account showed recurring transactions on one side only, and his earning capacity was at zero. There were not many Espindulas in the community, and no more hotels to be completed. After casting about for some while, and measuring against each idea the limits of his purse, the thought came to him swift as a dream "why not return to Demerara." As rapidly came his decision and, "Demerara had it." It suited his purse and pleased his inclination; for, as a boy, he had long harboured the hope of return to the land of his birth, and, who can tell: if the scalpel had been applied to his soul, deep down might have been found disinclination to go far from the woman who held leash of his heart: even though he would stifle and trample upon the least show of evidence.

On Captain Markham's return home that evening Harold apprised his friend of his decision. At first the genial seaman would not hear of it:

- "Live it all down, boy, live it down!" was his vigorous advice; but Harold had made up his mind, and in a few days he found himself embarked on one of the liners that connect Trinidad with the Great Land of Promise which had given birth to Harold, and centuries before, had sent death hurtling to the throat of the swash buckling Raleigh.

Forty hours after leaving Trinidad Harold's steamer was threading its way over the great Bar that lies at the mouth of the Demerara and Essequebo Rivers. As he watched the good steamer slowing, steaming past the old Fort William Frederick, he found himself first figuring how much water must have flowed past it since his mother had taken him outwards, so irrelevant is human nature, and then next wondering what fortune the city held for him. At least, thought he, the Church would cease to persecute, for in Demerara the Jesuits control her destiny; and what the Dominicans persecute, the Jesuits protect, so that their time honoured differences of opinion may be reflected to the greater glory of their respective Orders.

Scanning the serried ranks of river Warehouses and Wharves, ranged like a Macedonian phalanx, he gave full rein to his fancy and pictured unto himself an honoured old age in the land of his birth. Harold had no friends to greet him, so he disembarked alone, and, leaving his little belongings to the care of the good natured Customs officials, he set out on the aimless task of wandering about the fair city of Georgetown. If the view from the bar, when he could see nought but a couple of chimneys, had been unprepossessing, his new impressions were now enchanting. It seemed as though he had forced an entry into some forbidding cavern, to find the interior one vast fairyland. What spacious streets; What open spaces! While Port-of-Spain could boast of some few more examples of ornamental architecture, Georgetown was still ahead, and certainly filled with less of the meagre type of home sacred to the middle class of Port-of-Spain. Wandering from place to place Harold came at last to the foot of Main Street and stood spell-bound at its fairy like loveliness. Two broad avenues, paved with terra cotta, formed parallel borders to a wide stretch of water; in which grew profusely the graceful Victoria Regias and other aquatic plants, all in flower. Separating the canal itself from its terra cotta borders were well kept trees with wide overhanging branches: their trunks standing at even intervals and suggesting the columns of some sylvan cathedral or place of ancient rite. To add to the scene of early morning enchantment, the overhead trees were in riotous blossom, and carpeted the green sward underneath and the adjoining road, with flowers of purple and gold and crimson. " A Marine Square etherealized!" was the mental comment of the traveller. Pursuing his course further afield Harold was charmed to find many other streets laid out in the same manner: the cooling effect of the wide canals on the tropical atmosphere, being particularly noticeable. Nor did the streets that ran on either side of these canals suffer anything in breadth from their presence, as each seemed wider than the streets of Port-of-Spain; thus producing an effect of avenues four times the width of those of the neighbouring colony.

Harold, pleased with the first impressions of his native City, hustled around to find cheap lodgings. This proved an easy task. and quartering himself at a third rate Hotel, he actually made daily excursions to the various points of interest in the ' garden city ' of the West Indies. The wide and spacious promenade on the sea front, where man's ingenuity had erected a huge barrier to the inroads of the sea, at once filling its defensive duty and providing one of the finest marine esplanades in the West Indies, filled his heart with joy. The magnificent and extensive Botanic Gardens: the long and shady Brickdam: the stately avenue of palms at Ruimveldt, each caught his fancy in turn. But pleased as he was with his native city it offered him very little practical hospitality: such as he sought. The industrial life of the place was at a standstill: possessing vast resources and unlimited wealth the colony nevertheless marked time, awaiting the advent of the adventurous and the energetic; so it seemed that there was very little hope of securing any commissions in what Harold now came to regard as his profession: he therefore commenced to search for employment in the ordinary avenues of life. Every effort however seemed to bring him disappointment: In one place he would be confronted with his utter lack of training; in another he would be up against his absolute inability to produce any credentials.

Long after he seemed to have exhausted every avenue of employment he struck up casual acquaintance with Jack Engledow, and in the course of exchanging confidences let on the quandary he was in to secure a job.

Jack Engledow was Deputy Manager of Pln. Waterloo on the East sea Coast of Demerara, and he at once grasped at the opportunty to secure a worthy recruit to his staff of overseers, and, incidentally, to do his new found friend a turn. It was thereupon arranged that Engledow would represent things to his manager and communicate results to Harold.

In three days came a letter advising Harold of his appointment to the staff of " Waterloo," and bidding him make the necessary purchases, consisting of saddle and riding gear, bedroom furniture, etc., and to come up by first train available. Harold had not bargained for such a strain upon his exchequer, so he now had to weigh this inroad on his funds against employment for perhaps only a while. Weighing the matter for the space of a full minute he concluded that no other course lay open to him, and then set out to boldly plunge into the expenditure.

Jack Engledow came of a good white colonial family; failing at an early age to secure a footing in the local civil service, he, adventurous by nature, took to overseeing and by dint of some native ability and his family influence eventually rose to the position he now occupied. He had never married. Struggling through the early days of his calling with half of his wages permanently hypothecated to his manager " for board " he never could have thought of taking unto himself a wife. And, had the slender residue of his salary even permitted it, it would have been impossible for him to have taken a woman of his class to the rough lodgings which the Estate assigned to its overseers. During the last couple of years he had indeed risen to separate quarters, and, perhaps, the right to claim his board allowance: but he had been adrift so long that he now found himself entangled in relationships, some secret, some otherwise, which precluded all idea of marriage in other directions.

In a few months after Harold had established himself at Waterloo he discovered the whole lie of the land. The entire atmosphere of the place could be summed up in two words, " Sex " and " Gin." The fierce competition among the immigrants for the women of the place, and the occasional poaching of the overseers on the same were as evident as when Edwin Hamilton lived at ' Never Out.' Constant troubles, back biting, news carrying: work scamped, pay lists falsified; each and every one could be traced back in some way, remote or otherwise, to the influence of some woman. Where the one influence left off, the other took it up, and Gin played its part in just a lesser degree among the overseers. Harold in his time saw young men, indentured out from England, offering the highest promise; men who should have proved a most valuable nucleus in the colonization of the country, " lose, under the double temptation . . . ., what elements of the ' Gentle life ' they gained from their mothers at home." So wrote Charles Kingsley of this class fifty years ago, and so it is as true of to-day. No home life, no social element, no anything—save gin and coolie women. What wonder that these young men are so frequently to be found strewn along the byways of the country. Throw out of the employ for which they were indentured, and now unfitted for anything else, they become, instead of a gain to the country, a charge on their more fortunate brethren, and a disgrace to themselves.

There was young McGregor, as clean cut a young Scotsman as ever signed indentures. He was now on his fourth estate. He had completed his indenture to one, and " chucked " under some fancied slight, which was really only a disciplinary measure. The second and third had " chucked " him; and now, by dint of his pleasing address and wonderful wit, he had induced the Manager of Waterloo to take him on, despite the drawback of booze which had been writ large on his previous engagement at least. McGregor, once established, was the life of the place. His wit sparkled and effervesced around every subject imaginable. A row or a strike ; a wedding or a funeral ; all came as common setting to some inimitable comment of his. The immigrants, free and indentured, salaamed and smiled as he passed; for if he had no quip ready, they had some very recent one to remember. His brother overseers delighted in his company; and it is to be feared that this general demand, from each room in turn, from the time when he first set foot in quarters every afternoon—" to disturb the swizzle stick," as he put it—only helped to feed the weakness which grew upon him. To hear " Mac," as he was generally known, exchange " love greetings " with the driver, at 5.30 in the morning, when that gentleman did his matutinal rousings at the overseers' quarters, was a treat. To hear and see " Mac " apostrophise his mule, after a bad night, and before he mounted the sometimes peace loving but always wilful brute, to set out on his day's duties was a study in comedy. But, to see him at the Manager's table preening his neck from out of his collar and telling the butler, " thet whisky !" defied description.

Through all his good humour however there was one person whom Mac solemnly disliked; if it is possible for a nature such as his ever to really dislike, and that was the manager's wife. She was spare and angular in look, manner and speech. Her husband she ruled with a rod of iron, and, of course, she presided over his table, at which sat all his overseers. But so far as the introduction of any social element or feminine softness was concerned, she might as well have stayed away. The whole staff of overseers regarded her as a cheat of the first water. They claimed, and not without reason, that their board money was deducted from their salaries to feed them, and not to clothe her, or her bank account; and many were the growls heard in connection therewith. Occasionally a particularly loud growl would reach old Constant, the manager; but he, good man, was helpless, and all the sign he ever gave was a more liberal offering from the font of Bacchus, when they foregathered together.

It was on a night such as this that McGregor came over full charged, and as serious as an owl : and it was not always easy readily to observe when Mac was full. By the time they were all seated the manager had already supplied two swizzles, and the whisky bottle was early in evidence and moving briskly to and fro. My lady boiled inwardly, for she well knew that such were the outward and visible signs of some covert and wicked grumblings, of a particularly virulent type. She also had heard them, and that evening had planned something by way of a peace offering in the shape of a special menu: there was venison and chicken: blanc mange, iced pears, and some other inexpensive delicacies that they only saw at Christmas; so she fretted inwardly at the "double expense." Something of her manner seemed to communicate itself to Mac, for he grew taciturn, and "thet whisky" was not even to be heard. The tension however reached its climax when Mac, boldly discarding his knife and fork, took the wing of a chicken between finger and thumb, and was gnawing it with gusto. Whether the face of my lady showed disgust at his manners, or whether it was merely a reflex of her general annoyance, will never be known; but, as Mac lifted his head to take breath, their eyes met. Mac thereupon exploded :

"Ye be wanting this noo?" he cried: and then threw the remnants of the bone straight aimed in the lady's face.

To those who know the gulf separating overseers from "the manager's wife," the enormity of the offence will be understood: to those who do not, it might be explained that action like that may be regarded as if an obscure member of the House of Commons threw his boots in the face of the Speaker. In an instant there was a general upsetting of chairs : like a flash Jack Engledow was upon McGregor.

"Look out, man!" he cried, and, adding a savage "buck up," had Mac by the collar and pulled to his feet. Mrs. Constant, covered with shame and in tears, had instantly withdrawn and her husband after one scathing "How dare you? Sir," had followed in her wake to soothe her ruffled feelings. The rest of the staff, sobered by the coarseness of the jest, stood silent awaiting events. Engledow had hustled Mac out of the dining room on to the lawn and was heading him direct for the overseers' quarters, when old Constant returned.

"Gentlemen," he said, "of course there can be but one course open to me."

All murmured assent, and dinner was completed in a grave and solemn spirit. But, when once the fellows were out of sight and hearing of old Constant their hilarity knew no bounds. The comments and chaff were unbridled and merciless ; none seemed to realize that Mac's career was at an end, and that he must join the army of " P. B. O.s" who haunt the streets of Georgetown; frequently unfed and mostly without hope.

Gathered together in Mac's room the crowd took the nature of a triumph to a hero of ancient Rome. Mac's sole defence and excuse was:

"Dom it all lads, she wanted the bone, and I gie it to she."

And there were fresh explosions of laughter. Late into the night that gathering worshipped at the shrine of the grape; or to be less poetical and more accurate at the stool of the cane. All realized that Mac would be no more after the morrow; and so it proved.

Early next morning McGregor was given twenty-four hours' notice to quit Waterloo, and he had to make tracks elsewhere.

Nor was poor Mac the only one whom Harold saw, in a little while know Waterloo no more. Poor good-hearted Jack Engledow came to grief shortly afterwards. The successful covering up of the tracks of his amours had caused him to grow careless, and soon it was known on the q.t. that he took more interest in the fortunes of a free young female immigrant than was good for him.

What was known at first on the q.t. soon grew to common currency, and at last it reached the official ears of the Immigration Agent General. Soon followed the dreaded fiat that "John Henry Engledow was no longer eligible for employment on any sugar plantation employing indentured East Indian labour." In that bald sentence was the doom of a man. Every sugar estate that lays claim to be a sugar Estate employs indentured labour, therefore the career of "John Henry Engledow" was closed. And "John Henry Engledow" had to join the great army of "P.B.O.'s," for he was clearly unfitted at this time of life for any other employment. His savings had been nil: what little economies that could have been practised in his living expenses having been absorbed by Mrs. Constant, in her operations as professional boarding house keeper to Pln. Waterloo.

CHAPTER EIGHTEENTH.

As Harold stood one afternoon leaning over the balcony of the little barrack sacred to the overseers of the plantation, he wondered if all life held for him was this humdrum existence. Where were all his high resolutions and far reaching plans? His lectures: his guidance of the people? Was this the price of his sensational sacrifice? Indeed, there was still the necessity to earn his bread by the sweat of his brow; for he resolutely adhered to his determination not to touch a penny of his mother's money. Through his self communings seared the thought: " What had become of Marjorie?" Two months had passed since he had last heard from her. But, as always, he sternly ordered to heel all thoughts of his cousin. They were the thoughts and temptations which threatened his soul's further undoing, and must be forever held in leash.

Far at the other end of the gallery he could hear the boisterous laughter of young men: for the moment idle; for all time single. He could distinguish over it all the cheery swish swash of the swizzle stick, muffled in the lashing foam of gin and bitters, and broken ice. Now and again a shout would come for, " Walton, join in this?" But this afternoon he was out of tune. At other times he had joined the crowd and swallowed his swizzles with the best of them; though he had never again gone the length of that famous night out when he " saw red." Deep in his own thoughts, he scarcely heard the little telegraph boy as he ungrammatically challenged:

" You is Mr. Walton, Sah?"

The query had to be repeated and then Harold answered:

"Yes, but Harold Walton."

Harold expected no telegram and knew that there were other Waltons on the coast; though how they came, or who they were he never knew. And the ghosts of the past had never whispered that they held close blood relationship with his own.

"Yes, sah," answered the boy, irrelevantly, "is for 'Harold Walton, Pln. Waterloo!"

Stirred to a momentary interest in Jack Engledow, or poor McGregor, he reached for the orange coloured envelope and signed the acknowledgment. Languidly breaking the seal, he read a message that held his heart in one fell grasp for perhaps a second of time, then sent it galloping madly almost to the point of suffocation. And this is what he read.

"Your mother is dead. Meet me at Mrs. Wilson's . . . . . Main Street. Marjorie."

The double shock left his will paralysed and his initiative weak. For years his love for his mother had been quiescent. Wrapt in her devotions, she had merely performed her duties to Marjorie and himself as a conscientious warden of their future. He himself, steeped in the discipline of the Church, had obeyed literally the dictum of the scriptures to leave father and mother and cleave only unto Her. The momentous step of his life had widened yet further the open chasm of listless indifference which had existed between them. But now in one galvanic shock the breach was healed and he stood in fancy at her bedside while the gentle spark of life stole upwards from whence it came. Silently Harold withdrew into the single room awarded to each overseer; and there he shed silent tears for the fair mother who had once been his idol.

As the afternoon deepened into evening he heard the several overseers as they left their respective doors for the manager's table. Each in turn called to him to "gather for dinner," or "Come along for soup," and to each he made some different answer; "He would follow"; He was not up to concert pitch "; " He did not know if he would trouble," etc., etc.

When the rude barracks in which they all herded together had grown still, Harold took thought for action. To visit Marjorie to-morrow would be difficult: leave would have to be obtained, and it was now the grinding, and therefore the busiest, season of the year. After all, he concluded, the four miles separating Waterloo from Georgetown was but an easy cycle ride in the cool of the evening; and, lending action to his thoughts he set out to commandeer the first bicycle he came across in quarters. It was not long before he found one, and soon Harold and Marjorie stood face to face.

Marjorie was calm and self-possessed: robed in a close fitting mourning dress she looked taller than she really was. The black costume enhanced her loveliness, and the crowning glory of her raven tresses stood upon her brow like a diadem. Her radiant loveliness once again stood upon Harold, and held him spell-bound and speechless his blood tingled to his finger tips, and then flew back to his heart. Marjorie, in those soft evening lights, would have made the heart of a painter rejoice; but Harold was no painter, and her ravishing presence blinded his senses for the moment. Recovering his self possession he asked all in one breath.

" When did she die? Why did you come? Why did you not write?"

" Charming sort of greeting, Harold," Marjorie replied, " and three questions in one. To answer them categorically : Your mother died on Sunday last. I came because you and I will have to settle her affairs in Demerara. And I did not write because I feared you would move further on if I did."

Harold and Marjorie were soon in close conversation on all details. Accounting for her arrival at Mrs. Wilson's, she explained that dear Mrs. Keith would not hear of her coming to Demerara without a letter of introduction to Mrs. Wilson, who had been an old school fellow of hers in England.

Harold also learnt that his mother had never once roused herself to take an interest in anything, after the sensational news had reached her of his withdrawal from the Church; and she had sunk gradually, until she passed away as softly as a sigh. Thus had ended the life of the once graceful and brilliant Marion Walton.

Late into the evening the cousins continued their exchanges, and when Harold had perforce to take his departure it was arranged that he would return in a day or two to assist in the legal formalities. When Harold rose to go Marjorie accompanied him to the door, and as he took her hand in his for the usual formal farewell, Marjorie uttered the one plaintive word, soft as the breath of even amid rose leaves:

"Harold!"

Harold looked up and saw the love light soften his cousin's features; but, steeling himself once again, he barely bowed over her hand, and kissed the graceful finger tips.

Out into the night he rode, wondering what life held for him; and, what was to be the end of it all.

Next morning he paraded, with the rest of the staff, outside old Constant's window to receive the orders of the day as customary. On getting to Harold's turn the old man bade him remain behind as he had something to say to him.

Harold dreaming of nothing amiss sat at ease in his saddle, and awaited events. So soon as the rest of the staff had cleared the yard old Constant turned to Harold with more than usual fire in his voice.

"I understand, Sir," he said, "you left the estate yesterday without my permission."

"No, sir," Harold replied, "I rode as far as the East road, which I understand is our boundary, to warn that troublesome immigrant Gopaul that if he persisted in crossing the line, to go to Denvers after that woman Metharie, I should have him arrested as a deserter; but, though he sulked, he returned and I rode back."

"Don't hedge, or prevaricate, man," growled old Constant, "you know very well that I refer to your visit to Georgetown last night."

"You said yesterday, Sir," answered Harold, "I went to town last night after work was done ; and am here to begin with the rest to-day."

"Work done !" stormed old Constant. "Did you ever hear of work being done on a sugar estate, until a man was dead, or the estate abandoned ? Moreover, how dare you quit boundaries without my permission ?"

"But," submitted Harold, "I am not an indentured immigrant. Surely I may do what I like with my own time."

"Your own time, indeed," stormed the old man, who grew worse with every parry from Harold. "All your time belongs to the estate : day and night. And don't you know that overseers are as much bound by boundaries as coolies ?"

"I never knew that," replied Harold.

"You are a liar, sir," screamed old Constant.

"You *you* call me a liar. How dare you ! How dare you, Sir!" called back Harold, rising in his stirrups and blanched to the lips.

"How dare who, my fine gentleman," sneered the older man. "I call you a liar and will call anybody on Waterloo that way when I am so inclined. It seems, moreover," he added, "that I shall never have any peace until I am quit of the whole of Master Jack Engledow's gang. I give you twenty-four hours to pack your kit and clear. The book-keeper will settle with you for time."

"Twenty-four hours, Mr. Constant !" replied Harold, "I don't want twenty-four minutes, after your book-keeper has settled." And, without even a good morning he turned the head of his mule and rode for the Estate's office.

Arriving there he was accosted by the "buildings" overseer who happened to be there on some other business.

"Hallo Walton," he cried, "what's gone wrong ?"

"The sack !" answered Harold.

"Oh, no ! What for ?"

"Going to town last night without leave."

"What excuse did you make ?"

"I told him," answered Harold, "that I did not know I had to get leave."

"That sort of thing always makes matters worse," ventured the older man.

"What do you mean!" sharply asked Harold, "I tell you I did not know I had to get leave to go off at nights."

"I don't want to quarrel with you, old fellow," answered his companion, "but surely you have always seen the other fellows asking for leave to go off the Estate."

"Yes, I have; for the day time; or when a fellow thought he might be late for 'orders' next morning. But, hang it all, a man's master of his own time!"

"Not on a sugar estate, my boy. Engledow should have told you. But it is so generally known that I suppose he thought he had no need to bother. I am sorry."

"Keep your sorrow, old fellow," answered Harold, "thanks all the same." Saying which, and having completed his business with the book-keeper, he rode back to his room.

The task of getting his few "trappings" together was but the work of some minutes, and inside of his self-appointed limit he was ready to shake the dust of Pln. Waterloo from the sole of his boot. Passing the buildings he hailed Johnson, with whom he had just had the friendly passage of arms, and made the few remaining arrangements for his furniture and belongings to follow him: for, though the legend has it that an overseer is allowed " board and lodging " the latter barely consists of the four bleak walls of a room 20 ft. by 12 ft.; and, he may sleep on the floor, in the luxury of a brass mounted French bedstead; or "swing swang in a canvas bag," as his money or his inclination directs him. Hence, at every transmigration, and these as a rule are many and varied, the soldier of fortune has to flit with all his lares and penates.

That same afternoon Marjorie was overjoyed at seeing Harold's welcome form slowly wending its way up the garden walk of Mrs. Wilson's. If she was overjoyed at seeing him, she was nearly delirious with delight when she heard that he had left Waterloo and would be in Georgetown for some time yet.

"Best thing in the world," was her comment, "your income, from Auntie I am sure, will be quite sufficient to prevent you from going back to any other estate.

"I am not so sure," answered Harold, "that I will avail myself of my mother's money. I have a few dollars put by from my meagre pittance, and I shall doubtless find some way to augment it. Anyway, in the meantime we won't argue over that, but will get to business."

And to buisness did they get.

Later on Harold was introduced to old Wilson, the husband of Marjorie's landlady : and regular character he proved himself to be. He had lived forty years in British Guiana, and was one of the most inveterate talkers it was possible to meet. He spared no one and skipped no topic. He had hobbled into the room and pounced upon Harold as the proverbial spider on the fly.

"Ah, young man, glad to meet you—glad to meet you," was his fervid greeting. " Knew both your father and mother well. Many a day I sold laces and gloves to the dear lady. And how she did exile herself in that Robinson Crusoe's island, eh !

Marjorie having established Harold on a friendly footing with the head of the house, withdrew to make some changes in her toilet.

"Don't go until I return," she called to Harold before leaving and Harold laughed acquiescence.

"And how are you getting on in sugar planting?" the old man continued.

"Not getting on at all," answered Harold, " just getting off."

" Oh, indeed, I am so sorry," purred the old man. "Overseeing, it seems to me," he continued, " never does good to anybody, and I have always said it. Sugar is no such great blessing to the country : I have always held that. Give me the minor industries."

Harold, though reluctant to be drawn into a controversy, could not help replying.

"I think you are mistaken Sir : without Sugar you wi be nowhere. Overseeing may be its weak point ; but the industry itself is the mainstay of the country, and moreover, it is best suited to be the mainstay of the country.

"You think so, you think so," gleefully cried the old man. "I am glad to talk with you, sir ; just glad to talk with you. It is a treat to meet a man with colour in his opinions. As I always say, give me a man who knows his mind, and is prepared to speak it.

Harold deftly changed the subject to the one of the all engrossing subject of the drought from which the country was then emerging.

"Most extraordinary," the old man commented : "what a blessing they are so rare. There was a similar one many many years ago when I first came to the colony." And the old gentleman poured forth a deluge of reminiscences of the sixties. to which Harold listened with patience, and, even occasionally, with interest.

At last Marjorie made her reappearance, and Harold shortly after rose to go.

Mr. Wilson shook Harold warmly by the hand, and hard pressed him for a promise that he would dine with them another evening, to which Harold readily agreed.

When Harold left the old man turned to Marjorie.

"Very clever young man," he said, "very clever. Wonderful talker and very interesting. Be sure and make him keep his promise to dine with us. I'll have old Stenhouse to meet him, and a fine tussle we'll have. Wonderful old man is old Stenhouse. We don't agree always, but he knows his mind and speaks it," and so on the old man prattled ; while Marjorie looked down the shaded avenue after Harold's fast vanishing figure and wondered " What next?"

• That night after Harold had dined in the modest " diggings " which we had engaged for himself, he sallied forth : as much to drink in the beauties of the old Dutch town as to think out his plans for the future. His steps eventually took him up the wide Brickdam, with its brick red earth glistening dully in the moonlight, and its wide spreading trees on either side fanned by the soft evening air. Harold had not gone many yards when he espied in the distance a strangely familiar figure making headway in a more than unsteady gait. Tight gripped under his arm the lonely pedestrian carried a stout looking cudgel; which he seemed to grip as though it could give him support as tor anything else. As Harold drew nearer he discerned the unmistakable form of McGregor, the ex-overseer.

"Hallo Mac," Harold cried, as soon as he was abreast of the unsteady walker, " what's wrong ?"

Commissariat and defence laddie, cooed McGregor almost to himself. "Commissariat: cane juice: dinner. Defence: cane: strong weapon: club. Very useful in fight 'gainst men, dogs," and with that he unlocked a length of sugar cane from under his arm, and shook it mournfully at some imaginary enemy.

"Oh, I see," said Harold, "You are ready for a fight, if needs be; and then you will eat your weapon, when you get home !"

"Egshactly !" lisped McGregor. "See me hame, laddie. Nothing to eat for the day. Plenty to drink; and Mac invested last copper on great idea. Mac's cute, you know !

Harold listened to the monologue, half amused, half sad. Amused at the wit: sad to think that so many of these young men are brought from "home" to be broken and strewn on the streets of a more or less poverty-stricken colonial town. Men, who should be valuable assets of colonial settlement, left to struggle through a precarious existence: dining on a sugar cane, breakfasting on less: the butt of every gibe. Almost entirely because in their colonial surroundings there had been no element of home life; no refinement to keep alive the ideals of what they doubtless left their home full of, and, consequently, no check on their grosser selves and passions.

At length Harold got his erstwhile house companion to the unpretentious lodgings whither fortune had temporarily established poor McGregor; but McGregor refused to go further than the door-step, for there he declared his intention to " dine." Harold stood by and watched him for a few moments as he contentedly tore with his teeth at the stiff outer rind of the sugar cane : watched him as he methodically gnawed at each piece peeled off, that nothing be lost ; and compared this economical turn of mind, and the difference in setting, with the last time he saw poor Mac at dinner. He then bade him a cheery goodnight, and, receiving a bare acknowledgment, took his departure out into the night, pondering on the great tragedy of life.

CHAPTER NINETEENTH.

It was not many days after Harold had first visited Mrs. Wilson's when he concluded that if he would secure employment in Georgetown he must perforce widen the circle of his acquaintances; he consequently decided to give way to Majorie's constant pressing, and accepted old Wilson's invitation to dinner. A date was soon fixed, and Harold accordingly, when the day arrived, found himself at the appointed hour, facing the light and the glare of the Wilson's menage.

Old Wilson received him with an abundance of greeting. He was delighted: he appreciated the honour: and he hoped it was but the first of many. Harold acknowledged the greeting as cordially as his habitual reserve allowed him. After some moments "old Stenhouse" made his appearance. He was a regular character. Bred in the atmosphere of sugar cane and sugar, he could see no ill save in Continental bounties and the blindness of the British people in allowing the threatened extinction of the British cane sugar industry.

Old Wilson was delighted at his arrival: "Just wondering if you would fail me, sir," he cried, "but, as usual, your word is your bond, eh!" He then shook hands impressively with the new comer and led him towards Harold.

"Shake hands, my dear sir, with 'Honest John' Walton's son," he said.

"Indeed I am very glad to meet him," replied Mr. Stenhouse, "I had heard that he was in the colony; and am as I said, glad to meet him."

Harold acknowledged the introduction, and meanwhile the minutes flew and dinner was announced. A preparatory swizzle was swallowed, and then a general move made for the dinner table : men seemed to appear from everywhere, and soon the board was filled to its limit. A desultory conversation helped along the hour, until at last various members of the company, making different excuses and apologies, commenced to take their departure. A few minutes more and the function was completely at an end.

Old Wilson lost no time in disentangling himself from the crowd of remaining men. Button-holding Harold and old Stenhouse, he led them, one on either side of him, to the far end of the verandah and begged them to be seated, meanwhile rubbing his hands with glee.

"Ah ! Mr Stenhouse," he cried, " here is a young man for you. Regular ' chip of the old block'; been quite making history too in Trinidad : but been making sugar in Demerara, recently. Regular tartar, sir ; bearded me in my own den, the last time he was here, and challenged the gospel fact that the salvation of British Guiana is to be found in mixed cultivation and intensive farming."

" My dear Wilson," answered Mr. Stenhouse "you will go down to your grave a heretic. I have little against mixed cultivation, and less against intensive farming : but, as I have always told you, those won't run to hundreds of thousands of tons : Very well in their way, but, after all, a mere chopping of wood, and selling to one another. To get into big business you must touch one of the major items of the world's products . and, particularly, what is eaten. Timber is all very well ; but a shipload remains in existence forever, whatever use it is put to, or how many hands it passes through : you cannot sell the same quantity over again for the identical purpose : you must look out for another job going on"

" Oh yes, yes : I know," laughed old Wilson, " All the old thread bare arguments. Give us something modern. You cannot sell ' another shipment for the same dock gates,' but you can sell plenty more shipments."

" Certainly ! " briskly answered Mr. Stenhouse. " But what I want to tell you people is that when one shipload of flour is sold it passes into smoke and air : you can't find it the next day; and the stomachs that absorbed it are as hungry again to-morrow. You can sell another, and another, shipload to the same people. So you can grow wheat every day, and send your shiploads into the markets of the world as soon as they are ready. Timber you must find your contract for."

"Ah, my dear sir, but what about Cotton and Cocoa and Coconuts? answered old Wilson.

"All good, my dear Wilson," answered Mr. Stenhouse they always grew affectionate in inverse ratio to the extent of their differences. "But those after all are only "'accessories.' A hungry man neither wants a shirt nor a bon bon. Feed the people, sir, feed the people, and grow rich. We can't grow wheat, so get into the next biggest "eat line" we can. If we could produce ten, twenty, fifty times the sugar we now do, we could sell every punt load that was ready, as soon as it was ready, and at big money, if only the English Government would give us justice."

"There you go," replied old Wilson, "why should England upset her policy of "natural selection" to please the cane sugar industy? I know that you will say she is a fool not to abandon that policy, because if she lets the cane sugar indutry go to the wall, she will be at the mercy of beet; and then the jam industry will have to pay, through its nose. But believe me, Stenhouse, England was once at the mercy of cane sugar; and cane sugar did not treat her as a philantrhopist would have. However, never again could those prices be reached: the world's production of sugar has grown to dimensions that will forbid that: and the beet growing nations are fiercer competitors among themselves than they are against cane."

"Brother Wilson," pathetically exclaimed old Stenhouse, "don't you believe in Imperial preference?"

"Most certainly," answered the other man, "but I don't talk foolishness enough not to be able to see that Preference and Protection are two different things."

"What rubbish are you getting to now?" snapped old Stenhouse, "who ever asked for protection: we ask for justice."

"No rubbish at all," answered old Wilson "but preference is one thing : reversal of a policy, to offer protection to one industry, another ; even in the name of supposed justice to it ; for there will be but one step from protection in the name of justice, to protection in the name of expediency. Then you will have every section of the Empire with some tottering industry less worthy, perhaps, I admit than cane sugar, clamouring for protection. No, sir, if the cane industry wants to grow big it must do so on natural conditions ; and not on the ephemeral help of an artificial tariff. Otherwise let it make room for something else."

"Make room for what, old man," cried Stenhouse, " what else ; what else ? The cane sugar industry, as you put it, dosen't want to grow big: what does the industry care whether it is big or small.? It is the people who ought to want it to grow big. And, as to the tariffs, do you think that Europe created a Beet Sugar industry on natural conditions? Do you think that, if they did not see all things in a sugar industry that I have been just telling you about, they would have built up one on an artifical basis ?"

"Yes, my dear sir," exclaimed the enthusiatic Wilson, "but you forget that your industry is no infant one like Beet. You have been a hundred years at it and can't hold your own yet."

"That's just it. That's the way all you people talk," savagely replied old Stenhouse, "rank prejudice : rank prejudice. If there is a villain, he is a sugar planter. If there is a fool, he is a sugar planter. But I tell you what, a sugar planter can teach a lot of you people a lot about your own business."

"Ah ! young man, what do you say," exclaimed old Wilson, turning to Harold, "listening to two old men, eh ! Mr. Stenhouse must be your ideal by now."

Harold would fain have stayed out of the discussion but that he felt that it was growing dangerously warm, and, perhaps, if he joined in, the current would get less turgid ; and the discussion less acrid.

"Not exactly," he answered, "still there is a lot of truth in what Mr. Stenhouse says. There is far too much prejudice against the sugar industry here. No one out of it seems to have a good word for it. But that is, I think, due to a mistaken policy on the part of the planters. The sugar industry is now an alien industry: as alien, and as misunderstood, as ever Roman legions were in conquered territory. You have an alien labour supply, disliked and misunderstood: and you have, as overseers and superintendents, a class of men as naturally alien to the common life of the country as the Eunuchs of old; or as though they came from the planet Mars."

"I don't understand you, young man," chimed in Mr. Stenhouse, "where are we to get our labour supply from? To produce one hundred thousand tons of sugar, we have had to build up an immigrant population of one hundred thousand people. If we wanted to produce one million tons of sugar where are the labourers to come from? You have not twenty thousand native agricultural labourers in the place, outside of these people, if you drained every other industry in the colony. As to overseers being as alien as you say; you are evidently drawing on your imagination. Is a creole alien? Is a Scotsman a eunuch? Or, is a Lancashire man from Mars?"

"Good, good," ecstatically cried old Wilson, between the puffs of his pipe, "give him the reply," though he had no more idea of the reply than the forty-fifth proposition of Euclid.

"You misunderstand me, sir," answered Harold, ignoring old Wilson's interruption, "I see, and know that an alien labour supply is inevitable in an unpopulated country. But I do not see why your overseers should be artificially translated into an alien caste, so soon as they become planters. Overseers seem cut off from the social life of the colony: there are no ties betwixt them and the other classes, consequently there is no sympathy. Here and there an acquaintance is made between boon companions, only to be later severed, when the overseer drifts to the wreckage of city life—when no one cares to know him. There are no family ties, no interests, no community of thought, between planters and people, such as would counteract the feeling of alienship created by your labour supply."

"That's all theory and book talk, my good fellow. Overseers are as friendly as anybody else, perhaps too much so," cut in Mr. Stenhouse.

"That may be; but as long as you divorce them from the life of the people by denying them marriage———"

"Good Lord! we don't deny them marriage" cried Mr. Stenhouse.

"No, you don't, in so many words, but you make it impracticable, none the less. If you had overseers marrying into the families of lawyers, and doctors, and merchants, and had those people finding wives among the families of planters, you would create a community of thought, and an identity of family ties, each of which would become a medium for the dissemination of principles, and a clearing up of prejudices. At present no one knows or hears of the troubles and difficulties of a planter, but a planter; and, even, were those troubles trumpeted from the housetops, they would fall on ears that hear not: or on minds that are prejudiced and indifferent. Everybody's sympathy goes out to the farmer and the gold miner; but the bowels of compassion are closed to the planter; because he and his industry are alien to the thoughts of the people."

"But, my dear sir," sneeringly answered the planter champion, "who gives a damn for the sentiments or sympathies of the people; give us justice in the markets of England, and we will give bread to the people, with all their prejudices. Your precious sympathy and community of ideas won't give us bread; neither will they make two stools of cane grow where only one grew before."

Harold was now well into his stride. Not for nothing had he been classed among the most eloquent preachers of his day; neither was it without reason, as an exponent of thought, that he had been called the "twentieth century Savonarola."

"There you err," he continued, "this self-same lack of sympathy and absence of community of interest cost the sugar industry thousands and thousands of pounds. This identical prejudice has attenuated your labour supply; it has denied, or at least failed to demand, shipping and transport facilities for you in many instances; and it has imposed taxation on wha may be classed as raw material, and which ought to be free."

"Oh, I see you are one of those who believe that marriage will solve nearly every difficulty under the sun : a sort of quack prescription for growing canes cheap."

" I don't know whether marriage will solve every problem under the sun," answered Harold, " but, I do know that it could solve many problems," saying which he felt a lump rise to his throat : mastering the threatened exhibition of his emotion, and further warming to his subject, he continued. "And, I tell you what, sir, this self-same question of marriage is of greater importance than you think ; take to-day, sir, how many really able planters have you got ?"

"Youngster!" exclaimed Mr. Stenhouse, "you almost tempt me to be rude. They are spread all over the colony."

" Keep your temper : keep your temper," purred old Wilson, who was having the time of his life in listening to the discussion, " the boy is climbing high. Give him a chance!" and he rubbed his hands together gleefully.

Harold, taking little notice of the interruption, turned to Mr. Stenhouse.

" Have you really?" he asked, " I should not have thought so, judging by the way in which employers tumble over each other's necks in the scramble for the service of one or two men. Indeed the measure of these men's incomes, and the number of Estates contributing to those incomes, would seem to indicate that there was great scarcity of similiar ability."

" My God," almost shrieked old Stenhouse, "can marriage produce ability?"

" No, assuredly not," answered Harold, " but that is just how you miss the point. At present there is enormous wastage in the raw material which should go to recruit the higher ranks in planting ability ; and, it too often happens, that it is the best and most promising of the youngsters who get weeded out through entanglements with wine or coolie women. Unhappily the righteous and the upright are too often the fools of the family. How can you, in the course of natural selection, secure the giants of intellect with such a shocking wastage in those with the best initiative and imagination."

"Man, you are a dreamer," laughed Mr. Stenhouse.

"Dreamer or no dreamer, I go a little further and tell you," continued Harold. "that you never effectively tap a most promising source of ability. You have an excellent supply of well educated men of mixed colour; men who must assuredly combine the intellect and dogged determination of the white man with the fertile imagination and enthusiasm of the negro, but who taboo the sugar industry; apparently, solely because they would be denied their ordinary social privileges. Of course I refer to the best of them: you can always pick up the wastrels; and, unfortunately, you judge the remainder by those samples. Remember Chas. Kingsley said these men would be the painters and musicians and authors of the future; aye, and I add, inventors, because of their keen emotions and lively imagination, born of their blended intellects. Your sugar industry is a strangled one. Strangled for lack of intellect. What are the inventions recorded for the last hundred years? What generations have you had of boys and men, bred in the atmosphere of agriculture and sugar; generations from whom an Arkwright or an Edison could arise? Where are your families of "in and in" bred planters? None! Each generation sees a scratch team of raw Englishmen, who have never seen a cane field in their lives—and often not even a hop or a potato field—of rawer Scotsmen, and of broken Creoles. Death or dismissal closes all the effort and study of their minds; they bequeath their thoughts to no offspring; the barren die, and those few who rise to positions of affluence, and, are blessed with sons see that they take to the learned professions. to the Army or Navy, and to every other walk of life except planting."

"Young man, don't talk nonsense," sneeringly put in old Stenhouse. "Do you mean to tell me you want us to breed planters as we do Derby winners or hunters?"

IN BONDAGE.

"I don't say," answered Harold, "that the Planters' Association, or anybody else, should set up in the business of breeding planters, in stud farm fashion; but, I do want to make, that present conditions reduce to nothing all possibility of producing a planter—reared genius. And you will never compete in the markets of the world until inventions have played their part in your industry; until some one has taught you the sciences of manuring, of tillage, and of cane cutting, as these have never yet been learnt. Until these things have been, you will remain a mere fleck in the sugar market, dwelling in horror on every drop in price, and hoping that every rise will be succeeded by another."

"Oh, tell those things further west, lad," cried the older man, "our sugar industry will be a great one if we could produce as much cane to the acre as Cuba, or if we had the limitless protected market of Porto Rico."

"I am afraid, sir, you speak with too great a lack of true perspective. You may not be able to produce as much cane to the acre as Cuba, yet had you the service of a couple of generations of an imaginative people studying the utilization of waste and the questions of fertilisers, you cannot guess what might not have happened. You also forget that thonsands of tons of cane rot in the fields of Cuba when the market goes below a certain figure; your great canals of transportation are lost to Cuba. The Porto Ricans might lose their protection in the U.S. markets, as everything now seems to indicate, and then they might be faced with a ruin more complete than the West Indies ever saw, if their industry has not been built on a sure foundation. I tell you, sir, your industry suffers, more than you will ever admit, because the heart of the country is not with it; and, because it is alien in thought and being. But I am afraid I have allowed my feelings to run away with me and I must cry off."

"Oh, dear, dear no," cried old Wilson, reluctant to ose his treat, "Stenhouse, I told you so, a Tartar: a real Tartar. Dear me, how he does run on," and patting Harold on the back he added, "right, boy, right; things I have thought myself but have never been able to express."

"Well, well," sighed old Stenhouse, "there may be no fool like an old fool; but I should give a lot to have seen John Walton listening to his own flesh and blood. Most of what you say is far fetched: yet I don't deny that there may be germs of truth here and there: but it is too funny for words, to hear of men breeding inventors and planters as they do their platers and their porkers."

"Don't badger the youngster," said old Wilson; "when all is said and done, you must admit that there is a whole world of unconquered ground for the planter to cover. Refined sugar, direct: Mechanical tillage; and what not."

"Oh, don't you try it on now," exclaimed old Stenhouse, "It doesn't sit well on you. A lot of you doctrinaires don't know that solving mechanical tillage will create problems of labour at reaping time."

"Perhaps. But, nevertheless, quite as capable of solution as mechanical tillage itself: as English hop picking: or as wheat harvesting in the Canadian North West. There is nothing that the West Indian labourer loves so much as casual work. But we have had enough for to-night," at last admitted the head of the house, "so not another word, but the weather."

Once again all melted into good humour; and by the time the two visitors were ready to depart they were in close terms of friendship. So much so that old Stenhouse tramped all the way home with Harold, and showed a most cordial interest in his life; discussing meanwhile many phases of a planter's calling.

CHAPTER TWENTIETH.

The next day found Harold with his worries thick upon him. The old tuggings at his heart strings commenced all afresh. The problem of how to earn a living, without touching his mother's money, stared him in the face with savage persistence, and there seemed to be nothing but desolation of opportunity on every hand. All through that day, and the next, and the next, he worried. Seeing Marjorie daily, he yet so succeeded in keeping their relations as he would have them, that the radiant Marjorie paled, and pulled and chafed at the leash. She struck with her impetuous hands at the barriers which denied her the heart's desire ; but they stood rigid and unyielding.

Eventually Harold decided that he would call on his erstwhile friend, Jack Engledow, and hear again of the opportunities in "the bush," which he had so often heard him tell about ; and that day saw him ferretting out Engledow in the suburb where he lived. When Harold found the unpretentious cottage of his search, Jack Engledow was unmistakably glad to see him, and said as much. The whole history and fortunes of Pln. Waterloo had, however, to be threshed out afresh, before the real business of the day could be reached. Then Engledow "plumped solid" for Gold.

"Gold, my boy, is the thing," he said, "glad to come with you meself, if you'll have me. Make you rich in six months, if you strike the right thing,"

"Or poor in less, if you strike the wrong;" added Harold, " still, I don't dislike the idea," he concluded.

It was finally arranged that next day they would call on a friend of Engledow's who had been phenomenally successful in his gold ventures: and, who at that time had his quarters at the Palatine Hotel. Next day, accordingly, Harold was punctual to appointment, and Engledow and he set out for the Palatine.

On entering the well appointed place the visitors were shown to the suite of rooms occupied by the Gold King. That morning Messonier, for that was his name, was surrounded by a bevy of boon companions. The gay McGregor was there. Messonier had knocked up an aquaintance with him in some drinking bouts, and had taken quite a fancy to him. Mac had brought to the gathering a young tenderfoot overseer who had recently been broken on the wheel of the Immigration laws; Mac had extended his patronage to the youngster, and was as solicitous of the young one's welfare, as his own precarious existence would allow. There were also gathered around the "King" sundry others in various stages of fortune. The advent of the new comers was the signal for a fresh relay of drinks; and the imperatively summoned waiter had once more to make the round of guests. The "tenderfoot," from force of habit on the Estate, asked for gin and bitters, but McGregor, with masterful authority, countermanded the order to beer for both. When the waiter had withdrawn Mac whispered in the ear of the tenderfoot:

"Drink beer, you fool: beer is food!"

Which, being interpreted, meant that neither had breakfasted, nor saw any immediate hope of rounding up such a meal. Such were the fortunes of these men, broken in a great cause: buffeted by adverse winds, too proud to beg, too honourable to steal: breakfasting on beer, and dining on disappointments. A mystery to the uninitiated and a horror to themselves!

Everybody seemed to make himself comfortable in his own way, and, in the midst of the short confabulation proceedings between Messonier, Engledow and Harold in one corner, one of the company called aloud from the depths of a Berbice chair, whither he had retired behind the columns of a daily paper:

" Which one of you fellows wants a job, and is architect enough to do it? Brickdam Cathedral. Tower work; ' None but a competent workman need apply.'"

Giving which cryptic information the speaker once again lapsed into silence. The announcement however, had been like the sound of a trumpet to Harold. "Brickdam Cathedral." "Tower work." "Competent man." Was he not an architect? Had he not learnt the work from the bottom, and was he not workman as well as master?

Having made a business appointment with Messonier, for early the next morning, before his satellites would gather in full force, the new comers withdrew, leaving Mac and his tenderfoot to " breakfast on beer " to their hearts' content.

Harold's imagination now ran riot. Brickdam Cathedral, with its graceful tower standing bold and white against the sky line, was to give him a stepping stone to other things. But there were doubts. Would the Jesuit Fathers recognize and refuse to employ him? Abstention from persecution, and direct patronage, in the very church itself, were two vastly different things. However, he concluded, they could not murder him for applying, and, so soon as he got free from Engledow, he determined that he would make direct for the Presbytery and run his chance.

All his bold communings, notwithstanding, it was with something of a beating heart, that, free at last from his companion, he stepped once again on consecrted ground as he boldly entered the enclosure on the Brickdam which held the Presbytery and Cathedral of the Immaculate Conception. The name brought up memories of his college days in Port-of-Spain, and he almost contemplated abandoning the venture when he was greeted by a cheery " Good morning " from one of the " fearsome Jesuits." The good-morning was so full of cheer and grace, and human kindness that it dissipated every fear, and disputed the accuracy of his mental description.

The good Father, on learning his errand, admitted that there was work to be done, but that he had received hundreds of applications. None of the applicants, however, seemed to have any knowledge of even the elementary principles of architecture. He was now delighted to hear how familiarly Harold conversed with him on Cornices and Corbels, and on

Consoles and Chaptrels. Drawn into the question of details, the good Father never even stopped to enquire the name of his visitor; soon they stood within the sacred edifice itself, and, climbing the stairs within the tower, discussed the proposals, phase by phase.

The end of it all was that Harold was engaged to commence work at 7 a.m. next day; and he heaved a sigh of relief as the representative of the world famous Order withdrew, without having once turned to the subject of his name or antecedents.

Friday, the 7th of March, 1913, dawned in all the intense loveliness of the tropics; not the most confirmed pessimist could claim to have had premonition of the ghastly tragedy at hand; and the heavens itself seemed to smile down peace and benediction. Harold set to work as arranged, bright and early, and soon he was high up in the graceful white tower grappling with electric wires and soldering irons; guarding against short circuits, and generally full of the thousand and one details of the job in hand. By half past nine the bracing morning air, racing high above the city, had him as hungry as a hunter, and he decided to climb down and get to breakfast; at the same time he would pick up in the Business Street one or two odds and ends which he badly wanted.

Harold, having breakfasted and completed his purchases in Water Street, sauntered slowly up the Brickdam revolving in his mind many plans and theories for the work in hand; when, casually he raised his eyes, and—horror upon horror! —he beheld in the distance something uncommonly like smoke, issuing from the tower of the Cathedral. Like a flash came the false hope that it must be some cloud of smoke from elsewhere passing the tower. But the hope was a vain one, and the blood froze within his veins, as he saw another and another. For an instant he stood rivetted to the spot, gazing at the horrifying spectacle: then he saw scattered groups of men and women, flying all in one direction, with the awesome and whispered words on their lips:

"Good God! the Cathedral is on fire!"

IN BONDAGE.

Alas! it was but too true: and in less time than it takes to tell, tongues of flame licked in and out of the smoke, and twined and twirled around the delicate wooden architecture of minaret and frieze. Harold utterly unstrung could only murmur to himself:

"God in heaven! Can this be the work of **my hands?**"

Regaining the power of locomotion he rushed, as fast as his hurrying feet could carry him, to the spot. Arriving there, he found the Fire Brigade already in charge: a fire brigade consisting of practically the entire Military police, and boasted of for personnel and efficiency throughout the West Indies. But what a travesty on a boast, and of what avail was its presence? There was a shortage of water pressure, and the feeble jets from each nozzle rose pitifully for a few feet and fell to the ground, while the flames grew in volume, and raced up the sides of the tower. There never was a more pathetic spectacle of human helplessness; and women, aye, and even men, wept and wrung their hands in impotent despair. Harold stood amidst the crowd, cold and shivering as in a winter's day. In another instant he had sunk on his knees, and throwing his hands high up to heaven, cried aloud:

"Oh Lord! spare the Church! Oh God! visit not the sins of an infidel upon a defenceless people! Oh Almighty Master," he continued, "Spare the faithful this frightful desolation, and stay the wrath of Thy vengeance."

The frantic earnestness of the man, whom no one seemed to know, and the agony plainly visible on his features diverted the attention of the crowd from the burning tower to the burning fervour beneath: suddenly, a black man, for the moment belonging to no religion save epediency, cried out:

"Bass, dis no time fo' pray: dis a time fo' fight. Git up!"

The rugged practicability of the words, urged in no spirit of banter, but rather musical with love and understanding, roused Harold, and springing to his feet he cried:

"Then fight you, all of you. Why stand gazing? Fight! Do something. Save the Church!"

Wild as one demented, he rushed into the Church; by this time the water pressure had improved and jets played on all sides. Seizing a nozzle, and a policeman with it, Harold urged the two up the smoking stairs of the tower, but the Negro policeman, overcome by the clouds of rolling smoke, swirling down from above, desisted, and Harold pushed upwards alone.

No human endeavour however, was of the slightest avail. The Presbytery and school, both built of wood and within the same compound, were soon alight; though willing hands fought in every direction. Harold was here, there and everywhere: but where danger threatened most there was he.

At last the futility of effort dawned on every worker. The tower, the pride of the people, had come crashing to the ground. Harold, begrimed and exhausted, saw that all hope was lost, and through his surging brain came the thought of the execration of the multitude, when they learnt of the part he had played. Then assuredly would come a raking up of his Trinidad renouncement of the Church; and, quite possibly, he would be charged with wilfully setting fire to the sacred edifice. Like one who had seen a spectre he stood fast, and his eyes stared into empty space; for an instant he stood thus, and then rushing from the burning compound he sought oblivion; he knew not whither.

Suddenly, he remembered the good ferry boat "Amy." How had he loathed that name as he had read of frequent suicides from its deck. Many a time he had read of worn out souls, who had thrown themselves from the deck of that boat into the dark, swift, running waters of the Demerara River, and had shuddered at their hopelessness. To-day, he longed for the moment when the dark waters would close over him once and for all; thus communing, he hastened down Brick-dam to the wharf at its lower end, which berthed the old paddle wheeler to and from the short trip across the rivier.

IN BONDAGE.

Harold boarded the little steamer and threw himself into one of the wicker-work chairs without so much as a glance at his fellow passengers. One of these, a quiet browed man, took a seat near to Harold, and slightly nearer the rail; without appearing to notice anyone, he placed his hands on his bosom, extending his finger tips and joining them, apparently in the most supreme self satisfaction.

The quiet featured passenger was variously known as "Parson," "Doctor," or plain "Boss" St. Aldwyn; he too, strange to say, was a clergyman unfrocked by his own desire. Chafing under the trammels of another sect he also had lain aside his Cassock and Gown, though he had done so less dramatically than had Harold. Now he prosecuted the double avocation of medical practitioner and land surveyor. His studies in astronomy had even raised some comment; but, he was nevertheless known as one of the most level headed and kind hearted of men, though his views on religion were admitted to be somewhat bizarre and unconventional, and he had won for himself every manner of description from Atheist to Roman Catholic.

As the little steamer swerved in the sweep of the tide and helmed upwards for the landing stage on the opposite bank Harold sat upright, but Dr. St. Aldwyn gave no sign; when the steamer reached midstream Harold made one surge for the side, and was almost clear of the rail, when he felt caught in a grip of steel, and in another moment he was stretched at full length on the upper deck, which bore no other passengers but these two.

"How dare you?" Harold hissed.

"How dare *you*?" answered the stranger.

Harold lay exhausted and undetermined for the moment and his companion added:

"Let us talk it over; and, after that, I will allow you to make the return trip alone and in charge of your own fate."

Harold, nerveless and physically weary from his strenuous morning, curtly replied, "Agreed."

The stranger then helped him to his feet, and resting a hand affectionately on his shoulder bade him be seated again. He then said:

"I am Dr. Shenstone St. Aldwyn: yesterday a clergyman; to-day a medical practitioner, and to-morrow I know not what. Now what's wrong?"

"Yesterday a clergyman!" echoed Harold, "And are you no longer one? This is very strange," he added without waiting for a reply.

"No, not very strange: and there would be hundreds like me if only they had the courage to be sure of earning a living otherwise. But let us discuss other matters. What about you? What's wrong, man?"

"I, too, am a clergyman who 'also ran,'" whimsically answered Harold; and Gaston de Garcia came to his mind, as the familiar idiom of his erstwhile friend came unbidden to his lips. The Gaston whom he had betrayed. Then, like a sword suddenly unsheathed, flashed the thought to his mind, "Had he betrayed Gaston, or had prior right belonged to him, and Gaston had only crossed his path unhappily?" Then, he continued aloud, "But unlike yourself, perhaps, I sinned grievously and the face of God is now turned definitely and forever from me. My footsteps are dogged by misfortune, and a great desolation has come upon me."

"Oh, nonsense, man," cried Dr. St. Aldwyn. "Buck up. You are the architect of your own fortunes and the master of your own destiny. Don't you forget it! Come straight home with me. I live over there. Let us have lunch and talk it out. If at the end you still want to 'take the *Amy* ticket' I have given you my word you will be free."

"You talk about being master of my own destiny, but I was not much master just now," faintly replied Harold.

"There you are. No man can be master of anything, unless he takes masterful precautions to be master. You should have taken precaution to see that you were free to act as you would, before trying it. You forgot that you came on board smoke-begrimed and wild-eyed; and, at once I knew your intention. Yes, sir, that is one of the things that gave the last knock to my pretensions as a clergyman. I realized to its full, that precaution was better than prayer. How could I teach people to pray for rain when I knew that it was better to teach them to take precautions against drought—because the stars teach me the drought *must* come."

"What then, do you mean?" cried Harold, "Do you neither believe in God nor in prayer?"

"Hush, lad," replied the elder man, "always approach those questions in the profoundest awe and reverence. Only a fool ventures to answer the first part of your question rashly: and only a most profound thinker can dare to answer at all. To some men there is a God: to others none; and to yet others there are many Gods. Before you can get an answer to the principal part of your question, you must first define what is God. The Creator of the universe, in its Great First Essence, Whom no finite mind can define, and to Whom your prayers are as unavailing as if addressed to the law of gravitation? The Great Spiritual God, or the Cosmic Consciousness, which has as little control over the germination of a seed as you or I? or the 'God of nature who is the God of Love? Which? Are they, can they all be one and the same? I confess I know not: and my earlier professions, while I was in bondage, seen all a labyrinth of vanishing chambers."

Harold sat up; the reaction from the severe strain of the morning was complete, and he had neither the power nor the inclination to combat these strange doctrines.

Dr. St. Aldwyn scarcely heeding even the presence of his profound listener, proceeded:

"Prayer is a different matter, and more easily explained. Although I have just told you that precaution is better than prayer: I yet believe in prayer—of a kind. The Christian Scientists come very near the truth. Montgomery in defining prayer, in a beautiful poem full of imagery, if not fact, said 'prayer was the soul's sincere desire, uttered or unexpressed.' Prayer, in fact, is an inward communion; and, again, a communion with the Cosmic Consciousness. In the former it may be possible to will away certain ills of the flesh, by the greater control of mind over matter; and in the latter it may be possible to conserve the Cosmic Consciousness either for good or evil. It has been said, possibly with immeasurable truth, that the radiations from the eminently kindly and lovable soul of the Czar of Russia have been more responsible for his immunity from violence than all his trained legions. Yet, as I speak, the radiations from the fiercer wills of the Nihilists may overcome his, and send him silently hustling through the Great Valley of the Shadows. Prayer is but a radiation of the mind, and even the great Psalmist himself did not desist from praying for great evil, in some of his vitriolic psalms; and for all we know he succeeded tolerably."

"But," at last protested Harold, "even in these days we have highly trained intelligent men who are earnestly sure of a personal God: take John Henry Newman, Gladstone and the German Emperor. Each a different calling: each highly intellectual and each representing a different type of religion."

"And possibly each worshipping a differend God," added Dr. St. Aldwyn. "It does not seem that He can be the same to all three. In Newman's case his God is most exquisitely portrayed in his "Lead Kindly Light." The "Light" which led him into the arms of the mother of heresies, and to the forsaking of the religion which Gladstone clung to with all the tenacity of his masterful intellect. With Gladstone it is more difficult for me to describe his God; but He seems to be more Evangelical. With the Kaiser he worships and leans on the Great War God of his own heart. When he kneels and wrestles in prayer for guidance he is conducting a great military reconnaisance with his own heart, in a sort of circumspective introspection; and it is said that he never rises until he is full of guidance: and it is even, correct guidance, so far as his own interests are concerned. But I cannot conceive of each of these Gods being one and the same personal God."

A rude jolting of the steamer informed the strange companions on life's great ocean that the journey had been completed; and, as they disembarked and walked to the residence of the elder man, Dr. St. Aldwyn exerted himself to gain the complete confidence of his companion.

By the time the shadows of the trees had lengthened to the measure of the setting sun, many things had been told between the two men. Harold had told all there was to tell of his short life, even to the fatal night of temptation: omitting only such details of time and circumstance as would have given any clue to the identity of her who had held the Golden Chalice to his lips; and whether she was married or single. Then he had come right down to this day of desolation, and his part in it; and how, feeling that the face of God was forever turned from him, he had decided to plead in person at the foot of the Great White Throne.

The counsel that Dr. St. Aldwyn gave, kindled hope in Harold in every direction, and warmed his heart to the rising sun of the future.

"You owe reparation," Dr. St. Aldwyn said, "in two directions. First there is the young lady, or young matron as the case may be: I ask not which. If she is unmarried your duty is to marry her: your vows are probably only vows to the Church, and not to God. The Church may release you: God certainly will. If she be married, then your duty is more difficult, but just as clear. Help her to the Light. Help her in her duties to her children or to her husband; but leave her not alone to struggle in the burden of her guilt. And, if you serve and sacrifice together, there yet may be no sin in it."

"Your duty next," he continued "is to the community. You have destroyed a great edifice, and feeling will possibly be very bitter against you. You are an architect, and possibly, with your great suffering, your vivid imagination, and your intense nerve power, which I readily see, you should be able to design a Cathedral which shall be a Great Glorification to the God whom you worship. You are not a pauper, and you may be able to make sacrifices such as will be taught by your own heart."

The result of it all was that Harold took the last ferry boat for Georgetown, and on arrival, went straight to Marjorie, and took her as far into his confidence as he dared. Time enough, he thought, to speak of the subject that was dearest to his heart when he had made peace with the Church.

CHAPTER TWENTY-FIRST.

Early next morning and far into many days Harold and Marjorie took counsel with each other for the future; and, in particular, for the plans towards reparation of the great evil which had fallen on the people at Harold's hand. Once, when the day had melted into evening, and Harold could contain his soul no longer, he took Marjorie's hand in his and led her gently to the rose-covered entrance leading out into the garden. There he stood and looked earnestly into her eyes.

"Marjorie," he said, "if our plans come off and the Church accepts all my penance and sacrifice, I shall ask His Holiness to grant me dispensation from my vows, and then ask you to marry me."

Marjorie was scarcely audible in her reply.

"And, suppose His Holiness refuses?"

"Then God help me," answered Harold.

A lit match thrown into a powder magazine would not have been more rapid in kindling the slumbering pelts into violent explosion.

Marjorie stormed.

"What do I care about the Church? Or, who asked you to do me the honour of your mumble jumble service for bringing two people together. The Church is but for a time. What is fifteen hundred years in fifteen million? Who is this parvenu? this usurper, that shall tell me do this, or do that?"

"Hush Marjorie, I did not———" tried to venture Harold.

"Hush, what?" she cried, "men and women lived and loved, struggled, fought and died for hundreds of thousands of years before this precious Church reared its stupid head. I will not be chained by her!"

And, stamping her foot, she flung past him into the cool tropical night.

Harold humbly followed, and, as he caught up with her, she turned on him as imperiously as she had done on that memorable morning on the seashore of St. Seriol's bay.

" Leave me!" she almost hissed, " with your greatness of intellect, and your narrowness of view."

Harold left her, and went slowly once more out into the cold world; but, now, he headed for the East and the rising sun, as on that other day he had helmed his ship to the West. Are these little things auguries or determining factors?

Next day, and for many more after, Harold kept himself busy drawing lines and making circles upon circles. He knew little and took less heed of the thread of local feeling; he had not even called at the Wilson's, where he might have heard of the overt hints against his good name. Some subtle agency was at work; and did not hesitate to spread, as it had possibly initiated, the rumour that Harold had set fire to the great edifice of set design. Eventually, one newspaper, bolder than its contemporaries, openly stated that it would be best for the man, and the country, if " a certain incendiary P.B.O." were to shake the dust of the place from the soles of his feet. The term " P.O.B." originating in a very kindly effort, had degenerated into a term of opprobrium for " poor broken overseers," and they flung it as one that they felt would wound Harold most.

That same evening had Harold decided to make his peace with Marjorie. On his arrival at the Wilson's the old man was profound in his sympathy—more shown than spoken— and Harold could hardly account for his extreme solicitation.

Her kinsman could not have chosen a more opportune time to make his peace with Marjorie than this day. In the face of public attack all differences between them were healed, and to her again he stood a hero. Her own rebellious attack on the Church was forgotten. She remembered only the little parish Church in Tobago; and again she remembered that tragic morning of the fire; how Harold had prayed and fought in his bonds; and how he had risen from the hour of temptation; all of which he had told her simply, without vain glory or excuse.

When Marjorie greeted Harold there was no sign or vestige of the circumstances under which they had last parted; and when she drew him into one of the bay windows which looked out into the tropical garden, she was as affectionate as a crooning mother.

"Harold," she said earnestly, "why don't you put a stop to all this nonsense? Why don't you action them for libel?"

"Libel!" echoed Harold, "I am not aware that anyone is libelling me. In any case, I am in no mood for lawsuits. But, to what do you refer?"

"Why, to those wicket charges against you, of course."

"Wicked charges: what charges?" asked Harold in amazement.

"Do you not know," tenderly began Marjorie, "that you are being charged daily, with having, in some inhuman frenzy or the other, set fire to the tower of the Cathedral?"

"But, that's nonsense, of course; and no one will believe it," replied Harold, "why, as you know, at this moment I am trying to gather my brains together for the architectural plans of such a Cathedral as no Western city has ever seen. And, as you also know, I propose to devote my mother's fortune—or at least my portion of it,—" at this Marjorie smiled, "towards making some reparation for an act of mine that I can neither understand nor explain. How that fire started is a mystery to me," he added as a sort of after thought.

"Yes, Harold," replied Marjorie, "You and I know all these things, but who else? Have you seen His Lordship, the Bishop?"

"No, I have not," replied Harold, "What is the good of rushing matters? There is no need to hurry for some days, or even weeks. Why, I scarcely have a line of my plans ready. I seem not to be able to work; and that brought me here to-night. What do I care for a few whispering tongues?"

"The few tongues are growing to the many," claimed Marjorie, "and they must be silenced. Even the newspapers are growing bold, and referring to you as the 'incendiary P.B.O.'"

"What!" cried Harold, as his face grew livid, "are they calling me that?"

Harold then experienced all the paroxysms of rage it was possible for one of his temperament to feel. He resented bitterly and vehemently the foul aspersions, and it was with difficulty Marjorie could restrain him from immediately setting forth to wreak summary vengeance on the Editor of the offending paper. But Marjorie's greater influence held him in iron bonds until, at least, the worst was past.

That night, before they parted, the cousins laid final plans for the morrow and immediate future. First, it was decided that next day would see Harold calling on the Cathedral authorities to make the offer which both felt would rehabilitate him with the people; and, to Harold, it also meant bringing himself nearer to the other great plan of his heart. Steps were also taken that Harold should take up quarters at the Wilson's menage, where he would have two rooms in which to live and work; one would be fitted up for the work in hand, and he would thus be able to secure Marjorie's valuable assistance; for, though she was no architect, she was an exceedingly apt pupil at most anything; at figures she was exceedingly quick, and as a water colour painter she was above the average.

Next day, according to the overnight plan, saw Harold waiting on Bishop Dare, the prelate who held jurisdiction over the Roman Catholic hierarchy in British Guiana. On being received by that devourt, but far from bigoted man, Harold explained his mission and briefly referred to recent events. He proclaimed himself an unworthy instrument, but His Lordship averred that none were unworthy; neither was it for mere man to declare unfit or unclean, instruments which his Master, in His infinite wisdom, may have chosen.

Harold soon began to thaw under the influence of the Bishop's kindliness. He felt indeed a personal attraction to the goodly prelate, and soon explained that he had formulated his plans the very evening of the great disaster, but that he had hoped to mature his drawings before he submitted the idea to the Church. The calumnies, however, to which he was being subjected determined him to make his offer at once, in order to allay doubts and to silence forever the cruel hints that were being circulated. His fortune amounted to somewhat over £10,000 and that, also, he purposed to make a free sacrifice of; in order to push forward the work of reconstruction, and make some signal reparation for the evil which seemed to have been somehow unwittingly done by his hands. The money gift would be quite unconditional, and, if his architectural plans were not worthy or equal to any that might otherwise be submitted, he would withdraw them, and yet leave the fund already referred to in the undisturbed possession of the Church.

If His Lordship had been kindly and well disposed in the first instance, he now became cordial and even affectionate. He expressed himself as profoundly grateful to Harold, and full of admiration for the nobility of heart which prompted the offers; finally he confessed himself thankful to the Great Giver of all things that all men's hearts were not desolate and full of deceit, but that there were yet many who reflected the goodness of their Creator.

During the entire interview not one word had been said on either side regarding that fateful evening in the Cathedral at Port-of-Spain, when Harold had practically left his vestments at the foot of the altar, in the presence of one of the greatest congregations that had ever gathered together in that splendid edifice. Harold had thought it unnecessary to broach the subject, and Bishop Dare, out of the delicacy springing from his great kindliness of heart, had abstained from making any reference to it. His Lordship shared in little of the mutual distrust that unhappily exists between the two great Orders of Loyala and St. Dominic, in their inner citadels; and yet, and although his was one of those calm, pure hearts that thought no evil, he was prone to think that "those French Priests" were not all that they should be; therefore, he was not going to hold up to odium one of his "own flesh and blood," who had thought it advisable to break with them: even though he abhorred the manner of the doing.

Harold eventually parted from Bishop Dare in receipt of a pledge that his offer would be forthwith transmitted to the Presbytery, and that His Lordship would take care that an early announcement was made, from the pulpit, of Harold's handsome offer, and thus stifle once for all the base calumnies that were daily gaining in currency.

On the Sunday following the interview, the Bishop took the sermon at the popular early morning mass, and preaching a most eloquent sermon on charity in all things, made the promised announcement of Harold's double offer. His Lordship dwelt on the generosity of the offer, and pleaded with his hearers to assist in getting rid of the vile charges which were in circulation concerning the noble hearted young man who had been placed in such a terribly trying position; but, who had done everything in his power to repair the evil, from the day of the fire on which he rendered such splendid services, down to to-day, in his most princely offer. Under the powerful advocacy of such a champion the entire congregation was swayed to charity, and many of those who had been most bitter in their hearts against Harold, left the sacred edifice full of forgiveness and the milk of human kindness. Again at the High Mass of the day the preacher referred to the subject, and once more at the evening service the generous offer was retold to the congregation of worshippers. By next day the news of this offer had been carried to the remotest corners of the city; and public sentiment unmistakably veered round to Harold and inclined to the acceptance of his offers; provided the architectural plans were up to the standard of the great edifice that all were agreed should replace the destroyed Cathedral.

By the following day, however, the hellish forces of calumny had grown bold again, and came forward in the guise of a leading article in one of the daily papers. That article was a masterpiece of craft. Headed " Incendiary P.B.O. Bribes Church," it proceeded to deal with what it was pleased to term an " alleged offer." The £10,000 was a " figment of the imagination." The capacity to submit plans of such a standard as to commend themselves to those alone competent to judge was declared to be of the same growth; and eventually the " would-be architect " was reminded that building cafés, and building cathedrals, were somewhat different propositions. In another part of the same paper was a paragraph headed " The Human Mind." In this, after dealing with various strange forms of insanity and hallucination, it proceeded to state that men had been known to commit the gravest crimes in order to prove some alleged gift, or to indulge some craving to be a genius at any cost. " It would also seem," it proceeded to state, " that a certain member of this community could stop at nothing to prove his capacity to build a greater tower than the one which had been confided to his care for a few brief moments (without any regard to his antecedents.) All the same," it concluded, " £10,000, if in being, is a pretty stiff advertising fee, anyway!"

Comments such as these could not fail to have their influence on public feeling, and soon the community was sharply divided into opposing factions: one faction firmly believing in Harold's innocence, and the other consisting of those who held him guilty of the foulest incendiarism. Soon these last were re-inforced by every species of opposition. There were those whose very breath of their nostrils was, that nothing good could come out of Nazareth; consequently. Harold never by any chance could be of the same calibre as a " home man; " because—it may be supposed—that one from home would be made of different flesh and blood. Then there were many who disliked the man: why, they knew not; some his style offended; others, disliked his father; and some barely opposed, because it was their nature to.

Amid it all Harold pursued his labours; at the first wave of opposition he had withdrawn himself entirely from intercourse with his fellows, and so had escaped some of the bitterest shafts. To Marjorie he had expressed the wish to remain in ignorance of all that was said against him; and she had suppressed the well nigh irrepressible Mr. Wilson, so Harold remained in peace. Marjorie, however, sought out every shred of comment, and digested every line of bitterness. Her sensitive nature chafed and tugged: and her fierce passions thirsted to come to grips with "the wretches." But, amid it all, the metal of her nature was passing through the furnace. and being beaten on the anvil of life.

Harold meanwhile laboured like a galley slave: in the stillness of the night he would rise from his bed with feverish energy. and, passing into the drawing office that he had set up in the adjoining room, work for hours together; and when the sun rose and the household got astir, he would creep back into his bed, broken and exhausted, and endeavour to catch up with outraged nature. When Marjorie remonstrated, he urged that he was not master, for when the ideas came crowding upon him, he had to commit them to paper or forever lose their current.

As the time drew near for the presentation of the plans the opposition grew more fierce, and the legions of the damned gathered together for one final onslaught on the Bishop and the architect. The Bishop "was weak ;" and, there was nothing too base to urge against Harold: the opposition did not hesitate to use some of the old title tattle about Harold's life•during the period he spent with good Captain Markham in Port-of-Spain. "Unclean," "Perjured," "Apostate," were among the epithets hurled at the unhappy Harold. "What was the nature of the offence which drove the 'priest-Architect' from his vows?" was a question propounded fre-

IN BONDAGE. 227

quently; and many were the grotesque and filthy suggestions made in answer. Again was it asked: "How could the Church hold communion with one who had declared such communion unclean?"

So acute and bitter had the opposition grown that the sole paper which had stood by Harold, and those who thought him innocent, had to confess that the best course of all was to submit the matter to the Holy Father and the Sacred College in Rome. And, to this course, at last, all parties consented, with the proviso that the reference should await the presentation of the plans; for, eventually, they might prove unworthy to the merest tyro.

CHAPTER TWENTY-SECOND.

The longest night must blossom into day. The dreary Arctic night, of one long, black pall of months of darkness, gives place to a world of sunshine. Yea, even the Great Long Night, what time the earth stood ligatured to the Moon in the womb of time, gave place to day,—and " there was Light." That " light " which is again subdivided into light and shade, sunshine and cloud, summer and winter; through which all creation lives, and swarms, and dies. And even as the earth, when its journey to the Sun has been completed, must experience one blinding day and after that the darkness of forever, so also is man's brief span of life. Commencing in the darkness of the womb he eventually enjoys the light of the day, which is again subdivided into day and night; and after that, the darkness : a state of bondage which none may escape. Following the simile further, so also is man's fortune. First of all the darkness of obscurity, then the day of fame, subdivided again into the days of despair and the nights of discontent : to some is accorded the short tropical night : to others the long arctic winter. But for each, life is divided into black and white; and morning follows night as shadow follows light. Napoleon, after Austerlitz and Jena, went down to Moscow and St. Helena; and then, all indifferent, his ashes are accorded a triumphal return to France, to the measured tramp of thousands of men and the brazen clashings of massed bands; now they rest pillared in porphyry and told of in stone, among the unforgotten dead and the glories of a great people. All, all is vanity!

Harold, in due course, his plans completed, opened his bosom and sallied forth into the open to take his place in the sun : but it was not yet near day.

The plans of the great Cathedral, which he had seen in his dreams and caught upon paper, were worthy of the great masters of the renaissance. Harold had sought to build not only a great Church, but a Church which would pulse of his native land and its people. Even as the Jews had brought forth the first fruits of their husbandry to the steps of the temple, so had Harold laboured to express in Glory to God the products of the country. Inevitably based on concrete and stone he had planned a superstructure of the world-famed colony woods. Sills of greenheart and columns of mora. Pillars of bullet wood and purple heart, castellated and carved, supported the high arched ceiling of cedar and crabwood; the chancel and aisles were worked into mosaics of the brilliant and multicoloured woods so riotously abundant in the forests of British Guiana. On the exterior had he also lavished of the glories of the high wooded forests. The stupendous tower which reared its head to the brilliant tropical sky stood girded with the sturdy woods that have made their name and stood the test of time.

Nor had Harold sacrificed beauty or grace to the expression of the colony's praise and homage to the Glory of God. The great tower which carried the statue of the venerated Mother of Christ challenged the grace and the beauty of the Campanile of St. Marks. The high mullioned windows proclaimed ecclesiastical sanctuary; and the carved pillars and columns which spread wide along the great frontal entrance may have been carved in Athens, or lifted bodily from some Byzantine temple. The wonderful arrangement of the principal doors gave the appearance, even when shut, that the House of God and Prayer was always open to those who would seek its refuge. On the whole, Harold's masterpiece entitled him to cease from his labours, and feel that architecture could demand nothing further from him. But what was his reward?

No sooner had the plans and specifications been placed in the hands of His Lordship than the whole riot of controversy was reopened afresh. Those few faithful ones who saw the charm and grace of the work mostly held their peace : the Vatican and the Sacred College would decide, and to them they would go. None but the wholly prejudiced could deny the excellence of the work, and as neither the Vatican nor the Sacred College would be composed of such persons, the level headed, who saw merit in the plans, looked forward undoubtingly to a verdict in Harold's favour.

To the remainder, who certainly were the more numerous party, nothing was too cruel to urge; no shaft of wit too coarse, no criticism too bold. Persons who could scarce build a stable, blossomed into learned architectural critics. Many who scarcely knew the difference between a buttress and a battlement, swelled the army of critics and helped to throw stones at the "boy architect." "Pagan Temple," "Theatrical effect": "lifted front from some Parliament House"; were among the epithets and jibes flung at the plans of a great edifice.

Then drew near the day appointed for the transmission of the offer and plans to Rome. Even then, despite the solemn compact at the commencement, a pronounced and determined effort was made to prevent "such a crowning humiliation to the colony." The Bishop, however, maintained his early attitude and "to Rome did they go."

But it must not be thought that the master spirits of the opposition were to be outmanoeuvred or outgeneralled in any way. In a very short while a private fund was started for the purpose of bringing out an architect from "Home." Then the cry was started: "A stone, a stone cathedral, at any cost." Certain commercial interests immediately saw a possibility of greater business in a stone or concrete building; and so commerce found itself in the camp of the opposition. The result of it all was, that the same mail which took the papers to Rome took instructions from the "insurgents" for the coming of an architect.

Although tide and time wait for no man, neither do they hustle; and Harold had to possess his soul in patience for many a long day before any sign came from Rome. In the meantime *THE* architect had arrived. He was dined and wined, and feted to his utmost capacity; and he, poor man, was soon praying for some respite in which to get down to business and tackle the job in real earnest.

Harold's heart felt no bitterness at this treatment of his rival; for though Marjorie had bitterly charged him with narrowness of view, his was really a lofty soul. On the other hand Marjorie felt nothing but gall and wormwood; and her fierce combativeness chafed for opportunity to tell them all what she thought of them. To be frankly candid, after all, the architect was of no great outstanding ability: he had good papers and letters behind his name but he had never even built one of the great Railway stations of the greater world; nor had he, (even like unto Harold's "great monstrosity") had a talked-about cafe to his credit; yet was he feted and fed before he had drawn a line; while Harold with his life blood in his work, and genius breathing from every column, was a renegade and an outcast to be abused and execrated. Verily, what fools these mortals be!

At long last came the fateful words from Rome and Harold was summoned to hear them. The kindly Bishop Dare himself undertook the task assigned by Rome, and read to Harold the terms of the despatch from one of the Papal secretaries. The Holy Father, the letter stated, admitted the excellence of the plans; but, for the present, declined to consider them on their merits, as he could not lose sight of the fact that the architect was a priest of the Church, still defying his Superior. Nor had word reached the Holy Father that the architect had returned to communion with the church, even though not to his Order. The Church, the Holy Father desired to say, must remain pure and undefiled, and not avail itself of pagan efforts; no matter how pronounced their excellence or praiseworthy their supposed intentions. The instrument must first be converted to Rome. So far as the father-architect was concerned the Holy Father could not lose sight of the fact that he was an erring son of the Church whose sin, at least, was disobedience; a sin, particularly in one who had taken the solemn vows of his Order, which the Church could not but regard as very grievous and mortal. The Holy Father the despatch writer continued, could not conceive that one of such devout intentions and pronounced ability, could be guilty of such serious crime as to preclude him from return to Holy Orders ; therefore His Lordship was directed to counsel and command the erring Father, in the name of the Apostolic See, to make confession and return to his vows as a priest. The Holy Father was quite prepared to make great allowances for one so young, and evidently moved by such goods intentions ; and if his very regrettable steps in the Diocese of Trinidad were due more or less to his surroundings, or differences of a personal nature with his Superior, the Holy Father would consider, under proper representation the granting him of a Mission in His Lordship's Diocese. When the young Father had adandoned his apostasy, and returned to the fold of the Church, the Holy Father would be pleased to consider the matter again. But if the architect persisted in his error then His Lordship must take some other steps for the repair of the ruin which had fallen on the faithful in British Guiana. The despatch then proceeded to state, that the tragic experience of the 7th of February could not fail to impress upon the faithful the grave danger of utilizing pagan efforts in the service of the Church, and, to go further, in the same direction, in the face of such a lesson, would be but to court afresh the Divine Vengeance.

Thus was expressed the giant determination of Rome, a determination which meant to Harold divorce for ever from every hope of marriage with Marjorie. As the kindly old Bishop read the salient features of the communication, Harold bowed his head in silence but made no answer.

" My son, " gently asked His Lordship, "Is your sin one against the Holy Ghost, that it divorces you forever from the Church ? "

The old man had given language to Harold's unexpressed thought about " divorce forever, " and it had caught his imagination. The one had spoken of his Church : the other thought of his love. A whimsical smile flitted across the corners of Harold's mouth as he remembered a couplet on the fly leaf of one of Lord Byron's poems :

> Under which King, Benzonian ?
> Speak or die!

"Sin ? Divorce ?" echoed Harold ; " it seems "— then he paused, and added, almost as an after thought, " I crave leave of your Lordship to give thought to the subject."

"And I willingly give it my son," answered Bishop Dare. " May you take it all to God, in prayer and earnestness. My own prayers will be with you."

As Harold rose and bowed himself from the Prelate's presence, the good man was almost inaudible as he whispered :

" Benedice !"

On leaving the Bishop's place Harold felt that night had again descended on his hopes. The offer from Rome offered him peace and honour : above all it offered an opportunity of seeing his great life work take shape and being : he would see it raise its loftly timbers to the sky ; and, he doubted not would lead many men to God. For in a personal God he yet believed, despite the confusing theories of Dr. Shenstone St. Aldwyn. Had the Bishop, whom he had just left, been a less winning personality probably he would have rejected the offer from Rome without leaving the Bishop's house. But Harold felt a personal love and loyalty to Bishop Dare. He could not help being touched by the generosity with which the Bishop had stood by him all through the controversy which had raged round the subject. Gladly would Harold have obeyed the order of the Church, and thus bring joy to the heart of the old man. But he felt that to the Church he could not return. In the long walk home to Marjorie he revolved and re-revolved the conflicting questions in his mind. On the one hand stood his vows ; the personal interest of His Holiness the Pope—which might mean the highest preferment in the Church ;—his loyalty to the good Bishop Dare ; the joy of seeing a great cathedral reared to his mind's creation. And each and every one called to him in clarion voice, to yield to the command of the Church. On the other, silent as a sentinel, stood his conscience, and his outraged vow : but, back of it all stood—Marjorie ! Disguise it how he would : Marjorie ! in the joy of her youth, and the splendour of her beauty !

The English mail which had brought the despatch from Rome had been delayed from early in the morning into late in the evening; and by the time Harold reached his apartments, where Marjorie sat and waited impatiently, the soft shadows of the evening had deepened into night. As Harold entered what he called his work room, Marjorie, impetuous to a degree sprang from her chair and cried,

"What news ? "

Harold, without any answer to his lips passed dejectedly into the inner room, and, divesting himself of his blouse, sank into the chair which stood at the foot of his bed, and heaved one deep drawn sigh.

Marjorie who had closely followed her cousin knew at once that all was lost : she therefore asked simply,

"What did they say."

Patiently and softly Harold told the tale as it had been read by Bishop Dare; omitting no particular. Marjorie listened without comment, until Harold reached the view that the destruction of the old Cathedral had perhaps been a rebuke, from the Creat God whom she worshipped, for the employment of a renegade.

"Good God," she cried, " is it possible that so much evil can be thought and done in Thy name ? Indeed, it is no wonder that the Church and her Prelates drive short thinking men to deny Your existence. I would, indeed, rather believe in no God, than in the God such as they teach."

Harold waited gently for her to be silent and then he said.

"Marjorie, I am distraught. So much labour, so much love : must it be all in vain?"

" But what did you tell his Lordship ?" queried Marjorie.

" I simply asked time to consider the matter," replied Harold. " You, also, did so much of the work that it would not have been fair to act without consulting you."

"But what will you do?" persisted Marjorie.

"I scarcely know," answered Harold. "The Cathedral has been lost at my hands. I am morally bound to do everything in my power to assist in its reconstruction and the creation of a building that will be as graceful as the one that is lost. If I wash my hands of my responsibility and barely hand over the money to the Church I shall be left destitute, for I should scarcely have the energy to work again as an architect, after this great disappointment.—And yet, and yet!" he murmured.

The last murmured words went to Marjorie's bosom like a sword, and her heart welled in the maternal instinct, for the man she loved. In that instant she was resolved, and she rose from where she sat; drawing herself to her fullest height she crossed to where Harold sat. Once more blinded by the dazzling splendour of her beauty, Harold bowed his head on his hands as though he would shut out the vision of her radiance, and weigh the matter without sight of her disturbing loveliness.

"I, will tell you what to do," Marjorie cried; and speaking rapidly she continued, "Let them chase themselves into plans of some musty old barn of a church. Give them the money—yours as well as mine. We shall keep a thousand dollars, the remainder will be more than £10,000, and with what we have kept we shall go to London. Shake the dust of the country from off your feet; for a prophet is not without honour, save in his own country. We shall not want: I have not been idle all this time, and my pen is even now credited with being as sharp as a sword. Under my Mother's name of Ursula Singh my contributions have been largely commented upon, and, I shall wrest tribute from the Great London. My freshness of outlook, the Editor of the Daily Post says, will startle London Editors; and my criticisms shall make the world and the Church pay, and pay dearly for to-night's bitterness. Come," she coaxed, "a thousand dollars will carry us some distance, and we shall not want. We shall hunt out Jack 'the shooter,' and make a little Tobago Colony in London. You shall win back your love of work and you shall build palaces for the rich, and temples for the poor. Come Harold," she cried again, "I can close my eyes and see the world before me. And this self same Church that has made us suffer, when my steel is proved, and my blade made sharp, I shall measure swords with ; and she shall sup in bitterness."

Harold, roused under the enthusiasm of his young kinswoman, raised his head and asked slowly and sweetly :

"And you and I, Marjorie ? I have lost my freedom, which I expected." The old Marjorie again flashed out :

" I tell you Harold, I am not in bondage to this Church : never have been, and never will be." But in an instant the new Marjorie had returned : lowering her voice to the softness of a caress she added, " Harold, at St Seriols we stood together at the Great White Altar : what more do you want?"

Then, laying her hand on his, she murmured " Come, son," and raising him to his feet she folded him to her bosom.

Harold, as in a dream, raised his head and looked full into the depths of her eyes ; and then their lips met in one long, lingering caress. Soft as night, and sweet as death.

* * * * * *

The great white topped waves in the 'sandy bay' at St. Seriols in far off Tobago curved and curled and lashed themselves to foam on the wide stretch of sand, as they had done for ages before. For generations to come they will curve and curl and lash themselves to foam again and again. Man's heart in its rise and fall, is as changeless as the tides of the sea; on the banks of the Nile, the Euphrates, or the Ganges : on the Tiber or the Thames, under the white peaked tops of the Himalayas, or by the sunny waters of the Caribbean : those that are not as well as those that be in bondage.

* * * * * *

Swift on wing the Recording Angel rose from earth to heaven, bearing close writ reams of papyrus; and he would be a bold reader who would venture to say whether there was therein written more of sin or sacrifice : for even I, the author, venture no further than to record the incomings and the outgoings of some of the children of men—those that are not, as well as—

THOSE THAT BE IN BONDAGE.